Out of Habit

Kathleen Dutton

Inks and Bindings
888-290-5218
www.inksandbindings.com
orders@inksandbindings.com

CONTENTS

OUT OF HABIT
Kathleen Dutton
April 21, 2017

BOOK REVIEW

Secrets from the past threaten a young woman's future in this debut novel. Allison Weston overcame a traumatic childhood to build a promising career as a teacher of hearing-impaired children at St. Ives Institution in South Harbor, Michigan. An orphan, she has lived at St. Ives since she was 10 years old. She remembers little of her past or the circumstances that led to the death of her mother. Deeply committed to the institution, she plans on becoming a nun; however, her guardian, Sister Margaret, wants her to live on her own before taking her vows. The prospect of romance is the last thing on her mind until she meets photojournalist Ryan Harper. Handsome and sincere, he is drawn to Allison and embarks on a campaign to win her love and trust. Just as she is starting to reconsider her future, she is tormented by reminders of the past. A series of anonymous letters hints at her involvement in a murder, and she begins to have horrifying nightmares. Desperate to help unlock the secrets of Allison's past, Ryan begins his own investigation. As the threats escalate and hit close to home, Allison and Ryan find themselves in a race to discover the truth. Dutton's tale is solidly entertaining, with engaging characters and a plot that successfully weaves together a tender love story and an unpredictable mystery. The novel is anchored by Allison, a gifted teacher discovering life outside the institution that sheltered her for more than a decade. She is well-matched with Ryan, and their romance unfolds at a gradual but believable pace as Allison struggles to decide whether she should pursue a relationship with him. The strong supporting characters include Allison's neighbor Holly Kiefer and Maria Giovanni, the rectory housekeeper and the heroine's closest confidante. Setting plays a key role, and Dutton does a fine job of bringing South Harbor to life, from lively summer festivals at St. Ives to Allison's favorite lighthouse. The love story is well-balanced with the mystery, which offers suspense and valuable insight into Allison's background.

A satisfying combination of romance and mystery.

OUT OF HABIT
Kathleen Dutton

Reviewed by Tony Espinoza

Having an understanding of the past is a crucial thing not only for us individually, but for us as a people as well. Only by learning from the past mistakes can we create a brighter future. By facing our pasts, whether they be filled with bright memories or haunted ones, can we move on with our future. As Maya Angelou once said, "I have great respect for the past. If you don't know where you've come from, you don't know where you're going. I have respect for the past, but I'm a person of the moment. I'm here, and I do my best to be completely centered at the place I'm at, then I go forward to the next place."

In author Kathleen Dutton's Out of Habit, the past and present collide. A young woman named Allison has been sent out into the world by the nuns who raised her at the St. Ives Institution, told to live amongst the people for two years to see if she still wanted to become a nun after escaping her sheltered life. Haunted by her past, she hopes to find safety in the life of a nun, but finds her world turned upside down when she meets a reporter named Ryan. Both living in a small town, Ryan sees the potential for a story in Allison, but doesn't count on falling in love with her in the process. As they work to unlock the secrets of her childhood, they must tread carefully through her trauma and their growing relationship as the past comes roaring back with a vengeance.

This is a truly engaging story! The author found the perfect balance right away between suspense and romance. The character growth immediately set up this balance in the first couple of chapters, showcasing each protagonist's story and personal struggles and highlighting the tenuous relationship which begins for each of them as they meet in a chance encounter. The haunting story of Allison's background and how it comes back to her present life is gripping and shocking, especially when the climax of the narrative hits, and secrets are revealed that put everyone in danger.

This was a perfectly written fictional novel, especially for those who enjoy romance with a blend of suspense and thriller narratives. As a fan of all of these genres, I was so impressed with the author's blend of subtlety and descriptive writing that really painted the perfect image of this story and the small town it took place in. I could really picture the jarringly different views both Ryan and Allison had even of St. Ives itself, each getting a vastly different feeling from the building in their initial meetings.

A masterful, entertaining, and gripping suspense and romance novel, author Kathleen Dutton's Out of Habit is the perfect summer read for 2021! A chilling yet heartwarming story of trauma, opening ourselves to possibilities, and facing the past to move on into the future, this book is a truly emotional and brilliant read.

Prologue

I'd stopped fighting when the pain ceased and the sound of my scream was only a muted echo. I floated in the narrow space between sleep and wakefulness, a place where I could find shelter. Where I could hide from the terror.

It was like the time I'd slipped under the water in my friend, Carly's lake. At first I fought like mad, driven by panic to reach the surface, but I was out of breath and much too spent to struggle. An eerie calmness engulfed me as I surrendered to the realization that I was out of time. I let my body float in the peacefulness. It really wasn't so bad.

Then, Carly yanked me by the hair to the surface and I coughed and sputtered until my lungs filled with air. When I told her how glad I was she'd saved me because I sure didn't want to miss the chance to make Smores, we fell into a nervous fit of giggles.

But this time was different. As I fell into the suffocating darkness, I had nobody to pull me from the terror.

"Hurry," a small voice called to me. "This way."

I squinted to focus, but it was too dark. "Who are you?" I asked. I was afraid it was only a voice I'd made up so I wouldn't feel so alone.

"Follow me. We don't have much time," she whispered. "I'll show you where we can hide."

Her voice was urgent, yet reassuring, so I followed until I saw the small shadow of a girl. She motioned for me to keep up before she turned to run.

"Wait for me," I cried and reached for the shadow's hand.

The shadow stopped and placed a finger over my lips. "We must be very quiet so he can't find us." I understood the gravity of her words, nodded my head and together we ran into the darkness. Just the shadow and I.

"Come back," another voice called to me. "Don't go."

I dropped the shadow's hand and turned toward the tearful voice, toward the light behind me.

"I'm afraid I can't go with you," I said to the shadow.

She shook her head and grabbed at my arm. "He'll hurt us again." Even though the shadow whispered, her voice held a forbidding tone.

I looked to the shadow, then toward the other voice that called to me. I needed to go back and when I lifted my heavy eyelids, gentle fingers stoked my brow. "Close your eyes," the soothing voice prompted.

I wanted to talk, but my throat burned. I gasped for air, but couldn't breathe. On the floor beside me, I saw the broken wing of an angel and crimson drops of blood. In a terrifying instant I knew it wasn't a dream.

The shadow coaxed me, but her voice faded in the distance. "Come with me before it's too late."

I turned away to shut out the terror and pain and the sinking sensation of sorrow. I closed my eyes and slipped into the darkness toward the shadow.

Chapter One

As soon as the heavy oak door was closed and locked behind her, Allie regretted her hasty decision to decline Mrs. Carson's offer of a ride home. She hugged her backpack close as the wind drove the rain so hard she could barely see ten feet beyond the marble steps of the South Harbor Municipal Library.

She paused under the entrance awning, her mood as unsettled as the storm and waited for a break in the downpour long enough to dash to her bike at the side door without getting soaked. She scowled as a roar of thunder rippled across the sky, as if to will the storm into submission. Yet, the hard rain persisted, so she pulled up the hood of her rain slicker, muttered under her breath and darted into the chilly night. A bolt of lightning crashed so close, she jumped and shielded her face from the blinding flash.

She leaned against the building to catch her breath, and wondered if there was any merit to Sister Margaret's nagging. Perhaps getting a car with the trust money she would inherit after graduation wasn't such a bad idea.

Allie cursed and berated herself for having such weak thoughts. She'd be damned to hell before she'd touch the money. She didn't want to know where it came from. She didn't want or need a car. What she wanted was her life to remain simple, uncomplicated. She couldn't be bothered with the details of obtaining a driver's license, plates, paperwork and maybe, just maybe, the possibility of finding out who she was and where she'd come from.

She rushed to her bike, determined to endure hundreds of similar storms without the luxury of a car rather than risk opening doors to her past that were welded shut years ago.

She fumbled to open the security chain from the bike and began the two-mile journey to her apartment through the quaint resort town of South Harbor, Michigan.

Another boom of thunder rolled closer, so she peddled faster against the hard driving rain. It wasn't long before her energy was spent and she considered stopping at St. Ives for shelter.

For the past twelve years, St. Ives had been her home until a few months ago when she turned twenty-two. She peered through the darkness toward the institution and even though she couldn't see the fortress, somehow knowing it stood strong against Mother Nature's fury lifted her soggy spirits. She fought the urge to turn her bike toward St. Ives, but didn't want to cause alarm. She loved her guardian with all her heart, but knowing Allie was out in the storm, Sister Margaret would fuss and fret.

Caught off guard by loud barking and a distant voice, Allie flinched and whirled around.

"Sadie," a man shouted. "Get over here."

Allie gasped at the sight of an animal lumbering toward her so she swerved, only to land in the path of oncoming headlights. Her heart leaped to her throat as she narrowly avoided the car, but before she could gain control of the bike, she rammed up and over the curb and smashed into a lamppost.

Dazed, she lay on the soggy grass. Brakes squealed as the car spun and skidded to a stop. She cried out when the dog leaped on her chest and planted sloppy kisses on her face. She blinked against the blinding headlights and started to rise until a dark figure rushed toward her.

"Sadie, sit," the stranger commanded, his voice sharp as he knelt beside Allie. "Are you hurt?" he asked, his fingers digging into the flesh of her arm.

"I hit my head," she said and touched a tender lump above her eyebrow. She blinked to focus on the stranger who hovered over her. "I'm okay."

With strong hands, he lifted her to her feet. "I'm sorry about Sadie." His deep voice was edged with a hint of worry. "I'm watching her for my neighbor." When they looked at Sadie, she thumped her tail on the wet grass. "She's still a pup who hasn't learned proper manners yet."

"You should be more careful," Allie scolded the puppy, but couldn't resist a smile as she patted the dog's head. "I'm glad you weren't hurt, Sadie." She turned when she heard a car door slam.

"Lady, what the hell were you doing in the middle of the road?" The driver's angry words boomed over the deafening thunder. She glanced at his imposing figure, but his features were obscured by the glow of bright headlights as he walked toward her.

"I swerved to avoid the dog," she said and stepped forward.

The driver looked at the dog then back to Allie. "Are you stupid?" he yelled and planted clenched hands on his hips. "I could've killed you."

She caught a whiff of alcohol and grew wary, but before she could react, the stranger stepped in front of her to confront the driver. "It was my fault," he said. "The dog got away from me and chased her into your path." He crossed his arms, his broad shoulders blocking Allie's view of the driver.

As if seeing the stranger for the first time, the driver backed away. "You need to keep your mutt under control before someone gets hurt," he snarled and stomped back to his car.

"Nice guy," the stranger mumbled as the car pulled away with another squeal of tires. He held the dog's collar in one hand and slipped his other around Allie's arm. "Let's get out of this rain so I can look at your forehead."

"It's nothing." She pulled her arm free and turned toward her bike. The front tire was bent at an odd angle and the handlebars twisted in the opposite direction. "Oh, great," she murmured and stretched to touch the mangled frame.

The stranger carried the bike and pulled the unruly pup toward a nearby house. "Don't worry about your bike. I'll get it fixed."

"That's not necessary." She followed him across the street to retrieve her bike. "I can take care of it myself."

"I'm responsible for the damage. I'll fix it," he repeated as he set the bike into the bed of a pick-up truck. He hauled Sadie to the house and opened the door. "Inside," he commanded. Sadie looked up at him with mournful brown eyes and before he closed the door, Allie heard a faint whimper.

He dashed back to the truck and opened the passenger door. "Get in. I'll give you a ride."

Allie stood in the driveway to consider her options. She was wet, cold, exhausted and her head throbbed. She could say no to the nice stranger and drag her bike over a mile to her apartment or accept his offer. "Thanks," she said and climbed into the truck. Out of the corner of her eye, she caught a flash of a smile and her stomach muscles knotted. She said a silent prayer. If she made it home safety, she'd go to confession early and for good measure, she promised not to argue with Sister Margaret all week.

He slid into the driver's seat and started the engine. "I'm Ryan Harper," he said and offered his hand.

His voice was calm and reassuring, yet she hesitated before returning the handshake. "Allison Weston," she replied as her gaze fell to the warm, strong hand wrapped around hers. She pulled away and shoved her icy hands into the pockets of her raincoat. He studied her for a moment then put the clutch into reverse.

"Where to?" he asked.

She pointed out directions and when her teeth began to chatter, he clicked on the heat to full blast.

"Why were you riding a bike in this weather?" he asked. "That is kinda crazy."

"I don't have a car," she said defensively and indicated a left turn. "My apartment is the second building on the right."

When his truck came to a stop, he switched on the dome light and leaned close. Allie grabbed the door handle and balled her other hand into a fist. She didn't relax, even when she realized he was only examining the bump on her forehead.

His questioning gaze fell to hers. "You're sure you don't need to have that looked at?"

"I'm sure." Awkwardly, she cleared her throat.

"Do you live alone?"

Allie narrowed her eyes as a glint of apprehension coursed through her. "That's really none of your business."

"Hey." He held up his hand in a gesture of peace. "I'm only asking because you could have a concussion."

When she realized the frown on his face was from concern, not because he was some deranged psychopath, wariness turned to confusion. Raindrops trickled along the side of his dark stubbled face and she fought the urge to smooth a lock of dark, wet hair that fell across his forehead. His chin was strong and his lips were firm, except for a hint of a smile, which accented a small dimple at the corner of his mouth. His eyes were dark, but expressed trust. He was tall and solidly built, but not bulky like some of the guys at college who spent too much time at the gym. In contrast, Allie felt small, but oddly comfortable and for the first time, she realized how sheltered her life had been living with the nuns at St. Ives. For the first time, she understood what women found attractive in a man.

Her mouth went dry when the dimple deepened with his smile. Her cheeks radiated heat, certain the blow to her head had caused her thoughts to run amok. "I'll be okay," she said and opened the door. "Thanks for the ride."

"Where do you want me to return the bike?"

She chewed at the rough edge of her fingernail. "I. . . I'm not sure," she stammered.

He pulled a card from his wallet. "My cell phone number is on my business card. Give me a call so we can make arrangements."

Allie slipped the card into her pocket. "Thanks again." She shut the door and rushed toward her apartment.

Once inside, she ran warm water for a bath and peeled off the damp, cold layers of clothing. She groaned when she examined her forehead in the bathroom mirror, mortified by her appearance. The smudged mascara under her eyes gave her a ghoulish appearance. "No wonder I scared the poor guy," she mumbled. Her fingers tangled in her wet, matted curls and she thought her best feature was the red, throbbing bump above her eyebrow.

She closed her eyes and sank into the steamy bubbles to soak away the tension in her body, but the tranquility only lasted until the image of Ryan Harper's confident gaze lingered in her thoughts.

A lazy, treacherous smile tugged at the corner of her mouth when she recalled the way he studied her. She bolted upright in the tub and reached for the soap to scrub her arms, as if it would erase his image from her mind. What was she getting so worked up about? She'd just met a guy. It was a simple thing that happened to ordinary people every day.

She held her breath and sank under the water to cleanse thoughts of him from her mind. Once she got her bike back, she wouldn't need to see him again. It was clearly that simple. Her body began to relax when she convinced herself that she was above being distracted by romantic notions. She wanted to become nun for goodness sakes. As she closed her eyes once more, she was acutely aware of the uneasiness that settled in the pit of her stomach.

* * *

Ryan thought about Allison on the drive to meet some of the guys from his softball team. He didn't get a good look at her, and from what he saw, she resembled a drowned rat, but something about her intrigued him. He towered over her and although she wore a shapeless rubber raincoat, he detected soft, delicate curves. She never let down her hood, but he caught a glimpse of stray, wet curls that framed her heart shaped face and even though she had her guard up, she couldn't disguise the depth of emotions in her eyes. The moment he leaned close to look at the bump on her head, she flashed a warning that spoke volumes. She was scared, yet defensive, vulnerable but wary. Never had he seen such a conflict of emotions from just one glance. Maybe it was his investigative nature, but the invisible barrier she'd forged between them appealed to the reporter he was by trade. He was certain there was a story in those eyes.

Maybe it was basic attraction, but he couldn't shake the jolt of chemistry that crossed between them when he shook her hand.

Allison Weston was still on his mind as he entered Mac's Bar and Grill, sponsor of his softball team. Most of his teammates were coworkers from the local newspaper, *The South Harbor Herald,* where Ryan was new to the staff. His hometown was hundreds of miles away in a small farming community in the thumb area of Michigan, so he'd joined the team to make new friends.

He knew what a lucky break it was to land the job as a photojournalist at the Herald, but deep down he also knew the job was a stepping-stone for higher goals. Someday he'd work at a large press, but in the mean time, the job at the Herald would give him a start in a field nearly impossible to break into and would allow him to pursue his hobby of wildlife photography.

"Over here, Ryan."

He waved to Craig Kulik, one of the copy editors at work and Mike Vetrano, a South Harbor police officer. With a quick smile, he moved through the crowded bar to join them.

As he slid into the booth, Craig poured beer from a pitcher into a beer mug and set it in front of him. "Thanks," Ryan said. "Where's everyone?"

"Phil and Steve already left and Carl hasn't been here yet," Mike shouted over the noisy crowd. "Where have you been? I was just about to leave."

Ryan took a long drink. "I was helping a damsel in distress."

Craig smirked. "Was she cute?"

Ryan grinned back. "What I could see of her sure caught my attention." Craig's eyebrows rose in question, so Ryan continued. "My neighbor's dog got away from me and chased a lady riding a bike. When she swerved to avoid the dog, a car almost nailed her. She wasn't hurt, but her bike's a mess."

"What's her name?" asked Mike.

"Allison Weston."

Craig sipped his beer. "I think the paper did a piece on her recently. Doesn't she live at St. Ives?"

Ryan shook his head. "I dropped her off at an apartment in town."

"She moved out of St. Ives a few months ago," Mike informed them and leaned across the table. "Are you sure she's all right?"

"I offered to take her to the hospital, but she said she was fine." Ryan frowned at Mike's concerned expression. "How do you know her?"

"My family has strong ties with St. Ives. I've known Allie since she was a kid. She teaches hearing impaired children at St. Ives Elementary and my niece, Lisa, works as a student assistant with Allie."

"Man, she doesn't look old enough to be a teacher." Ryan felt a sense of relief. "I can't put my finger on it, but there's something intriguing about her. What's her story?"

"Allison was raised by the nuns at St. Ives since she was ten," Mike said. "She's probably having a tough time adjusting to living on her own."

Ryan frowned. "That might explain why she seemed so distrustful of me."

Mike gulped down the last of his beer and placed some money on the table. "I think I'll drop by her place to see how she's doing."

* * *

A knock at the door interrupted Allie as she wrote notes for class. Who'd be calling at this time of night?

She ran her fingers through her damp hair, secured her robe around her and smiled when she saw Mike Vetrano crouched under the overhang to shield himself from the rain. She worked with Mike's niece at the library and knew his dad, a retired police officer. The family resemblance was striking in the tall, muscular build and dark features.

"Come in, Mike," she welcomed him. "What are you doing out in this weather?"

"I heard you got hurt and wanted to see for myself that you are okay." Mike's frame filled the doorway and his dark, serious demeanor could be intimidating, but Allie had known him for so long, she considered him family.

"I'm fine," she said, touched by his concern. "Word sure gets around fast."

"It's the price of living in a small town," he said and pointed to her forehead. "What happened?"

"I was riding home from the library and a dog chased me into the path of a car," she said. "Can I get you something to drink?"

"No, thanks," he said and shook his head. "I'm on my way home."

"How did you find out I was hurt?"

"Ryan Harper is on my softball team."

"Is he?" she asked, her interest piqued. She waited for Mike to continue, but he didn't so she changed the subject. "You don't need to worry about me."

"It's my job to worry," he said. "You need to be more careful. Have you thought about getting a car?"

"You sound like Sister Margaret." Allie raised her eyebrows. "Are you sure she didn't send you over to check on me?"

Mike laughed and shook his head. "Sister Margaret does her own dirty work," he said. "But, if she thinks you need a car, I'd have to agree with her."

"I'll think about it," she promised.

When Mike turned toward the door, Allie stepped forward. "How well do you know Ryan Harper?" She cringed when Mike's eyes glinted with humor.

"Why? Do you want me to set you up with him?"

"No," she said. "You know I'm not interested in dating." She frowned when his smile deepened.

"He moved to town recently and works at the newspaper. He seems like a great guy."

While Allie watched Mike drive away, she was determined to get Ryan Harper out of her head. She thought about Sister Margaret asking her to leave St. Ives to discover what life was like outside the institution before making the decision to become a nun. Allie sighed, the bite of disappointment still strong. Margaret was convinced that Allie's desire to become a nun was based on the wrong reasons.

Allie closed the door and made a silent vow to endure the next two years, stick to her plan and then prove she was worthy of taking the vows.

* * *

When the shrill blast of the alarm jarred her awake the next morning, Allie opened her eyes with a groan. The knot on her forehead pulsed and all she wanted to do was hide under the covers to sleep away the morning. With a sigh of resignation, she moved to the window and lifted the shade, pleased to discover the rain was replaced by a breathtaking sunrise that decorated the sky with fingers of pink and blue.

While she dressed, she reviewed the day's schedule. First, there was a class with a new student at St. Ives. After the session, she needed to rush across town to campus and then to the library for a story session with a group of hearing impaired preschoolers. When she planned to study for a test, she didn't know, but one thing was certain, she needed her bike.

She gulped down the last drop of coffee and grabbed a bagel to eat on way to St. Ives. It wasn't until she was out the door when she remembered the card with Ryan Harper's phone number. A small pang rumbled in her stomach when she tucked the card into her pocket.

A sweet, gentle breeze drifted in from Lake Michigan, and as Allie approached St. Ives, she closed her eyes to inhale the fresh, clean fragrance of April. Spring had arrived early, only to tease the senses, for the unpredictable weather could turn freezing by noon.

Allie loved the warm spring days and wished she could steal a few moments to sit under a tree to catch her breath. She had a habit of moving in a million directions all at once. It was her choice to stay busy, but wouldn't it be nice to do absolutely nothing for a change?

She entered St. Ives and ignored the prickly sensation on her skin. This had been her home for the past twelve years and she didn't understand why the cold, stone corridors still intimidated her.

Allie hurried through the halls to the administrative office, stopping to smooth her hair and slacks before she entered.

Sister Margaret sat posture perfect at her desk and typed on the computer keyboard. At first glance, Sister appeared small, almost frail, but Allie had seen first hand how Margaret could reduce someone twice her size to tears.

Margaret's silver hair was cut into a neat bob and she wore no makeup, but the twinkle in her hazel eyes could light up the room. She peered over half glasses and her smile faded when Allie entered the office. She stood to examine the bump on Allie's forehead. "What happened to you?" she demanded.

"I ran my bike into a lamppost," Allie admitted, having learned long ago Margaret's ability to smell a lie and how she could whittle out the truth without much effort.

Margaret crossed her arms and continued to observe her. "You know how I feel about that bike," she declared. "The minute you graduate, I'm taking you to the bank so you can open your trust to buy a car."

Allie set her hands on her hips. "You kicked me out of here so I could learn to stand on my own. Now you're fussing over me as if I were a child."

"Don't take that tone with me. I didn't kick you out," Margaret huffed while she studied Allie's forehead.

Allie felt her smile wane. "I wish you'd let me come back home."

Margaret's eyes shone with love as she patted Allie's shoulder. "I know you do, dear, but you've been much too sheltered here. You need to discover there's more to life than the walls of this institution."

"I don't want anything more." Allie looked away and bit her bottom lip.

"I'm going to be firm about this, Allison. If you choose to become a nun after two years, then I'll gladly help."

"Two years is a lifetime," Allie muttered and rose from the chair. "I know you think you're doing this for my own good, but I still don't like it."

Margaret placed an arm around Allie's waist and walked her to the door. "In time, my dear, you'll thank me for helping you make this decision."

"I didn't make this decision," Allie grumbled in the hall on the way to meet with her new student, Jessica Morgan.

* * *

St. Ives Elementary School served the parishioners with private classes from preschool through the sixth grade. There were several hearing impaired children, like Jessica, who required special instruction in addition to regular classes. Jessie was one of three children who lived at the Cottage House on the grounds of St. Ives.

Allie slipped into the room to observe how Jessie interacted with the other students and spotted the little girl forming clay shapes while the other students played together, Jessie seemed content to sit alone.

Mrs. Cleburne, the preschool teacher, joined Allie at the door.

"How's Jessica doing?" Allie asked.

"I was hoping she'd be more outgoing by now."

Allie had hoped the same. "It's only been a few weeks. She's been bounced around the foster care system most of her life. It will take some time." Allie felt an instant bond with the little girl, knowing from experience how harsh and uncertain life as an orphan could be.

Allie sat in a small chair across from Jessie, but the little girl didn't look up until Allie reached for a piece of clay. Jessie was four years old and small for her age. She turned to Allie with sad, brown eyes and then looked away.

Allie's heart sank, but she smiled and tapped on the little girl's hand to gain her attention. "It's time for our class," Allie signed.

Jessie followed the sign language and watched Allie's lips, then put the clay away.

* * *

At lunch, Allie sat at a picnic table on campus away from the other students. She had never dated or joined clubs. She'd never been part of a group and was always invisible to her peers. She wanted so much more for Jessica. If she had any influence at all, she'd help

Jessie gain self-esteem so she didn't spend her life cursed with the isolation Allie had endured.

As she munched on an apple, a young couple seated across the lawn caught her eye. From the way they gazed at each other, it was obvious they were in love. Allie held her breath when his arm slipped around his girlfriend to draw her close. With her head resting on his shoulder, they appeared to face the world as one.

Allie looked away and scolded herself for being rude, but then she saw them kiss and her mouth went dry. As the kiss deepened, an unfamiliar yearning began to stir at the base of her stomach. Never before had she considered getting involved with anyone. Still, she frowned at the sudden emptiness in her chest. She shook her head to clear her thoughts as confusion quickly turned to anger when Ryan's easy smile crossed her mind.

She marched to a trash bin and tossed in the apple core. Why must she suddenly remind herself that she was going to become a nun? She needed to get a grip on her emotions and stop acting like one of the starry-eyed girls in her class.

She pulled the business card from her pocket with Ryan Harper's phone number and hurried to find a pay phone, determined to get her bike back and put a stop to these wayward thoughts.

* * *

With a groan of disgust, Ryan kept one hand on the steering wheel while he groped for his chirping cell phone. He hated the intrusive sound of the damn thing, but knew it was the only way to stay in touch with the office since he was often on the road covering assignments. He parked his truck and gathered his camera gear, then headed toward the track field and returned the call to the Herald.

"This is Ryan Harper." He checked his watch when the receptionist put him on hold.

"Just a minute," he interrupted when she returned to the line. He searched his pockets for a pen, wrote down the information and smiled when he stared at Allison Weston's phone number. Again, he checked the time and dialed the number, his mood suddenly lighter.

He leaned against the fence and drummed his fingers on the phone when the person at the South Harbor Municipal Library put him on hold. After a few moments of listening to sappy music, his senses came alive when a soft voice responded. "This is Allison Weston."

"Hi, Allison. It's Ryan Harper." He detected an unsteady sigh.

"Hello." The softness in her tone faded. "I was wondering when I could get my bike back."

Ryan sat down on a nearby bleacher. "It's still at the shop, but I can give you a call later to let you know when it'll be ready."

"The library closes at nine," she said. He didn't know why, but he was certain she chewed on a fingernail. "Can you call before then?"

"Sure. I'll check on your bike and call you back at this number."

Ryan disconnected the call, grabbed his gear and raced toward the field before the track events were over.

* * *

Allie stared at the phone and wondered why she allowed herself to become so rattled at the sound of his voice. He had such an easy confidence, which seemed to emphasize her uncertainty. She despised the effect he had on her.

She didn't have time to dwell on her thoughts, for the first of the kids in her reading group entered the children's section at the library. She smiled and signed a greeting as she walked toward the little girl to begin the weekly story hour for hearing impaired preschoolers.

* * *

Ryan dropped off two rolls of film at the Herald and began to write the article on the track and field event before he called Allison. By the time he was done with his final draft, it was close to nine o'clock. Hoping he hadn't missed her, he dialed the library.

"This is Allie."

"Allie." He smiled as he said her name. "This is Ryan. Your bike should be ready Saturday morning. Can I drop it off at your apartment?" he asked.

"Well," Allie paused before answering, as if she weren't certain about the arrangement. "I guess so."

"What's a good time?" he asked.

She hesitated. "I'll be home in the afternoon."

"How about two o'clock?" He inhaled deeply and waited.

"I suppose."

He wrapped the phone cord around his finger, not ready to end the conversation. "Do you need a ride home tonight?" he asked.

"Thanks, but I already have a ride."

He had a hunch she wasn't being truthful, but let it pass. "I'll see you Saturday then."

Again, she paused as if she wanted to say more, but said a quick thank you and goodbye.

Ryan stared at the phone and wondered why she made the simplest conversation sound mysterious. With a shrug, he placed the completed article on the editor's deck and headed to the gym.

Chapter Two

ithout her bike, Allie was forced to jog from one end of town to the other. Between work at St. Ives and the library, exams, classes and finalizing a research paper, she could barely stay awake during lectures.

After her Saturday morning class, she had just enough time to catch a nap before Ryan returned her bike. She set the alarm, but when she closed her eyes, she couldn't seem to get comfortable. She tossed every which way and finally sat at the edge of her bed.

She stared at the clothes in her closet and groaned. Everything she owned was out of date and plain. After more thought than she'd ever admit, she settled on a simple pair of jeans and a sweater which were standard dress on campus and stood in front of the mirror with a critical eye. There was a frown crease between her eyes, which made her look cross, so she attempted to soften it with a dab of lotion.

Maybe a little make-up would hide the effects of lack of sleep. When she was finished, she scolded herself for making a fuss over seeing Ryan.

* * *

"Allison?" Ryan inquired when the door opened.

"Yes," she said.

"I hardly recognized you." He detected the familiar clash of wariness in her eyes, but the rest of the package was foreign. He stood at the door, not speaking. Not prepared for the impact of how soft and creamy her skin appeared and the way her wavy hair fell past her shoulders and shone like honeycombs in the sunlight until a slight breeze suddenly whipped it into a riot of soft curls. He nearly lost himself in the deep blue of her eyes with shades of gray that reminded him of an unexpected storm over Lake Michigan on a hot summer day. She was taller than he'd thought, but the top of her head barely reached his chin. Her frame was small, but she had just enough curves in just the right places.

"It's me," she said, which jolted him back to reality and he closed his mouth when the color deepened on her cheeks. "That's not my bike."

"The frame was totaled on your bike, so I brought this as a replacement." He cleared his throat while she examined the bike in silence. "It's slightly used, but in excellent condition."

She shook her head and turned to face him, her hands planted on her hips. "I. . . wish you hadn't bought this," she said.

"I wrecked your bike, its only right I replace it." He watched her shoulders slump as if repaying his debt was a huge crisis. "It's only a bike." He smiled to reassure her. "With no strings attached," he added because he thought she'd want to hear it. When her mouth lifted into a slight smile, he knew the first hurtle had been crossed.

"Thank you," she said.

"Have you ridden a ten speed before?" When she shook her head, he jumped on the bike. "It rides different than your old bike."

He demonstrated how to change gears, speeds and how to apply the brakes. When he circled around and stopped beside her, she looked uncertain as she bit her nail. Hell, she looked younger than his seventeen-year-old sister. "Give it a try," he coaxed. "It's easy."

She climbed on the bike and began to pedal. He leaned against a tree to watch, thrilled when her mood lightened as she became more familiar with the bike. When she stopped next to him, a relaxed smile transformed the cloudiness in her eyes. "What do you think?" he asked.

"It's much easier to ride than my old clunker," she exclaimed. "Please let me pay you. My old bike wasn't nearly this nice."

Ryan shrugged. "The guy at the bike shop has a son who plays baseball. He gave me a good deal if I'd snap a picture of his son for the paper." Ryan laughed when Allie's mouth dropped open.

He retrieved another bike from the bed of his truck. "In fact, the bike shop was having a special so I bought myself one as well. Let's go for a ride." When she frowned, he didn't give her the opportunity to refuse. "You need to make sure you know how to work all the gears." He was already riding toward the street when he called back to her. "You can show me around town."

* * *

Allie pursed her lips, uncertain about whether to follow Ryan as he pedaled away. Why didn't he get the hint? She jumped on her bike, determined to make it clear that she wanted nothing to do with him.

He smiled when she pulled up next to him. "Looks like you've got the hang of it." He nodded to the bike as she led the way, down the winding side streets to point out the mix of Victorian and farm style homes.

They rode by the library, past the college and to St. Ives.

"See the stone house?" She stepped off her bike to point out the Cottage House in the distance. "I grew up there."

"It reminds me of a house from a fairytale," he said.

She studied him to judge his reaction, as if it were a test and she silently dared him to say something negative, but he didn't.

"What are the other buildings?" he asked.

"That's the elementary school where I teach. The rectory is there." She pointed out a two-story house adjacent to the church. "The convent is on the other side of school and the rest of the buildings are for storage and maintenance." She watched as he studied the ivy-covered buildings.

"Great architecture," he commented. "I'd like to take a closer look sometime." He narrowed his eyes and frowned. "I wish I had my camera."

Allie followed his gaze and tried to see the institution through his eyes. "I always thought it was cold and. . ." She stopped, having revealed more than she cared to and began to peddle toward the road.

"Where do you like to hang out?" he asked as they rode the scenic drive along Lake Michigan.

Allie glanced at him for a moment, puzzled. "I love the water." They parked the bikes. "My favorite place is the lighthouse. I like to watch the boats and freighters from the control room." She led him to a path that wove through steep rock formation to the beach below.

The wind was heady at the shore and drove through her sweater. They stood at the water's edge and gazed at the magnificent body of water. She closed her eyes and drew in a deep breath. "This is where I hang out."

"Do you come here often?" he asked.

She nodded and spotted a freighter in the distance. "I avoid it during the tourist season, though. It gets pretty crowded during the summer."

"I know what you mean. I went to college across the lake in Chicago," he said and pointed west.

"When?" she asked and followed his gaze.

"I graduated four years ago, but I go back once in awhile to visit friends."

"What brings you from Chicago to this small town?"

"It's the only place that would hire me. My first job out of school was developing film at a drug store. It's hard to break into the field of journalism with a job that pays the bills."

"What do you write about?"

"I cover high school sports and some of the college games. I'm also a photographer which helped land me the job."

She hugged herself as a gust of wind went right through her sweater and when he started to remove his jacket, she turned toward the steps. "Maybe we should head back."

On the ride through town, Ryan sped past her. "Race you back!" he shouted.

Allie watched him disappear over the hill. She wasn't a match for his athletic strength and knew when he slowed, it was to allow her to catch up. They raced down the hill and by the time they stopped in front of her apartment, they were winded and laughing.

He leaned against the porch rail and smiled as if they were long time friends.

"I haven't laughed like this since Sister Celeste told me about the time she snuck out of the dorm at school by climbing down a tree with a cigarette dangling from her mouth and landed right in front of Mother Superior."

He laughed. "Now that's a picture." His deep laugh put her at ease, as if they'd shared a private joke only close friends would understand.

"Do you want some iced tea?" She cringed as the words formed, but had to admit that she wasn't ready for the visit to end.

"Sure," he said and followed her inside the apartment.

Allie wanted to kick herself for making the offer, but he was already seated at the small table in the kitchen, so she poured two glasses of tea.

She watched him take a long drink and studied his strong hand wrapped around the glass. He seemed larger than life in the cramped corner of her breakfast nook. Sunlight filtered in the room and created auburn highlights in his dark brown hair. His gaze met hers when he set down the glass.

"Tell me what you like to do for fun."

"Fun?" She couldn't think of an answer that wouldn't make her sound like a real loser, which bothered her more than she cared to admit. She concentrated on the frown line across his forehead.

"You do have fun, don't you?" he asked.

"Yes," she hesitated. "I have fun with my students." The dimple deepened at the corner of his mouth, which only added to her discomfort as she fidgeted in her chair and bit the corner of her nail.

"I mean grown up fun."

Allie pushed away from the table to open a box of crackers and passed them to him. He shook his head and waited. "I'm really busy and don't have enough time to sleep, let alone have fun" she stated, annoyed that she felt the need to defend herself. Annoyed that she sounded like Sister Margaret who never took any time for fun. The cracker stuck to the roof of her mouth like sawdust, so she took a long drink of tea and returned the box to the counter.

"Want to go out with me tonight?" he asked. She started to choke on the cracker and he stood to pat her on the back. "You okay?" he asked.

She nodded, took another drink, but spilled tea down the front of her sweater. When he passed her a towel, she blotted the stain. He placed his hand over his mouth and she knew he hid a smile by the amusement that danced in his eyes. "I have a big project I'm working on for school and a test to study for." It was the perfect opportunity to tell him about her plans to become a nun. *Tell him.* Ryan followed her into the living room as she pointed to the stack of books and papers spread on the desk. "There's my fun."

"Sounds to me like you're much too serious. I managed to get through college and have fun doing it." His eyes sparkled with mirth and she could only imagine the hidden meaning. He stood at the door and watched her so intensely she had to remind herself to breathe. "Maybe another time," he hinted.

Allie was certain there wouldn't be another time. Certain he'd already come to the conclusion she was the biggest geek ever. Certain she couldn't risk seeing him again because he sent her mind wandering. Like how would it feel to hold his strong hand? Or what if he held her close so she could discover exactly what it felt like to lose herself in his strong arms.

She shook her head to clear her mind and stood in the open doorway to watch him walk to his truck. "Thanks for the bike," she called out and didn't understand why she felt the sudden impulse to stop him.

Ryan folded his arms across his broad chest, leaned against the truck and winked. "My pleasure."

Allie gulped and shut the door. Even though she closed her eyes, his easy smile lingered in her mind. Her heart rate was up a notch or two, so she leaned against the door to compose herself. She wasn't sure what had happened, but she felt more alive than ever. The tea stain on her sweater stuck out like a flashing light and she covered her face with her hands and groaned.

She made a face at the papers stacked throughout her apartment. "Fun," she snorted and found herself looking out the window in time to see his truck disappear around the corner.

* * *

The following week, whenever Allie thought of Ryan, a funny rumble would settle deep in her stomach and she'd bury herself further into her tasks to block him from her mind. The last image of him leaning against his truck was particularly difficult to shake. His broad shoulders and long muscular legs left a lasting impression. The hardest thing to forget about him was the way he looked at her as if she was the only person around for miles. Her mind usually reasoned in logical measures. All she had to do was pretend he didn't exist. But, the fascination she felt for him wasn't logical.

Just the other morning in class when she should have been writing notes during Professor Kendall's lecture, she imagined how it would feel to kiss Ryan's smooth lips, which always held a hint of a smile, or run her fingers along the strong line of his chin to discover the texture of his five o'clock shadow.

What possessed her to dwell on such thoughts? Was it because he was the first man to make her senses come alive? She folded her arms, determined to drive him from her mind.

Whatever had her hormones in an uproar would pass. After all, she had no intention of seeing him again.

She inhaled deeply and stared out the library window as frozen rain hit the pane. She attempted to convince herself that the weather was the cause of the hollow ache in her chest, not the thought of never seeing Ryan again.

Lisa Vetrano, her student assistant, looked up from the computer. "What are you thinking about, Allie?"

Allie frowned and glanced at the clock. "I was wondering how I'm going to get home."

"My mom's driving Jessica and Kara back to St. Ives. We can give you a lift on the way."

"That would be great."

Allie had given the girls crayons and stickers to keep them busy until story hour and she watched Kara help Jessie outline a picture. Allie smiled. "It's so good to see Jessie playing with another child."

By six-thirty, only three other children had arrived so Allie gathered the small group to begin story hour. Midway through the session, the kids started to fidget. It was clear they needed more activity, so Allie closed the book and signed instructions to play a game of Simon Says.

* * *

Ryan had debated whether or not to drop by the library to see if Allie needed a ride home. It was impossible to get her out of his mind, even though she'd made it clear she wasn't interested in seeing him again. But, he found himself standing in the entrance of the children's section at the library.

His gaze rested on Allie. Her hair fell in soft curls past her shoulders and she wore wire-rimmed glasses. Her smile was bright and she appeared relaxed as she played a game with the kids. She wore a plaid kilt and navy sweater with matching tights. If he didn't know better, he'd think she was the student rather than the teacher.

As he watched the interaction between Allie and the children, he wished he had his camera. Not a word was spoken, other than through sign language and mouthing the words for those who read lips. He studied Allie with the five small children and it was obvious how much she enjoyed her work.

When the game was over, one little girl pulled on Allie's sweater and signed something. Allie nodded, took the book the child held and motioned for the kids to sit in a circle.

Ryan found himself mesmerized by the communication he did not understand, but could easily follow. Watching Allie, he saw a relaxed, confident side she hid well. She appeared open with the children in their private world. Yet, around him she was reserved and uneasy. When the story time ended, each child said an affectionate goodbye to Allie and her helper. He noticed how comfortable she was with the mothers, but the moment one of the fathers approached, she stepped back and sent up an immediate barrier. Ryan longed to know why.

Allie and her assistant laughed as they straightened tables and chairs and set books on a cart while two little girls put crayons into a box.

When Allie saw Ryan approach, her laughter faded and she frowned. Then he caught a flicker of excitement flash in her eyes before she sent up the shield and turned to gather books from the tables. He knew that coming to see her wasn't a mistake. She might want him to think she's not interested, but that one flash of hope in her eyes told him otherwise.

"Hi, Allie."

She faced him, her face flushed and her smile forced. "Hello," she murmured as she pushed the cart into a chair, which caused the books to slide to the floor.

He detected a faint groan as she picked up the books and he leaned over to help, wishing he didn't have this effect on her.

"With the weather so bad, I thought you'd like a ride home," he said, stacking the books back onto the cart.

The young assistant walked over and signed to Allie.

"This is Ryan Harper," Allie said. "He's on your Uncle Mike's softball team." In the process of tucking a stray curl behind her ear, she knocked her glasses askew. "This is Lisa Vetrano, my assistant."

"Hi, Lisa." Ryan smiled and refrained from adjusting Allie's glasses.

"Hello," Lisa said, then signed something that caused the color on Allie's checks to deepen. Lisa laughed and walked over to help the girls with their coats.

"What did she say to you?" Ryan asked.

Allie averted his gaze. "She thinks you're cute." When he laughed, she pointed to a chair by the door. "You can have a seat over there if you'd like. I'll be finished in a few minutes."

Ryan opened a newspaper and tried to concentrate on the sports section, but found Allie much more interesting to read. Once or twice their gaze met, but she'd look away.

He liked the way she watched him when she didn't think he noticed. So what if she said she didn't want to date. His gut reaction told him otherwise. Besides, he couldn't do a damn thing about the unspoken connection between them. He wanted to find out what made her tick. He wasn't sure why she fascinated him, he hardly knew her, but he wanted to learn everything about her.

When she approached, she covered her uncertainty with a shaky smile. A little girl held her hand.

"This is my student, Jessica," Allie signed and spoke out loud. "This is my friend Ryan."

Jessie watched Allie's lips and hands form the words. She didn't look up, but she waved. Allie knelt down and buttoned the little girl's coat and helped her slip mittens into place. "I'll see you in the morning, Jess," she signed.

Jessie waved and ran to the door where Lisa waited with another little girl.

"Cute kid," Ryan admitted.

"She's my first official student," Allie said with a smile. "I'm graduating next month, so I'm pretty much on my own."

Ryan opened the door and they stepped outside. "Do they need a ride?" He nodded to Lisa and the girls.

Allie shook her head. "Lisa's mom is driving them home."

They stood under the awning. "I'm parked over there." He pointed through the freezing rain.

Allie was the first to dash toward his truck and slipped on the sidewalk. By reaching out to steady her, he pulled her close. So close he could feel her uneven breathing. Light from the street lamp shone down and a flash of lightening reflected in her eyes. Or was it fear? She had no idea how close he came to crushing his mouth over hers until the wall between them crumbled. She stepped away and opened the door.

As he started the car he turned to face her. "This reminds me of the night we met." He sensed her wariness and kept his voice light.

"I . . .I don't expect a ride home every time the weather's bad." She stared out the window and practically hugged the door.

"I don't expect to be here each time," he answered, fighting to keep the edge from his tone.

There was silence for several seconds. "I'm sorry," she said. "I didn't mean to sound ungrateful." She turned to look out the window once more. "Why did you come?"

He stopped the truck in front of her apartment. "I wanted to see you again." He noticed the death grip she had on the door handle. "To ask if you wanted to go out this weekend."

"I can't."

"Do you have a boyfriend?"

She shook her head. "I've told you I don't date, but you keep asking."

"You said you're too busy, but I'm sure you can take a night off once in awhile." He went on before she shot him down. "We can go out as friends."

"You're very persistent," she said and crossed her arms.

"I'm used to getting my way." His gaze met hers and the edge around her softened as a hesitant smile touched her lips.

"You make it sound so easy."

"What's so difficult? How about Saturday night at seven-thirty?"

She opened her mouth, he was sure she'd say no. "All right," she answered and looked at him with huge uncertain blue eyes.

He swallowed hard and resisted the urge to touch the smoothness of her cheek. "I'll see you then." He watched her race to the building and when she stopped at the door to wave, his heart lifted.

Chapter Three

*A*fter her morning session with Jessica, Allie followed the irresistible scent of cinnamon to the rectory. She leaned against the doorframe and her heart swelled at the sight of the rectory housekeeper, Maria Giovanni, glazing warm rolls with icing.

Maria was short and stocky, but possessed an energy someone half her age would be hard pressed to match. She wore a simple cotton shift and her long silver braid was coiled into a plump bun at the nape of her neck. Her olive complexion and dark eyes were as warm as espresso. When she spoke, her words were heavily laced with an Italian accent.

"Umm. Smells good," Allie said and walked around the large farm table to embrace her long time friend.

"Mio caro." Maria laughed and opened her stocky arms.

"Maria," Allie said and kissed Maria on the cheek. "It' so good to see you."

Maria held her at arms length and clucked her tongue. "You need to eat." She pulled Allie to the counter and placed a cinnamon roll on a plate and poured milk into a glass.

"These are the best," Allie mumbled and licked the warm icing from her fingers.

"Why you stay away?" Maria asked. "I save you meals and you never come."

"I've been busy," Allie said and took a sip of milk. "I'll visit more often when school is over."

"You too skinny," Maria scolded. "I stop by your apartment and we cook together, si?"

Allie nodded. "You're welcome any time."

"Tell me what new."

Allie met Maria's gaze. "Not much. You know, work and school." She dragged her finger along the plate to scoop up the last drop of icing.

"You hide something," Maria scoffed. "I know when you pretend it nothing."

"I met someone," Allie confessed in a whisper, as if ashamed.

"Multo buono, caro." Maria's face beamed with pleasure. "Why not happy?"

"All of a sudden I'm not sure what I want. He confuses me."

"Una piccolo confusion `e buona per lei." Maria's deep, infectious laugh brought a smile to Allie's lips.

"You lost me," Allie said.

"You so organized, caro." Maria beamed. "A little confusion good for you."

Allie stared out the window in time to see a pair of robins land on a cedar bird feeder. "He's not like anyone I've met before."

"Buono, Alicia. I meet him soon?" Maria grinned.

"We'll see." Allie rinsed off the dishes and hugged Maria. "Thanks for breakfast."

"We'll see, eh," Maria mimicked. "Don't be stranger, Alicia."

Allie wasn't due at the library for several hours, so she waited for Sister Patricia in the science room and flipped through a magazine to keep her mind off her date with Ryan. Even though he skirted the issue with the guise of friendship, it was a date, plain and simple.

"Hi, Allie," Pat called out as she breezed into the room to set a stack of books on the desk. "I'll be right with you."

Allie closed the magazine and watched Pat outline a formula on the blackboard. Her thick brunette hair fell to her chin and her almond shaped brown eyes cast an exotic air to her appearance. She was taller than Allie and kept in shape by taking daily walks around the grounds. Although her license stated her age at forty-two, she appeared years younger. She was Allie's closest friend. "What's up, kiddo?"

Allie fidgeted with her watch. "I have a date tomorrow night," she grumbled. "I was hoping for some advice."

A broad smile brightened Pat's face. "Well, isn't that something?" She set down the chalk and rubbed her hands together. "Why do you want advice from me?"

"I don't know." Allie ignored the humor. "I know you dated before you became a nun."

"What about the kids on campus? It's been a long time since I dated."

"Please help me," Allie pleaded.

"You look as if you're going to a funeral." She leaned across the desk to punch Allie's arm. "A simple date shouldn't be so painful."

"I wasn't interested in dating, but this guy won't take no for an answer." Allie stood and began to pace in front of the desk. "Besides," she said. "I like him."

"Why does that makes you so uncomfortable?"

Allie turned to face her, annoyed with the twinkle she saw in Pat's eyes. "I don't want to like him." She frowned when Pat burst into laughter. "It's the last thing I want," she reemphasized and chewed on a nail.

"Girl, it's exactly what you need. Is he cute?"

"I guess." Allie shrugged.

"Which means he's gorgeous."

Allie attempted to stifle a smile, but it was too late. "He really is." She beamed as she eased into the chair. "We've agreed to go out as friends." She saw the frown on Pat's face, but continued. "I have no intention of getting into a serious relationship."

"So what do you want to know?"

"I don't want to make a fool of myself." She stood to pace again. "Heaven knows why I agreed to this date."

"Oh, come on," Pat said with a gleam in her eyes. "Just act naturally and you'll be fine."

"Acting naturally is the problem," Allie said. "I've never done anything like this before. When I'm around him I turn into a first rate klutz. I don't know what to say or how to act."

"Oh, dear. It sounds more serious than I thought." Pat continued to smile. "Lighten up, Allie. Go crazy. Have some fun for a change."

Allie nodded her head and swallowed hard at the thought of going crazy with Ryan.

"Where are you going?"

"To dinner and a movie."

"What are you going to wear?"

"I don't know." Allie groaned when she looked at the sensible sweater, khaki slacks and loafers she wore. "Will you help me pick something out?"

Pat rolled her eyes and checked the time. "Meet me here in an hour. We can go shopping in Grand Bay."

"Thanks." Allie smiled and hurried to the door. "You're a life saver."

* * *

All Allie wanted to do was catch up on some sleep, but the racket outside was making it impossible. She lifted the edge of the blanket to check the clock. It was almost noon, which meant she'd only slept a few hours after studying all night for finals. Another loud thump had her off the couch and peering out the window.

She saw a young woman carry a box from a rental truck into the apartment next door.

Allie stumbled into the kitchen and while a fresh pot of coffee brewed, she rested her head on her hand at the table and closed her eyes.

The noise wasn't going to stop, so she gave up hope of going back to sleep, got dressed and carried two cups of coffee outside.

Her new neighbor walked out of the apartment and stopped when she saw Allie. "Hi." She smiled over the empty boxes she carried. "I'm Holly Kiefer."

Allie held out a cup of coffee. "I'm Allie Weston." She looked around and didn't see anyone helping. "You need a hand?"

"Thanks," Holly said. "I only have to move these boxes from the truck. My furniture was delivered yesterday."

Allie studied her new neighbor. Her shiny, black hair was blunt cut past her chin and her eyes were a vivid green. She was tall and slender. Even moving boxes, she looked like she belonged on the cover of a fashion magazine. Allie wanted to disappear into her apartment to fix her hair and change clothes, but the end result still wouldn't compare to Holly Kiefer's striking beauty.

"Thanks so much for your help," Holly said as they carted the last of the boxes into the apartment. "Let me fix you something to eat."

"Thanks, but I have to study for finals."

"Then have something to drink," Holly insisted as she refilled the empty coffee mugs. "What are you studying?"

"I'm finishing my degree in early childhood education for the hearing impaired. What type of work do you do?"

"I'm a registered nurse. Next week I start a new job at Bayside Hospital," Holly said. "Actually, I'm starting a new life."

"Are you from out of town?"

"I'm from the Detroit area. When I was a kid, my family used to vacation in this area. So, after a messy divorce, I couldn't think of a better place to relocate."

Allie watched a worry frown cross Holly's brow. "I hope things work out for you here," she said and gathered the mugs. "If you need anything, I'm right next door."

$$* * *$$

Allie thumbed through fashion magazines for hairstyles and fashion tips. Why she was going to so much trouble when she didn't want to get involved with anyone was a mystery. Her mouth dropped open when she came across an article that listed ten tips to make your man hot for only you and she shut the magazine. What was she getting into? Why couldn't she be honest and tell Ryan about her intentions of becoming a nun? Why did her pulse race at the thought of never seeing him again?

She sighed when the answer shouted in her brain. She wanted to be with him. Maybe Sister Margaret was right. Maybe she wasn't cut out to become a nun.

She wiped her damp palms against her shorts and stared at her reflection in the mirror. It's not like she needed to change her goals. This thing with Ryan wouldn't last long, because he'd get the message soon enough and move on without her. She might as well enjoy it while it lasted.

She became frustrated when her hair didn't turn out like the picture in the magazine. She bit her nail and started to pace. What did she know about looking snazzy for a date?

She changed into her new outfit, but still felt like something was missing. Then she thought about her neighbor, grabbed her makeup and hurried next door.

When Holly opened the door, she was talking on a portable phone and motioned for Allie to enter.

"What's up?" Holly asked as she disconnected the phone.

"I have a date tonight and wondered if you could help me get ready."

Holly frowned as her gaze analyzed Allie from head to toe. "What time's your date?"

"In an hour," Allie said.

Holly grabbed her by the wrist and hauled her to the bathroom. "We'd better hurry."

"Is it that bad?" Allie asked.

"Let's say you need some finishing touches." She plucked one of Allie's eyebrows.

"Ouch!" Allie shrieked.

"Lot of touches," Holly mumbled. "Haven't you been on a date before?"

Allie scrunched her face as Holly continued the torture. "I lived at St. Ives with the nuns until two months ago. I was never interested in dating," she said. "Until now."

Holly raised an eyebrow and plugged in a curling iron. "Well, you came to the right place."

Holly curled Allie's hair and applied makeup. "Don't over do it," Allie fretted.

"Have a look," Holly said and unplugged the curling iron.

Allie studied her reflection in the mirror and touched her hair. "It looks so natural. I was worried I'd look like a clown." She smiled, pleased with the results. Her hair was fluffy and stylish with just a hint of curls. "You'll have to show me how you did this."

"Now, what are you wearing?"

Allie smoothed the new black slacks she wore. "This?"

Holly rolled her eyes. "Do you like this guy?"

Allie nodded. "I guess."

Holly pulled Allie into the bedroom and rummaged through her closet. "You're shorter than me, but I have a great little dress that should work. Here it is."

"Little is an understatement," Allie muttered. "I can't wear that." She pointed to the low cut of the neckline and skimpy hemline.

"It's all the rage." Holly pulled the sweater over Allie's head.

"Really, Holly," she protested. "I'm nervous enough without having to worry if something vital is covered."

Holly narrowed her eyes at Allie's plain cotton bra and pointed to the black slacks. "Those have to go, too."

Allie shrugged. "What's wrong with these?" "It looks like you were dressed by the nuns."

"Actually, Sister Pat and I bought this outfit a few days ago," Allie admitted.

"Exactly." Holly shook her head. "I can see we have our work cut out for us. How's this?" she asked, holding a black sweater dress.

"Better," Allie admitted.

Holly slipped the dress into place. "Put these on," she instructed.

Allie stared at a pair of silky black hose and stylish black leather boots and once she was dressed, Holly closed the door to reveal a full-length mirror. "You look wonderful."

Holly continued to fuss with Allie's hair as she stared in the mirror. "Who's that?" she muttered.

Holly laughed and splashed on some perfume aptly named *Shattered*. "This should render him helpless."

Allie's gaze met Holly's in the mirror. "I'm not sure that's the effect I'm looking for."

Holly held out a pair of gold earrings. "These will look great on you."

Allie shook her head. "I don't have pierced ears."

Holly's eyes opened wide. "Besides my great-grandma, you're the only other woman I've met who doesn't have pierced ears. I'll take you to the mall next week and we can take care of that." She smiled, and Allie felt an instant connection between them. "Maybe you can get a tattoo to liven up your appearance." Holly pulled down her tee shirt to reveal a small butterfly tattoo above the purple lace of her bra.

"I don't think so."

"Come on." Holly laughed. "Guys go crazy over tattoos in discrete places."

"I can just image Sister Margaret's reaction if I show up at St. Ives with a little number like that." She laughed at the thought. "Thanks for everything, Holly."

Holly stood in her doorway. "I expect a full report tomorrow."

By the time Allie was back in her apartment the slight bit of confidence she'd experienced with Holly shriveled to self-doubt. She bit her nails and paced. By seven-thirty, she'd changed her mind and was ready to cancel the date.

When she heard a car door shut, she leaned against the wall, shut her eyes and ignored the knock at the door. If she didn't make a sound he'd go away and this ridiculous charade would end. As if faced with one of life's biggest challenges, she squared her shoulders and with a shaky smile, opened the door.

"Hi, Allie," Ryan said. The dimple at the side of his mouth deepened with the slightest smile.

She could listen to his deep, soothing voice for hours. She shook her head to clear her thoughts. "Come in," she murmured.

Allie hung his leather jacket and almost bumped into him when she turned around.

He was dressed in khaki slacks and a deep chocolate polo, which accented the warmth in his eyes. He wore popular attire she'd seen countless other men wear on campus, but never had noticed how broad other men's shoulders appeared. She swallowed hard when his dark eyes twinkled and she clasped her hands together to keep from devouring a nail. She exhaled a slow, shaky breath and placed her hand over her stomach to ease the bundle of nerves.

He cleared his throat, but didn't step away. "You look great," he said and continued to watch her. "Smell nice, too." She regretted wearing Holly's perfume when he closed his eyes and inhaled slowly.

"Thanks," she said and inched away to pick up a newspaper from the couch. "Here's the movie section."

"You seem a little nervous," he said. "Is something wrong?"

She eased onto the couch. "Me? A little nervous?" she asked and opened the paper to search for the theatre guide. "I'm fine." When the sports section caught her eye, she glanced up. "Are any of your articles in here?"

Ryan sat beside her and flipped the page to his piece on a high school baseball game.

Allie read the article and smiled. "I like your style." She felt her smile fade when his dark intense eyes studied her.

"Good, because I like your style, too," he said.

Her breath caught in her throat when he leaned close so she buried her face in the movie guide. "What do you want to see?" she asked, as the sections of paper slid from her lap to the floor.

He smiled as if he took delight in the turmoil he created. "It doesn't matter." He picked up a book on sign language from the coffee table. "Tell me why you decided to learn sign language."

It was silent for several moments and her heart thudded against her chest. "As a child, I was mute for a few years. I learned sign language at St. Ives." She held her breath as he watched her. "I've never shared that with anyone before." She wanted to run as far from him as possible, and as if he sensed her withdrawal, he set the book aside and covered her hand with his. Curiosity shone in his eyes, but he didn't speak. Allie watched a slight crease between his eyes deepen.

"Sign something," he coaxed.

She slowly used her hands to form words.

"You have beautiful hands," he said. "Except the way you torture your poor nails."

"Bad habit," she said and folded her hands in her lap. "Don't you want to know what I said?"

He nodded. "Tell me."

She repeated the message with sign and spoke the words. "Thank you for everything you've done."

"My pleasure." Allie resisted the strong urge to reach for him and frowned, confused by the intensity of the attraction that lured her to him like the tide at dawn. When she saw something more than curiosity in his dark eyes, her heartbeat quickened. She placed the paper on the couch next to him. "You pick," she said in a forced, calm voice.

He read the titles out loud, rejecting most of the selections. "I heard this one was all right." He read the movie log line about a romantic comedy.

"It sounds good to me."

Ryan looked at his watch. "We'd better go. It starts in twenty minutes."

He held Allie's coat as she slipped it on. She smiled when he held the door and almost giggled when he opened her car door. How could such simple acts cause her heart to swell?

She scowled on the drive to the theater, upset with her body for rebelling against her thoughts. Not only was he handsome and confident, but also a gentleman. She tried to think of one thing she didn't like about him. She'd just have to concentrate and find something so despicable it would be easy to walk away and forget they'd ever met.

The movie paralleled their fledgling relationship. The female lead wanted to remain friends and the male wanted more than friendship. Through a series of comical and touching events they finally fell in love. Allie narrowed her eyes at Ryan, suspicious he'd picked the movie on purpose in order to send a subtle message.

At dinner, the warmth from the candlelight enhanced the mellow glow she felt from one glass of wine.

"Tell me about your work, Ryan." She thought her grin was a bit lopsided, but didn't care because she'd rarely felt so relaxed.

"What do you want to know?" He started to refill her glass.

Allie covered her glass with her hand and laughed. "That's all for now. You don't want me to get silly."

"You're much too serious." His deep voice resonated. "I'd like to see you a bit silly."

She rested her head on her hand. "Tell me why you decided to become a reporter."

"I was at the University of Illinois on a full baseball scholarship when I slid into second base and tore the tendons in my right knee to shreds." He grimaced, as if it were still painful. "The injury forced me to get my priorities in order. I love sports and photography so I combined the two and majored in journalism."

She wanted to know how others coped when their lives were suddenly thrown into a tizzy. "Didn't it make you angry to have your plans changed so abruptly?"

He shook his head. "I believe things happen for a reason. It turned out perfect because I love what I do. Besides," he said with a twinkle in his eye. "I wouldn't have met you."

The relaxed sensation slipped away when she thought about things that happened for a reason and their chance meeting. "What do you photograph?" She reached for her glass and nearly tipped it over.

A slight quirk hitched at the corner of his mouth as he steadied the glass. "I spend most of my free time photographing a pair of nesting eagles."

"How exciting."

"If I'm patient, it can be. Want to join me sometime?"

She thought of several reasons to decline, but found herself nodding. "I'd like that."

Ryan thanked the waiter when dinner was served and Allie picked at her food, afraid she'd spill the entire plate of fettuccine on Holly's dry-clean–only dress.

"Don't you miss your family and friends?"

He nodded. "We get together as often as we can." She watched the fine lines at the corners of his eyes soften. "I have two younger brothers and a sister and tons of cousins."

"Tell me about them."

"My parents own an apple orchard, cider mill and gift shop back home in East Branch. I'm the oldest of four. My brother, Matt is starting his own architecture company. Jake just graduated from the Coast Guard Academy and my little sister, Emily is a senior in high school."

Candlelight flickered and caused his eyes to sparkle with warmth. "What about your family?"

She lowered her gaze to avoid the questions in his eyes. "I don't remember much about my family," she said. "I've lived at St. Ives since my parents died when I was ten. The nuns are my family."

Ryan set down his fork and caressed her hand. "I'm sorry."

She pulled away. "There's no reason to feel sorry for me." Her tone was short even though she knew he hadn't meant to be patronizing.

"I didn't mean. . ."

"I'm sorry," she interrupted. She missed the warmth of his touch, but stopped herself from taking his hand. "I get a little defensive about my past. People think I'm a freak because I was raised by nuns."

He frowned. "I don't think you're a freak."

When she looked into his eyes she saw compassion, not pity. Why didn't he just make a jerk out of himself so she could end this fruitless relationship?

"I'm not Catholic," he said with reservation.

She smiled. "I wasn't either until the nuns got a hold of me."

"Well, that's one barrier out of the way." He continued to watch her, and judging by the slight frown across his forehead, he was just as confused about the circumstances as she. It was the perfect opportunity to tell him about her plan to become a nun, but instead, she wondered why the dark brown of his eyes lightened just a shade and how his face became impossibly irresistible when he smiled.

He pushed away his empty plate. "I told some friends I'd try to meet them at a bar across town. Do you want to join me?"

She hesitated, but decided she wasn't ready for the night to end. "Sure."

* * *

Mac's Sports Bar and Grill was noisy and crowded. Not sure just how sheltered her life had been at St. Ives, Ryan held Allie's hand to guide her toward the back of the bar. "Let me know if this is too overwhelming," he shouted.

"I can handle it," she answered.

"What?"

"It's okay." She turned toward him the same instant he leaned close and smashed her nose against his chin.

"I'm sorry," he said.

She rubbed the tip of her nose and he saw color spring to her cheeks as a bright smile crossed her face. "You must think I'm such a klutz."

"You're the most beautiful klutz I know, especially when you smile."

The color deepened on her cheeks and when she began to bite her nail, he took her hand and brought it to his lips. He watched her eyebrows lift in question, but she didn't pull away.

"Hey." Mike walked over and nudged Allie. "It's good to see someone finally got you out on a date."

Allie smiled as Ryan guided her into a chair and sat next to her as Mike passed them a pitcher of beer. "Do you want to play a game of darts?" he asked.

Ryan turned to Allie. "It's up to you."

"I'll only play if you don't laugh." Her sweet smile hinted of shyness. He clasped his hands together to keep from drawing her close and crushing his mouth against hers to discover exactly how sweet. Instead, he showed her how to throw darts.

Allie gave it a shot and they laughed when she missed the bulls-eye by a mere fraction.

"Beginner's luck," Mike muttered.

"Good shot," Ryan said. When she threw the next two darts to double her score, she jumped up and down like a child.

"Allie?"

Ryan turned to see a tall brunette walk toward them.

"Hi, Holly," Allie said and turned to Ryan. "This is my neighbor, Holly Kiefer. This is Ryan Harper and Mike Vetrano."

"Nice to meet you," Mike said.

"Same here," Holly acknowledged and turned to Allie. "Come over and let me buy you a drink. I'm meeting some of my new co-workers," she shouted and pointed to a table near the window.

Allie nodded and when Holly walked away, she tilted her head toward Ryan. "I'm wearing her perfume."

"I like her already." Ryan smiled deeply.

Mike stepped over to Allie. "Who was that?" he asked.

"She moved into the apartment next to me yesterday."

Mike raised his eyebrows and searched the bar until his gaze rested on Holly. "Interesting," he said and stepped back to take his turn.

* * *

It was late when Ryan drove Allie home. "Did you have a good time?"

"Yes, I did," she admitted. "Thank you."

"What are you doing tomorrow?"

He detected a faint catch in her breath. "I need to study all day."

"Can't even take a break to go for a bike ride?" He stopped the truck in front of her apartment.

"I don't think so." Allie opened the door and hurried up the walk, but he matched her steps until they were at her apartment door. She turned and bit at a nail. "I enjoyed this evening, but I don't think we can see each other again."

"Why not?" Ryan felt the sting of her words. "I'm not asking for a lifelong commitment." He saw her cringe.

She met his glance and once more a storm brewed in her eyes. "I don't know," she whispered. "I wish it were different, but. . .I can't do this."

"Do what?" He searched her face for answers that were veiled by her uncertainty.

"You can't understand. It won't work." She stepped inside, closed the door and left him standing alone.

Ryan hesitated before he pounded on the door. "Allie, I can't believe you don't want to see me again. Tell me what's wrong."

The door opened a crack. "You are the most persistent person I've ever met." Her chin jutted out and her luscious mouth was closed in a tight line.

When her face clouded with uncertainty he fought the urge to hold her. "I'll be over tomorrow afternoon so we can go for a bike ride." He shut the door before she could decline and as he backed away, he scratched his head and wondered for the hundredth time what made her tick.

* * *

The next afternoon, Allie sat on the front porch step and smiled when Ryan parked his bike near the porch. She'd been waiting for him, as much as she refused to believe it was possible.

"Had your fill of studying?"

Allie searched his smile for a hint of mockery, but found only warmth. "Yes, I have. A bike ride is exactly what I need." She sat on her bike. "Want to ride by the lake?" she asked.

"Sure," he said. "Lead the way."

They parked the bikes and walked along the shore. She couldn't remember the exact moment he took her hand and she stared at their interlaced fingers. It seemed so natural, felt so safe and it scared her to pieces.

She guided him to a path overgrown with weeds that led to the lighthouse.

Inside, he followed her up the circular staircase. "How long has this been abandoned?" His voice echoed in the room at the top of the stairs.

"I'm not sure. The priests used to run the lighthouse, but it hasn't been used for years."

In the control room, Ryan wiped the dirty window with the sleeve of his sweatshirt until there was a clear view of the lake. "It's great," he said. "I wish I had my camera." He pointed to rusted beer cans on the floor. "Does anyone else come here?"

She shook her head. "Those have been here forever. This is private property on St. Ives grounds." Allie sat on the counter. "I've spent a lot of time here," she admitted, not certain why it was so comfortable to share her private world with him.

He sat beside her and took her hand. "It's a great place."

A small flutter in her chest caught her by surprise. "Just so you know, I was seriously thinking of becoming a nun." She watched the way his eyebrows lifted a mere fraction, the only indication of his surprise, but he remained silent. "Sister Margaret doesn't think my heart is into becoming a nun." Allie looked over the vast blue of the water and watched a tiny sailboat skim along the horizon. "She sent me away from St. Ives a few months ago to live on my own before I make the decision."

Ryan moved closer and she looked away, suddenly feeling a stifling closeness in the small room. "You used past tense when you said you wanted to become a nun," he said, searching her face.

"Did I?" she whispered. He was so close she could feel the warmth from his body.

"Does that mean you aren't sure what's in your heart?" His voice was rich with tenderness.

Allie's gaze fell to the firm line of his mouth and becoming a nun was the furthest thing from her mind. When a slight smile brightened his face, she knew her thoughts were obvious. She stepped off the counter to leave, but he caught her arm.

Surprised, Allie swung around. "I don't know why I told you." She pulled free and ran down the stairs.

"Allie," he called and caught up to her on the beach. "Why are you angry with me?"

"I'm not angry." Her words were choppy and winded from running. "I thought I knew exactly what I wanted until I met you. The plans I made were neat and orderly. Now I don't know what I want."

Ryan drew her close in a strong, protective embrace and she relaxed against him. "I'm glad you're confused," he whispered, his breath warm against her ear. "You can't take a road map and plot out your life. Sometimes there are detours."

She lifted her gaze and held her breath as his eyes brimmed with tenderness. "You'd be smart to walk away," she said, but bit her lip, dreading the thought.

In response, his arms tightened around her. "We'd both be smart to follow our hearts."

Chapter Four

*A*llie closed the text book she'd been reading, rubbed her tired eyes and stretched to ease her stiff muscles. A protesting grumble from her stomach was the first reminder she hadn't eaten a bite all day. Knowing she was long overdue for a trip to the grocery store, she didn't bother to open the fridge and as she spread peanut butter on a cracker, the door bell rang.

She tucked stray curls into a lopsided ponytail and groaned. Company was the last thing she expected. She smoothed the frayed wind pants she wore and a sweatshirt that was long overdue for the rag bag.

"Alicia," an impatient voice called followed by another bang on the door.

"Maria." Allie grinned as she unlocked the door.

"What take so long?" Maria grumbled and carried two grocery bags into the kitchen. "We make Chicken Cacciatore for la cena," she announced and held up two bottles of wine. "With Chianti."

"You only brought two bottles?" Allie laughed and helped unpack the groceries. "There's enough here for a feast."

Maria uncorked the wine and found two glasses in the cupboard. "We start with this," she said and filled the glasses.

Allie put her arms around Maria's shout frame. "What a nice surprise," she said.

"Caro." Maria smiled and brushed the hair from Allie's face. "I'm never far away."

"I know." Allie nodded and began to chop the onions Maria passed her way.

"How's il suo amore?" Maria inquired while she searched through the cupboards.

"Pans are in the oven." Allie pointed while she wiped onion tears on the sleeve of her sweatshirt. "If you mean Ryan, he's not my love and he's fine."

"Ryan." Maria sounded the name. "When I meet him?"

"Soon," Allie promised and sipped the wine. Before long the pungent scent of simmering garlic, onions and spices filled the kitchen. Allie placed a hand on her stomach and bit into a breadstick.

"While this cook, you change." Maria clucked her tongue. "What if suo amore comes over? You scare him."

"He's not my love," Allie repeated, but self-consciously smoothed her hair. "We don't have plans tonight, but I would feel better if I freshened up. Do you mind if I take a quick shower?"

"No, mio caro. You go."

When Allie came into the kitchen she closed her eyes and inhaled. "It smells so good. I'm half starved." She swept her hair into a twist, but stopped when she entered the kitchen to find Maria passing a glass of wine to Ryan.

"Ryan," Allie said. "I wasn't expecting you."

"I was on my way back from a soccer game and thought I'd check to see how you're doing."

Maria raised her glass and winked. "I like il suo amore," she said with a grin.

"What'd she call me?" Ryan asked.

Allie covered her lips with her fingertips. "She thinks you're nice," she said and glared at Maria. She noticed an empty bottle of wine. "I can see the two of you have been getting acquainted."

"Maria invited me to stay for dinner." Ryan's warm gaze met hers before he lifted a lid from the pan on the stove. A billow of steam floated to the ceiling and he inhaled deeply. "Man, this smells unbelievable."

Allie crossed her arms and watched Maria toss the salad while Ryan placed garlic bread on a baking sheet. Her heart filled to the brim with an unfamiliar sense of bliss. Something so strange and wonderful also drove a flare of foreboding through her thoughts. She frowned and placed her hand on her chest, as if to shield her heart from doubt.

Ryan's gaze met hers and the bright twinkle in his eyes faded just a bit when he stepped over and slid his arm around her waist. "What are you thinking?" He skimmed his fingers across her cheek and the cozy gesture brought tears to her eyes. "What is it?" he asked.

Allie blinked back unwanted tears. "Must be the onion," she whispered as he drew her close.

* * *

Allie didn't regret spending most of her free time with Ryan, even though she suffered a few sleepless nights to complete the final draft of her dissertation.

How could it be possible to change her dreams so quickly? Would she regret her decision in time, all because one person made her heart dance with a joy she'd never known? She struggled with her tumbled emotions every hour of each day. She fought with her conscious for having a weak heart that could falter so easily off course. It was difficult to admit how much she cared about Ryan and more baffling, how much he cared about her. He actually cared about her. She could tell by the way he watched her and how the strong bond forged between them. He wove a magical, wonderful spell around her and she embraced it with open arms. She was also deathly afraid of where it would lead. Would she string him along and in the end make her decision to take the vows after all? Or worse, would he grow tired of having to deal with her fragile emotions?

At the library near closing time, she searched the seat by the front entrance where he often read the paper as he waited for her shift to end. She looked up and there he was. Wasn't it exciting how she felt his presence before she saw him? Their gaze locked and her heart fluttered as she held her breath.

"Your young man is here, Allison," Mrs. Carson informed her.

"I know," Allie confided and felt heat rise to her cheeks. *Your young man!* Who would ever have thought she'd hear those three words? Her heart danced as she stamped the last of the book cards.

She lingered in front of the mirror by the lockers, fussing with her hair and makeup before rushing to meet him.

"Hi." His low baritone settled over her like a soft caress.

"How was your day?" she asked as he held the door.

"It's not over yet. I have to finish an article that's due first thing in the morning." He placed his hand at the small of her back to guide her to the truck. It was a simple gesture, but it was enough to send Allie's head spinning.

She looked at the bright stars while Ryan placed her bike in the bed of the truck.

Next to her, he leaned against the truck and followed her gaze. "There's nothing more spectacular than the evening sky." He placed his arm on the truck behind her and without giving it any thought, she leaned close to him. "There's a spot I go to up north where the stars are ten times this bright. You'd like it."

She turned to him and watched the patterns of light dance in his dark eyes. "I'd like to see it sometime."

"I'm going to try to get some shots of the eagles next weekend. Want to tag along?"

"I'd love to." She'd fret later for agreeing so spontaneously, but the desire to be with him overpowered all other options.

The scent of spiced soap and after-shave penetrated the cool night air and Allie closed her eyes to reel in the aroma. Warmth radiated from his body, even though they barely touched. Just standing next to him sent her nerve endings into high gear. She opened her eyes and her cheeks flushed warm when his smile deepened, as if to mock her.

With his arm wrapped around her, he pulled her against him and together they shared the magic of the star-filled sky.

* * *

On her way back from a bike ride to the lake, Allie saw Holly at the mailboxes.

"Hey, Allie," Holly called and sorted through her mail. "I ran into Mike Vetrano at the hospital. He asked me out."

Allie unlocked her mailbox and pulled out a stack of mail. "Did you say yes?"

"Of course," Holly scoffed. "He's pretty hot."

"Maybe I could give you some fashion tips." Allie laughed as they walked to the apartment building.

"That would be interesting," Holly said.

Inside her apartment Allie poured a glass of juice and looked through the mail. One letter caught her attention. The lettering appeared to be written by a child. She opened the envelope and unfolded the letter. It was a photocopy of a newspaper headline which only read. . . *IS CHILD HEIRESS. . .*

Allie frowned at the childish print on the envelope and read the message again. What could it mean? It made no sense at all. It must be a mistake or some sort of joke, so she folded the note, tucked it into a drawer by the stove and opened her book to study.

She scanned several paragraphs before she realized she couldn't remember one word. Dread settled over when her gaze rested on the drawer next to the stove and her pulse began to race.

* * *

I opened my mouth to speak, but couldn't utter a sound as I walked through a hallway toward an open door. Piano music played a light classical tune. People crowded the room, but I couldn't see their faces.

When the music stopped, I heard the low hum of voices. I didn't understand the words, but heard the sound of soft weeping.

The scent of perfumed candles and flowers and decay wafted through the room. A coffin draped in pale roses stood in the center and I covered my mouth to stifle a cry.

The mourners turned to face me and parted as I approached the coffin. My hand trembled when I reached to touch a single rose.

The crowd closed in around me and I backed away, toward the open door. I ran through the large room, through the hall and outside to the gardens. I slipped on the soft, damp soil, and tumbled down a small hill, soiling my pretty new dress. At the top of the hill, a crowd had gathered and my heart thudded so hard against my chest. As I hid in the garden, I wept silent tears because I knew my life would never be the same. Ever.

* * *

With a gasp of breath, Allie sat up in bed and wiped the tears from her cheek. She hugged her knees and rocked herself for comfort. The only sound in the room was her anxious breathing.

"No," she whispered. "Not again."

* * *

The next morning, Ryan was touched when Allie opened her door and fell into his arms.

"I'm glad you're here." Her voice was soft, but tense. Her unusual display of affection caught him off guard and he frowned when he saw worry lines mar her delicate face. "I just made a pot of coffee," she nodded toward the kitchen.

He poured a cup and looked at the stack of papers and books spread over the kitchen table. "How's the paper coming?"

"Slow," she said. Her hand trembled as she started to bite her nail.

"What's wrong?" he asked and reached to smooth a curl from her face. She glanced at him and he detected fatigue in her cloudy blue eyes.

"I didn't sleep well." She closed her eyes and rubbed her temple. "I have the start of a migraine." She was dressed in flannel pajama bottoms and a sweatshirt that hung on her petite frame. Her hair was pulled into a ponytail, but loose golden curls strayed everywhere. She resembled a lost little girl. "I haven't had a migraine in years."

Ryan led her to the couch. "You'll feel better if you get some sleep." He returned from her bedroom with a blanket and tucked it around her.

"Last night I had a dream I haven't had since I was a kid." Her eyes fluttered open, the uncertainty as clear as the stars on a cloudless night. "Will you stay awhile?" she whispered.

Nothing short of a tidal wave could move him. He wanted to kiss away the deep furrow from her brow. "Of course I'll stay." He sat next to her and a lump formed in his throat when she rested her head on his lap and placed her cold hand in his.

He ran his fingers along the side of her face and soon her body relaxed. There was no doubt in his mind she was hiding something. She was scared, yet she wasn't ready to confide in him.

He watched the steady rise and fall of her breathing and knew she was asleep. He twirled a soft curl around his finger as the desire to protect overpowered all other thoughts. A light sigh escaped her lips. He knew how difficult it was for her to confide in him. What little bit she'd revealed was a huge step. He wanted more. Damn, he wanted it all, but would have to be content to wait for her to share her secrets at her own pace.

"You don't have to face your nightmares alone," he whispered. At the same instant her fingers curled around his when he touched her hand, something wrapped around his heart.

* * *

Holly held two cups of steaming coffee and entered the apartment when Allie opened the door. "Looks like you could use some of this." She passed a mug to Allie. "Are you all right?"

Allie wrapped her hands around the mug to savor the warmth. "I studied late," she explained and ran a hand through her tangled hair.

"I came over to see what time you wanted to leave for the big game."

Allie frowned. She'd forgotten their plans to meet Ryan and Mike at their softball game. "I don't think I can make it."

"What do you mean?" Holly followed Allie into the kitchen.

"I have to study for finals."

"You've been cooped up in this apartment all week. It's not healthy." Holly marched into Allie's bedroom and gathered some clothes. "Get dressed. I'm not leaving without you."

Allie bit her nail. "How long is the game?"

"You'll have plenty of time to study later." Holly sat on the couch and sipped her coffee while Allie got ready.

"Better dress warm," Holly called out. "I swear it's going to snow."

Allie applied makeup in an attempt to cover the drawn out look of fatigue. She zipped her winter coat and reached for the knit hat and mittens from the closet shelf.

When they arrived at the ballpark, the game was already in progress. She sat next to Holly on the cold metal bleachers and scanned the field for Ryan. She didn't know the first thing about baseball and felt foolish when she asked Holly which position was shortstop.

Holly shot her an odd look and pointed to the player between second and third base. "Ryan isn't on the field. Our team is at bat." She pointed to the batting bench. "Mike's number is seventeen and Ryan is number twelve."

The players faced the field and Allie scanned the numbers on the backs of the uniforms until she found Ryan. He turned around and searched the stands and a smile brightened his face when his gaze met hers. Allie's stomach performed the little flutter it usually did whenever she saw him. He nodded and turned back to the game.

A strong wind drove clean through her jacket as she huddled under the blanket Holly had brought.

"I gather you don't watch much baseball," Holly said as she moved closer to Allie to share warmth.

"Not really," she said, not wanting to sound like a total alien.

Holly explained the basics and Allie found herself starting to enjoy the game. When their team took the outfield, she watched Ryan. He was quick to snag the ball and his aim and throw were near perfect. She couldn't deny how great he looked in the snug uniform. Allie glanced over and found Holly watching her.

"See why I like sports?" Holly's grin was wicked. "By the way, that was a double play Ryan just threw into."

When Mike was at bat, Holly stood and placed two fingers in her mouth and whistled. "Come on, Mike," she hollered. He swung and missed and Holly muttered an oath. On the next pitch, he hit a line drive for a double. "Ryan's up next." She pointed to the warm up circle.

A thrill traveled through Allie when Ryan stepped up to the plate. The score was close and there were two outs. He took a ball for the first pitch. The second pitch was a low strike and he shared a few choice words with the umpire. On the third pitch, Allie held her breath and stood when the ting of the metal bat resonated through the air. She yelled when he ran past first base. The ball sailed toward left field fence as he rounded second. The crowd stood and cheered when he crossed home plate. She laughed when Holly slapped her on the back.

By the time the game was over, Allie was hooked on softball. When they met the guys on the field, big flakes of snow were falling.

"It was a great game," Allie said as they walked to the parking lot. She started to shiver and Ryan put his arm around her.

"You must be freezing," he said and brushed flakes of snow from her cheeks.

"Want to join us at Mac's for dinner?" Mike called out from his car.

Ryan turned to Allie. "It's up to you."

"I really can't." She shook her head. "Finals are next week."

"We'll take a rain check," he shouted and nodded toward Mike and Holly. "It looks like they're hitting it off."

"They make a nice couple," Allie agreed. "Why don't you go with them?"

"I can meet them later," he said and dusted snow from the windshield of his truck.

A pristine blanket of snow covered town when he pulled his truck into the parking lot of a Chinese Restaurant. "I'll grab something for dinner."

* * *

They settled in Allie's dining room and dug open the cartons of food. Ryan passed her a fortune cookie. "I always read my fortune first," he confessed and grinned like a little boy.

Allie cracked open her cookie. "What's yours say?" she asked.

"*Get ready, good things come in bunches.*"

"Hmm," she mumbled and read her fortune out loud. "*Answer only what your heart prompts.*"

He watched her as they ate. "What is it?" she asked. "Do I have chow mien on my chin?"

"No." He laughed. "I was waiting to hear what your heart prompts?"

Allie set down her fork, the meal forgotten and moved to the window. Ryan stepped beside her and turned her to face him. "What's wrong, Allie?"

Her gaze rested on the kitchen drawer and she closed her eyes. "I don't know." It was true. She didn't have a clue why the dream and her migraines had returned. "I'm not sleeping." She pressed against him when his arms tightened around her. "Maybe after school is over next week I won't be so edgy."

He cupped her chin and lifted her gaze to meet his. "Something more than school is bothering you." A frown creased his brow when a sob caught in her throat. She wouldn't cry, certain the flood gates would open and she'd never stop. "You're shaking," he whispered. "Would you tell me if something was wrong?"

She closed her eyes and rested her head against his chest. With his strong arms around her, she could almost forget the note and the dreams. He was safe, not a ghost from her past. She never asked for anyone like him to come into her life, never asked for any part of a relationship. But, she ached from wanting him.

"I'm here whenever you want to talk." He stroked the back of her neck with his fingertips.

Reluctantly, she stepped back. "I know."

At the door, Ryan turned to face her. "Promise me you'll get some sleep."

She held his hand, fighting the urge to ask him to stay. "I'll try."

His gaze lingered on her lips and Allie struggled with the temptation to kiss him. He was so close, the desire of wanting him was so strong.

He opened the door. "I'll stop by tomorrow."

Allie straightened the collar of his jacket. "You don't need to check on me."

"It's not a matter of needing to," he narrowed his eyes and brushed his knuckles against her cheek. "It's a matter of wanting to."

* * *

After Ryan left Allie's apartment he couldn't shake the image of the haunted look in her eyes. If she wasn't going to tell him what was wrong, then he'd just have to find out for himself. He turned into the office to see if he could find something about her in the article Craig had mentioned at the bar.

At his desk, he switched on the computer and began to search back articles about St. Ives. There were several pieces about charity benefits for the school and its rich history. Then he came across an article written the previous year about the special talents of a student teacher for emotionally troubled hearing-impaired children. The interview was with the head mistress, Sister Margaret Collins. Ryan clicked the print button. Sister Collins raved about Allie's work, but gave little information about her personal life, other than she'd lived at the institution since she was ten years old.

Ryan stared at the screen. Allie told him she couldn't remember much about her life before she came to St. Ives, but she'd have to remember something before the age of ten.

He folded the article and shut down the computer. Maybe a chat with Sister Margaret might shed some light on the reasons why Allie had such serious commitment issues.

He drove to Mac's Bar and wondered if he was getting into something over his head. Allie was a complex person with deep seeded secrets. But, when her sad beautiful face flashed through his thoughts, he knew he was hooked and didn't have the choice to simply walk away.

* * *

The sun was warm and healing against Allie's skin as she raced to visit the sisters at St. Ives. She'd just finished her last exam and in a few weeks she'd graduate. She felt free and excited it was finally over.

She stopped at the chapel to say a prayer of thanks and ran toward the school office to find Sister Margaret.

Allie smiled when sister glanced up from the work on her desk.

"Allison, dear,I was just thinking about you," she said.

"I hope it was something good," Allie said with a half smile.

"It's always good when I think of you." Margaret stepped from behind the desk to brush a kiss on Allie's cheek. "What brings you by this time of day? Aren't you usually in class?"

"I'm done!" Allie exclaimed. "That's what I came to tell you."

Margaret glanced at the calendar. "How can that be?" she questioned. "I must've lost track of time."

Allie twirled in a circle. "I'm really done," she repeated as if it were just beginning to sink in.

"I'm proud of you." Margaret smiled at Allie. "This calls for a celebration."

Allie was never comfortable with the idea of being the center of attention. "Please don't go to any trouble."

"Trouble, indeed," Margaret said with an indignant grunt. "This is special. We'll invite the sisters and priests and your students, of course." She reached for a pencil and started to jot notes. "Sister Celeste makes the grandest cakes." She peered over her glasses at Allie. "Might there be someone special you want to invite?"

Allie recognized Margaret's ploy. "Maybe," she answered.

Margaret grinned. "Sister Patricia told me about your date." She paused and waited for Allie to continue.

Allie turned away. "If there was someone, and I'm not saying there is, I'd be crazy to bring him here so everyone could fuss over him."

"Oh, now aren't you the smug one?" Margaret smiled. "Do you really care for him?"

Allie sat on the corner of the desk. "I do care about him." Her tone grew serious. "I just don't know what I'm going to do about it."

Margaret placed a reassuring hand on Allie's shoulder. "You'll figure it out."

Allie frowned and felt the sting of unshed tears. "I wish I was so sure."

"Now that you're graduating, we need to go to the bank in Grand Bay to activate your trust," Margaret said. "I know how you feel about it, but it's your money."

Allie shook her head. "I don't want to know anything about it." Her words were sharp and she walked to the door. "I'll activate the trust and give it all away to charity. I don't want a penny."

* * *

It was still dark on Sunday morning, but Allie lay awake and waited for the alarm to sound. She wasn't able to fall back to sleep after a terrifying dream. Every time she closed her eyes, she saw images of faceless people chasing her through the gardens.

She finally gave up trying to go back to sleep and crawled out of bed to shower. The warm steam did little to calm her and her hands shook so, it was difficult to button her sweater. Ryan wasn't due for another hour so she started a pot of coffee.

While she styled her hair, an image reflected in the mirror. Allie couldn't breathe, frozen with fear. When the illusion held out her hand, blood dripped from its finger tips.

Allie dropped the brush, covered her mouth to stifle a cry and backed out of the room. She needed to breathe, to get away. She ran to open the front door and her hand fumbled on the lock. When she threw open the door, a muffled sob escaped when she ran smack into Ryan's open arms.

* * *

While Ryan drove, he kept a worried eye on Allie. She'd fallen asleep during the first few miles of their trip to Rock Falls, Michigan. Knowing she was exhausted, he kept the radio low. His heart sank, wondering why she was so shaken when he'd picked her up. Was it another dream? He'd held her at the door for several moments, but as usual, she wouldn't tell him what troubled her.

When he touched her hand, her eyes opened wide and she sat upright. Her gaze darted to him, then outside. "Are we already here?"

"We've been on the road over two hours. You slept the entire time."

Allie flipped down the sun visor and looked into the mirror to wipe sleep from her eyes.

He reached for her hand and felt her stiffen. "School is over now. You should be getting more sleep." She stared down at his hand, but said nothing. "Are you ready to see some eagles?"

She nodded and stepped out of the truck. "Is this to heavy?" he asked as he helped her into a backpack.

"It's fine," she said and picked up a small cooler.

"I'll carry the rest," he said. "I'm used to lugging all this gear by myself."

The wind kicked and she pulled up the hood of the down jacket he'd brought for her. "Are you going to be warm enough?" He sized up her jeans and lined hiking boots.

"I'm never warm enough," she admitted.

Ryan led the way along a path through a thick of trees. He pointed out the difference between deer and elk tracks imprinted along the trail.

"Did you study conservation?" she asked.

He shook his head. "I've always been interested in wildlife," he whispered as they approached a rustic blind which consisted of tree limbs set tee-pee style against a stand of trees. "I grew up in the country and there was always an injured or orphaned animal to care for. My dad used to take us into the woods for hours where we'd search for animal tracks and signs of wildlife."

He set the gear into the blind and motioned for her to come inside. "I bought my first camera when I was eight. Been taking photos ever since."

Allie watched him with a slight frown. "What was it like growing up in a big family?"

Ryan helped Allie remove the backpack. "We fought like crazy, but loved each other all the more. Still do." He searched her face and realized how different their back grounds were. "Was it lonely not having brothers or sisters?"

Her smile turned wistful. "I was never alone at St. Ives. There were always kids coming and going. The hardest thing was forming a bond with someone and then they were adopted or returned to their family." Her voice trailed off.

"That might explain why you have a hard time letting me get close."

"Maybe," she confided and averted her gaze.

Ryan fought with the uncontrollable urge to take her into his arms and help her face the hurt and loneliness she fought so bravely to hide. She shivered and he unpacked a blanket to wrap around her shoulders. He smoothed another blanket on the ground and set out binoculars and his camera gear. Allie searched the sky above the trees. "What are we looking for?"

He pointed to a clearing in the distance and adjusted the binoculars. "See the broken tree with the dead snag? You'll see the nest there." He held the binoculars for her.

She scanned the trees and he watched a smile touch the corner of her mouth. "It's so big," she exclaimed. "It looks like nobody's home."

"They probably took off when they heard the truck." He detected her disappointment. "If we're patient, they'll return." He poured two cups of coffee from a thermos and passed one to her along with a bagel.

"Thanks." She closed her eyes to inhale the steam rising. "You thought of everything."

"It can get pretty boring out here." He adjusted the focus on his camera. "Sometimes I never see anything worth snapping, but you never know when you might get the shot of a lifetime." He sipped coffee and refrained from kissing the tip of her nose that was pink from the cold. "Waiting for that shot keeps me coming back." He looked across the horizon.

The sun peeked out from behind a cloud and teased them before it disappeared. The lake had thawed, but the water was gray and choppy.

She searched though the binoculars. "Do you think there are eggs in the nest?"

"There might be. The eggs incubate for over a month and the eaglets make their first flight two and a half months after hatching. It takes the parents three years to raise the chicks."

When Allie turned to him, he placed his fingers to her lips and nodded toward the sky as an eagle circled over head and squealed a warning cackle. Allie uttered a surprised sigh. She beamed and watched Ryan as he snapped several pictures while the eagle landed in the nest.

"That's the male. I call him Henry." He chuckled when she suppressed a laugh. "The female is Grace."

"How do you know they're the same pair from last year?"

He watched for the other bird. "Eagles mate for life and they return to the same nest each year. I named them after my grandparents who've been married over fifty years."

When he glanced at Allie her eyes were bright. "Your family means a lot to you," she whispered.

He nodded and pulled her close. How he wanted to tell her what was on his mind, but he knew she wasn't ready.

"Look, Ryan." Allie nodded. "It must be Grace."

Ryan followed her gaze and grabbed his camera in time to snap a series of the second eagle, a fish clutched in her talons. Through his zoom he could see drops of water dripping from the fish.

"Isn't she magnificent?" Allie watched through the binoculars.

"You must be my good luck charm." Ryan smiled and snapped several pictures. "I'll have to bring you back when the eaglets hatch."

Her face glowed with excitement. "Promise?" she asked.

Her smile faded when his gaze lingered on her lips and he wondered if she'd run screaming out of his life forever if he kissed her. Although she made a poor attempt to act touch, she was so fragile he was sure she'd crumble at the slightest touch. It wasn't worth the risk. Not when he was just starting to gain her trust. He swallowed hard as desire charged through him like an electric shock. Her stormy blue gaze searched his and he cleared his throat. "You bet," he said, his words strained, even to his own ears.

Chapter Five

Ryan lost track of time as he worked in the dark room he'd set up in the laundry room of the house he rented. He selected two prints of the eagles as a graduation gift for Allie. He smiled as the photos came to life in the developing solution and recalled the wonder on Allie's face while she watched the eagles. One was a shot as Henry landed in the nest and the other was of Grace with a fish clutched in her talons.

Wouldn't Allie be surprised when he showed up at her graduation? She hadn't invited him. He knew she wouldn't, for she guarded her privacy intensely, but it bothered him all the same. He'd been open and patient with her from the start. He gave her the space she needed to come to terms with her past, but it seemed like she was buried alive. She couldn't move forward or back.

He studied the prints once more, satisfied with the quality and attached them to the drying line with just enough time to get ready for his softball game.

One thing was for certain, Allie needed to take the next step.

* * *

Allie dressed for the graduation ceremony with mixed feelings. She didn't want to attend, but the Sisters had gone to so much trouble she couldn't disappoint them. She slipped on a yellow flowered dress the sisters had given to her for the occasion. Allie loved the feel of the cool, sheer material as it floated around her. It fell beneath her knees and showed off her new yellow sling-back heels. She looked herself over in the mirror and decided that even Holly would approve.

When she heard a car stop in front of her apartment, she raced out to meet Sister Pat. "You look great," Pat called when Allie joined her in the car.

"Thanks to you," Allie said.

"Well, a girl has to look good on her graduation day."

At Symphony Hall, Allie slipped into her cap and gown and found her seat for the ceremony. After the speeches and awards and musical program, she crossed the stage to receive her diploma and smiled when her personal cheering section called out her name.

Afterwards, she met the sisters and Maria outside on the grassy entrance where Sister Pat snapped several pictures.

She smiled when Sister Celeste handed her a beautiful bouquet of flowers she recognized from the garden behind the rectory. "Father Kotalski won't miss them," Celeste whispered with a wink.

Allie's laugh faded when she saw Ryan approach and a tense knot formed in her stomach. She refused to connect the feeling with guilt because she hadn't told him about the ceremony. Or was it the fit of his dark gray suit tailored to perfection? Dark sunglasses shielded his eyes, but she braced herself for a confrontation by the firm set of his jaw and his rigid smile.

"Congratulations, Allie," he said and reached for her hand. "Surprised to see me?" He lifted the sunglasses and shot her a withering glance.

Allie clamped her mouth closed when she realized it hung open. "I didn't want anyone to make a big deal out of this," she explained and searched the faces of the nuns who were regarding

Ryan with varying degrees of interest. It was Sister Margaret who was the first to speak.

"You must be Allison's friend," she said.

He nodded and held out his hand. "I'm Ryan Harper."

"This is Sister Margaret, Sister Patricia, Sister Celeste and you know Maria," Allie said.

"We're having a celebration at the church. I asked Allison to invite you," Sister Margaret said. "I hope you can attend."

When Ryan narrowed his eyes at Allie, she wanted to crawl into the nearest hole. She flashed him an apologetic smile and informed sister she'd forgotten to ask him.

Margaret frowned. "Well, it's not too late," she said and gathered the nuns and Maria. "We hope to see you there."

Allie waited until the ladies disappeared before she faced Ryan. There was fury in his eyes and his jaw was set as if to keep from telling her exactly what she deserved.

"I didn't want it to turn into a party. I hope you understand." She tried to keep her voice convincing and reached for his arm, but he stalked away.

"Ryan," she called out. She was no match for his long strides, especially in her new sling-back heels. "Please don't be angry."

At his truck he opened the door for her, but remained silent. She jumped when he slammed the door and swallowed hard as he stormed around the truck to the driver's side.

Silence only added tension to the short drive and Allie didn't know what to say. He stopped the truck in front of the church and didn't turn to her.

"Won't you come inside?" she asked.

When he glared at her, she could handle the anger, but not the disappointment that simmered in his eyes. She'd do anything to take the hurt away. "I. . .I'm sorry," she stammered and cringed when he balled his fist and hit the steering wheel.

"Damn it, Allie," he shouted.

She looked down, ashamed for the way she'd treated him. After all he'd done for her. After all he meant to her. "I. . .I didn't want. . ." Unwanted tears stung her eyes.

He grasped her arms and pulled her to face him. "Can't you see how much you're tearing me apart?"

"I'd never do anything to intentionally hurt you." She blinked back the tears when his anger dissolved to frustration, then to sadness as he cupped her chin tenderly in his strong hand.

"Don't you know how much I care?"

She looked into to his for a split second and saw a future. A future she'd never dreamed possible. Reacting on impulse, she slid her arm around his neck and pulled him to her until his warm lips touched hers.

The kiss began soft and tender, yet Allie thirsted for more, as if she'd crawled out of the desert and he was a cool drink. He crushed her against him and pressed the kiss deeper until a soft cry escaped her and she pulled away, confused and shaken.

Ryan rested his head on her forehead, his breath fast and irregular. "What am I going to do with you?" he whispered.

"Come to my party," she pleaded. "Please."

A tender smile flashed across his lips as he brushed the trace of a tear from her cheek.

* * *

Ryan didn't know what to expect from a party hosted by nuns, but one thing was certain, he wasn't prepared when an elderly priest passed him a small flask. Ryan smiled, thanked the priest and took a swig. At first the liquid went down smooth, but when it hit the back of this throat it transformed into a fireball. Ryan's eyes welled with tears when he started to cough. "Holy Jesus, Father, what is this stuff?" he sputtered as the priest slapped him on the back.

Wrinkles on the weathered face of the priest deepened when he cackled and his clouded blue eyes sparkled with delight. "It's me own brew, lad. What do you think?"

Ryan choked on a laugh as he tipped the flask and braced for another assault.

Father slipped the flask into the sleeve of his robe. "No sense in upsetting the sisters," he muttered and plastered on an innocent smile as Sister Celeste approached.

"Father McLaughlin. Have you met Allison's friend?"

Father placed a hand on Ryan's shoulder. "We're just getting aquatinted, aren't we lad?"

Ryan swallowed hard to soothe his burning throat and nodded. "Indeed we are."

A group of musicians started a catchy tune and a younger priest escorted Allie to the center of the room.

When Sister Celeste walked away, Father McLaughlin uncorked the flask and nodded to the dancers. "Will you look at Father Kotalski trying to impress young Allison?"

Ryan watched Allie dance and waved off the offer of another drink. "No thanks. I'm beginning to feel as if I were the one dancing."

Father McLaughlin gazed at the dance floor with a faraway look in his eye. "Just looking at the bonnie lass does me heart good."

Allie's face was flushed with excitement and merriment shone in her eyes as she whirled to the Irish tune. Slender and graceful, she revealed a confidence Ryan had not yet seen. The rhythm of the music pulled at him with each step she took. The burning sensation in the pit of his stomach spread throughout his body and he knew the cause was not the whiskey alone.

Ryan choked down another belt of the priest's private stock. "I know exactly what you mean," he muttered.

"It's good to see the lass happy for a change." A dreamy expression softened Father's face. "If I were fifty years younger, I'd not think twice about turning in me collar and giving you a run for your money over that one."

Ryan joined in the revelry and clapped in time to the expert steps of the pair. They clogged and reeled in perfect time to the music of the fiddle and it was obvious they'd performed this routine before.

He glanced at the faces of the spectators and saw pride and love while they watched Allie laugh and curtsy when the dance ended. This was indeed her family and he'd never feel sorry for her because she wasn't raised in a traditional household. Ryan joined in the applause and shouted for an encore until the priest led Allie to him.

"Oh, no you don't." He shook his head. "I don't dance," he protested, but realized it was useless as the crowd began to chant. Someone dimmed the lights and a slow melody filled the air. He forgot about the crowd the moment he looked at Allie. Her laughter was winded. He'd never seen her look so beautiful and it took every bit of restraint to keep from kissing her again. Her eyes sparkled when a slight smile touched her lips. His throat tightened from wanting to tell her how much he cared, but was certain she'd retreat and he'd lose what ground they'd made so far. So instead, he was satisfied to hold her in his arms while a room full of strangers smiled with approval as if they could see the obvious.

His throat still stung from Father McLaughlin's brew and his heart threatened to burst from the effects of holding her. Damn. He was falling hard and all he could hope for was a smooth landing.

* * *

The next day, Allie fretted about the kiss. What had possessed her to act so impulsively? Well, maybe it wasn't impulsive, for she'd thought about kissing him so many times she'd lost count. She placed her fingers against her hot cheeks and cringed when she thought about how the kiss had left her wanting more.

She peddled the bike faster as if to do penance for her impetuous thoughts. She was late for mass and didn't think her conscience could handle disapproving looks from Sister Margaret.

Sister Celeste escorted the children into church single file and Allie rushed to help. When Jessica looked up, a slight smile brightened her eyes. She stepped out of line to join Allie, and hand in hand they found a seat.

After mass, she hugged Jessie goodbye and attempted to slip away unnoticed.

"Allison, I want to talk to you," Sister Margaret said as she rushed to greet her. Margaret locked arms with her to steer them toward the garden behind the rectory.

"What is it, Sister?" Allie asked.

"I couldn't help but notice how much you enjoyed the party."

Allie detected a twinkle in Margaret's eye. "I loved the party. Thank you for everything."

"Did your friend have a good time?"

Allie smiled, but wouldn't divulge any information about Ryan. "I'm sure he did."

"Well, good," Margaret said as she fussed with her habit. "He seems like a nice young man and it's plain to see he likes you."

"Do you think so?" Allie asked. "How do you know?"

"My lord, child, I may be a nun, but I'm not blind," Margaret huffed. "Even I can see how smitten he is with you."

* * *

Allie thought of Sister's words and hummed as she carted groceries back to her apartment and unlocked her mailbox to grab the mail.

She smiled when she discovered Ryan waiting for her at the door. She shielded her eyes from the bright sun and sighed when he moved toward her in his self-assured, easy manner. His smile was equally as confident and she inhaled slowly to calm the jitters his gaze created.

"I can't stay long," he said and took the bags from her.

She almost told him it was just was well, because she wasn't sure if she'd be able to control the pressing urge to kiss him again. "I'm on my way to cover a softball tournament."

She had trouble fitting the key into the lock. "Can you come in for a minute?"

He followed her into the apartment and she turned to face him. "Want some iced tea?" she asked. Her gaze rested on a large package he'd set on the kitchen table.

"No thanks," he said and motioned toward the table. "I brought you a graduation gift."

A small lump formed in her throat as she stared at the package wrapped in brown shipping paper. "You didn't have to get me anything."

He stepped to her. His fingers skimmed the line of her jaw and tilted her chin until it was impossible to avoid his gaze. "I rarely do anything because I have to." His touch was like fire against her skin. She wanted to step back, but her body wouldn't move. "Open it." He motioned toward the package.

Grateful for the diversion, she untied the twine with unsteady hands. He lifted the paper away and a surprised cry escaped her as she cradled one of the prints. "Oh, Ryan," her voice faltered. "They're beautiful." She glanced his way and caught a look of pride as she ran her fingers along the smooth wood frame. "You made the frames, didn't you?"

He nodded. "This one is Henry," he said while she studied the prints. "That's Grace."

"They're beautiful," she repeated. "Thank you."

He appeared pleased with her reaction. "It's good to see you smile."

She smiled again, even though tears clouded her vision. He cared enough to give her such a precious gift, made only for her. "No one has ever given me anything so wonderful."

"Never?" he questioned and set the frame aside to pull her close and lowered his head to kiss her. Her heart thudded against her chest when her lips parted as his fingers brushed the nape of her neck, traveled along her shoulders to rest at her waist. She folded her arms around his neck and her hands fisted in his hair to draw him closer. His hands tightened around her waist when the kiss ended and she opened her eyes to find a sly smile tugged at the corner of his mouth. "See what you started yesterday with that kiss?"

"You were so angry, I couldn't think of anything else to do." Heat rose to her cheeks as his eyes gleamed with pleasure.

"It worked just fine." His laugh was uneven.

When she laid her head against his chest, she discovered her pulse matched the strong beat of his heart. She didn't know how to tell him what her thoughts were because they were jumbled and crazy, but if it meant always feeling this safe and secure, she could stay in his arms for eternity.

"I have to go," he said, with a note of regret. "But I'll stop by after the tournament."

Allie's hands rested on his chest. "I'll cook dinner," she said. "Do you like spaghetti and meatballs?"

Ryan raised his eyebrows. "You bet, but don't go to any trouble. I'll pick something up."

"I love to cook. Maria and I spent hours in the kitchen together."

He brushed a light kiss on her forehead. "I'll be back as soon as I can."

Allie's heart soared as they walked outside arm in arm. He lingered at his truck to watch her for a moment and then his mouth curved with tenderness before he got into the truck.

Inside the apartment she leaned against the door and placed her hand on her chest. It was obvious they were headed for something more than a passing fling. Never had her heart's conviction to become a nun beat as strong as the desire to be with Ryan.

She hummed as she held the picture of Henry against the wall for effect. She'd borrow a hammer from Holly so the pictures would be hung before Ryan returned for dinner.

As she set out ingredients to make spaghetti sauce, the stack of mail on the table caught her attention.

One letter with childish print stood out from the rest and her hands went numb as she held it. She tossed it into the waste basket. She didn't want to read it, but while she crushed garlic, curiosity got the best of her, so she picked it out of the trash and tore at the envelope. It was another piece to the headline which read. . .*GUILTY OF*. . .

She gulped back a sob as she ripped the note to pieces and bolted from the apartment. She needed to think. To clear her mind and get a grip on what was happening.

She ran toward the lake and when she entered the control room in the lighthouse, the first sharp pain of a migraine stabbed her brain. She slid to the floor and covered her face with her hands.

Seagulls screeched their shrill, mournful call and the sound of the waves lapped against the shore. The rhythm quieted the hard pounding of her pulse.

There was such pressure in her head, she thought for sure it would explode as the wind howled through the rafters in the alcove high above the tower's peak.

"*Come with me*," a whispered voice rang through the control room. She sprang to her feet and gulped back frustrated tears when a mournful creak sounded on the hard wood planks below.

"No," her mind screamed as the words seeped through a fracture in her memory. Another creak on the steps was louder, closer and Allie leaned against the wall for support.

"Leave me alone," she cried and covered her mouth with her hand. She was truly losing her mind. She was alone in the tower of a lighthouse talking to the wind. If her head didn't pound so, she'd burst out laughing.

Instead, she sank to the floor in defeat, assaulted by a terrible sense of loss. How could she think she'd ever have a normal, loving relationship? It just wasn't in the cards for her. If she opened her heart for Ryan, then all the other ghastly memories would gush out. She couldn't let that happen.

* * *

With the last of the film rewound, Ryan tucked the roll in his canvas back-pack as he watched the losing team file into the bus. He gathered the remainder of his gear and hurried toward his truck. The game had gone into extra innings and had ended later than he'd expected. He wondered if Allie was still on for dinner so he could pick up where they'd left off.

He gripped the steering wheel as he drove to her apartment. He wasn't prepared for the way she'd responded to his kiss. Not that he hadn't thought about it every waking hour since the day she opened her apartment door when he returned her bike.

He knocked on Allie's door. It was dark inside when he checked the front window. He knocked again and when there was no answer, he reached for the knob, surprised the door was unlocked.

"Allie," he called as he stepped inside and flipped on a light switch. He checked the rooms to find the apartment empty. He followed the scent of garlic and onions in the kitchen and decided she must have gone to the store, so he sat on the couch to wait.

* * *

He jerked awake when the door opened and Holly led Allie inside and released a shaky sigh when he saw Allie's pale, tear stained face. "What happened?"

"I don't know. I just got home from work and found her sitting on the step," Holly said and looked into Allie's eyes. "Are you sick?"

Allie shook her head as Ryan took her icy hand. "Are you hurt?"

"No." Her eyes were clouded with pain and when he folded his arms around her, she pushed away.

"I'll leave you two alone," Holly said and closed the door behind her.

"What happened?"

"I don't know what's happening to me." Allie squinted at the light and held her fingertips to her eyes. Her face remained pasty white. She paced in front of him and when he moved closer, she shot him a warning glare.

"How can I help if you won't talk to me?" He clenched his fists and fought to keep his voice calm.

She whirled around to face him. Her face no longer pale but flushed with color. "It doesn't make sense," she cried and covered her face with her hands.

"Allie," he said and moved toward her.

She stepped away and hurried into the kitchen. "I can't see you anymore."

"Why?" Ryan ran his fingers through his hair and pushed away the queasiness in his stomach.

"I'll only keep hurting you."

She didn't look at him and he swore as he swung her around to face him. "Let me in, Allie. Let me help."

"I don't want your help. I want to forget," she cried and shook his hands free. "I was wrong to involve you in this."

Ryan stepped back, rocked by her words. "Is that how you really feel?" The hollow ache in his stomach intensified.

"I told you in the beginning. . ."

"Do you want me to leave?" he asked.

"Yes," she whispered.

He shook his head, desperate to clear his thoughts. "If you can't trust me enough to help, then I guess you're right."

Chapter Six

Summer fell over South Harbor like a warm, cozy blanket as if Mother Nature worked over-time one evening to open each and every bud so when the town folk woke, all the trees were in full bloom.

Allie avoided the beach as tourists arrived in droves like migrating birds.

She volunteered for extra shifts at the library and St. Ives to help cover vacations. She didn't have anything better to do, at least that's what she told the sisters and Maria when they lectured her about working so hard. She couldn't admit to anyone, especially to herself, that if she stopped moving, even for a moment, she'd think about Ryan.

No matter how hard she drove herself, her conscious caught up with her. At night, thoughts of Ryan would creep into her mind, just before she slipped into sleep. She was wrong to think her life would return to the way it was before they'd met. His absence left a hole in her heart the size of Lake Michigan and everywhere she turned she was faced with reminders of him.

After one rough, sleepless night, Allie dragged herself out of bed and outside for some air. She stared at two flats of colorful petunias Maria had dropped off and made a sour face at the sad, wilted flowers. The last thing she wanted was a reminder of how bleak her existence was in contrast to the bright blooms, but decided it would be easier to plant the flowers rather than face an eternal lecture from Maria for allowing them to fade away.

She changed into a pair of tattered shorts and a worn tee shirt and went to work.

The sun was hot and Allie welcomed a break when Holly came out of her apartment with two glasses of lemonade.

Allie placed the cold glass against her face. "Thanks, Holly."

Holly sat beside her on the step. "The flowers look great," she said, "but, I can't say the same about you."

"I'm fine."

"Mike wants to know when you're going to stop tormenting Ryan."

Hoping to wash away a tinge of guilt, Allie took a long drink. "I don't want to torment Ryan. It didn't work out between us."

Holly glared at Allie. "You can't fool me. I know you're miserable without him."

Allie shook her head. "No, I'm not." She thought she did a great job to make her voice sound convincing, but knew she failed when Holly rolled her eyes.

When Mike parked his shiny, new convertible at the curb and walked toward them, Holly gathered the empty glasses. "I'm not ready yet," she said and disappeared inside her apartment.

Mike leaned against the porch rail and examined Allie as if she was a suspect in a line-up. "How are you doing, Al?"

"Okay," she lied.

"We're going to the softball picnic if you want to join us. Ryan will be there."

"No, thanks."

"I'm all set." Holly joined them with a bright beach bag in hand and smiled when Mike kissed her.

Allie watched them stroll to the car hand in hand with their heads bent close in an intimate way and she scolded herself for allowing a rush of envy to sweep over her.

Mike opened the door for Holly and waved. "Sure you won't change your mind?"

"No, thanks," Allie called out. "Have a good time." She suppressed a sense of loss as she watched the car disappear around the corner and it took every ounce of effort to plant the remainder of the flowers.

She looked up when she heard a car door and cringed when she saw Ryan get out of his truck.

She tended the flowers, hoping he'd disappear if she ignored him, but out of the corner of her eye, she glimpsed sandals and tan muscular legs.

"Did Mike and Holly already leave?" he asked.

Allie patted dirt around the base of a flower and dug another hole. "You just missed them."

"How have you been?" The formal tone in his voice didn't mask his irritation.

Allie gritted her teeth. If one more person asked how she was, she might just break down and give them a blow by blow account of just how pathetic her life was. She carted the empty flats to the steps. "I'm just dandy."

"You look awful," he commented.

She glared at him through sunglasses. "Thanks," she said and wiped her dirty hands on her shorts.

"You should wear sunscreen," he lectured.

She touched her tender nose and his eyes danced with amusement as he brushed dirt from her cheek. She slapped his hand away. "Did you stop by just to insult me?"

Ryan continued to watch her, but the softness in his eyes was replaced by fire. "You choose to stay buried in the past," he said and followed her to the door. "You need to get over it."

Allie spun around. "You don't know anything about me."

"No kidding," he smirked. "You don't know anything about yourself." The truth hurt, but she raised her chin as he lifted her sunglasses. "Why do you set out barriers whenever I try to get close?"

She watched hurt and anger flicker in his eyes and she was so close to crying, she didn't dare speak. They were silent for several long seconds until she snatched the sunglasses out of his hand and stormed inside her apartment.

* * *

Ryan sat in a booth at Mac's bar and watched a couple seated in the next booth. There didn't appear to be a centimeter of space between them. He looked away when a stab of emptiness probed his gut and downed a shot of whiskey, in an attempt to purge Allie from his system.

It didn't help that the image of her sun kissed nose with a spatter of freckles invaded his thoughts whenever he closed his eyes. Everything was a painful reminder of her, the color of the lake, the scent of fresh spring flowers and the magical display of the stars.

He saw Mike enter the bar and felt a sense of relief. "It's about time," Ryan muttered as he looked at his watch.

"I got tied up with a routine traffic stop that turned into a past warrant." Mike raised an eyebrow when his gaze rested on two empty shot glasses lined in a row. "Looks like you got started just fine without me."

Ryan leaned back in the booth and stretched his legs under the table. "I'm doing my spring cleaning."

The waitress placed a menu in front of Mike. "I'll have a draft," he said. "Want something to eat, Rye?"

Ryan shook his head. "Just keep these coming," he instructed.

Mike glanced at the waitress. "Bring us a super nacho," he added and waited until she walked away, then pointed to the whiskey. "It won't make Allie go away."

Ryan folded his arms across his chest. "Maybe not, but it will give me a reprieve," he said and swallowed the bitter taste in his mouth with another shot. "What do you know about Allie?"

"I thought it was over between you two."

"I'm still concerned about her." Ryan shrugged. "I think she's in some sort of trouble." He saw worry lines crease Mike's brow as he leaned forward to give Ryan his undivided attention.

"Go on," Mike prompted after the waitress set their drinks on the table.

"Something from her past has her spooked."

"She's guarding something," Mike agreed. "What do you think it is?"

"I don't have a clue. I think she has flashbacks and dreams, but I don't think she remembers what happened."

Mike frowned. "My mom used to work in the office at St. Ives, I'll see if she knows anything about Allie's past."

"I'm going to talk to Sister Margaret," Ryan said.

When the nacho was set on the table, Mike dug in. "Be careful," he cautioned. "The sisters protect their own."

"What have I got to lose?" Ryan dipped a chip into salsa. "Don't say anything to Holly. Allie wouldn't be pleased if she found out I was snooping around her past."

"I won't say a thing," Mike nodded and took a long drink of beer.

* * *

School buses pulled away from the circular drive when Ryan parked his truck in the main entrance at St. Ives School. He closed his eyes for a moment, to still the pounding in his head from last night's binge. He hated to admit it, but Mike was right when he said it wouldn't make the memories disappear. He'd had a fitful night with haunting dreams of Allie.

The corridors were empty when he entered the building. He followed voices to a classroom down the hall and when he entered the room, a young girl and a teacher stopped talking.

"Can I help you?" the teacher asked.

"I'm looking for Sister Margaret Collins."

"I'm Sister Pat." A slight smile softened her serious features. "Aren't you Allie's friend?"

"Yeah, I'm her friend all right." The unpleasant sting of the sarcasm in his voice made him wince.

Sister Pat stepped to the doorway. "Sister Margaret's office is to the left and around to the end of the hall."

Ryan thanked her and followed her directions to the office. He paused outside the door, cautious about barging into the world Allie protected with a vengeance, but shook away the guilt and opened the door.

Sister Margaret turned to him with a look of surprise. "Hello, Sister," he said.

"Good morning." She set a stack of papers on the desk. "What can I do for you?"

"I'm Ryan Harper."

"I remember," she said and motioned to a nearby chair. "How's Allison?"

"I'm not sure." He eased into the chair and watched concern in Sister's eyes cloud with disappointment. "I wanted to ask you some questions about her."

She studied him with a wary frown. "What do you want to know?" Her tone reminded him of his mother when he was in trouble.

"What can you tell me about Allie's past?"

"If Allison hasn't told you, then I'm not at liberty to say."

He clenched his fists in frustration. "I don't understand why everyone who claims to care about Allie can't see how much their good intentions to protect her are causing more harm?"

Sister Margaret's expression remained cool as she rose from the chair. "Where Allison is concerned, the best approach is to leave well enough alone." As if she realized she'd revealed too much, she moved around the desk and opened the door. "Now, you'll have to excuse me. I have work to do."

Ryan placed his card on the desk. "In case you change your mind, I can be reached at this number."

Sister Margaret nodded. "Good day."

His steps echoed through the corridor as he found his way outside. Uneasiness crept over him as if he was being watched and he turned to see Sister Pat wave from a classroom window.

He stood for a few moments on the steps, hoping the bright sunshine would chase away the chill.

* * *

Allie bustled around the library, minutes before the scheduled time of her summer program. She arranged cookies and juice on a table in the children's section before the kids arrived.

She wiped away a smudge on the framed eagle picture and felt a catch in her throat. "How many babies do you have, Grace?" she whispered.

As if she expected Ryan to be seated in the chair by the front entrance, she turned in anticipation and placed her hand on her chest to soothe the ache of disappointment when she found the chair occupied by an older gentleman. She looked away when tears clouded her vision and concentrated on the summer program about endangered species of Michigan.

Bald eagles were the topic of the first session with a visit from Greg Slayton, nature expert from the nearby wildlife sanctuary and his special friend, Kawlin.

When excited voices of children echoed in the hall, Allie turned to see Sister Patricia leading three children from St. Ives into the room.

"Hi, Pat." Allie reached for Jessica's hand.

"I'm already exhausted," Pat grumbled with a slight smile.

"Hello," Jessie signed.

"Hello," Allie signed and smiled when Jessie gave her a quick hug then skipped away to join the other children.

"I'm so happy she's doing so well," Allie said.

By the time the children and parents found seats, the room was filled to capacity. She began the session with a video about eagles. A craft project followed until Greg Slayton entered the room with Kawlin perched on his gloved arm.

The kids gathered around Greg while Allie interpreted Kawlin's story. Someone had shot her and although she'd never fly again, she enjoyed her job as spokes bird educating the public about the preservation of wildlife. Allie laughed when Kawlin flapped her huge wings and the kids squealed with delight.

Afterwards, Pat and Allie straightened the room while they kept a watchful eye on Sammy, Kara and Jessie.

"It was a great program, Allison." Pat nibbled on a cookie as she cleared the refreshment table.

"I had to convince Mrs. Carson to allow the eagle," Allie admitted. "I'm glad it turned out so well."

She wiped off the tables and her heart lurched when she saw an envelope addressed to her. Allie grabbed the letter and hurried to the doorway before she ripped it open. The room twirled as she stared at the familiar newsprint that read . . .*MURDER?* Her mouth went dry and waves of nausea assaulted her as she pieced together the headline . . .*IS CHILD HEIRESS GUILTY OF MURDER?*. . .

She scanned the library, not sure what she searched for, but was certain the letter had been placed on the table during the program. "Who are you?" she whispered, but fought the urge to scream.

Footsteps sounded on the tile floor, so she folded the letter and slipped it into the pocket of her jumper.

Pat took one look at Allie and guided her to a chair. "What's wrong?" she insisted. "You look like you're ready to pass out."

Allie shook her head and closed her eyes. "It's nothing."

"Don't lie to me!" Pat scolded. "Tell me what's wrong."

Allie stood up, but the room continued to spin. "It'll pass."

Pat gathered the children and approached Allie. "Why don't you come to St. Ives for dinner?"

Allie nodded when she detected the concern in Pat's voice. "All right," she agreed and followed Pat and the children to the car.

The drive to St. Ives was quiet. Sammy, Kara and Jessie played in the back seat, and Allie closed her eyes to ease her throbbing head.

Inside the sunny kitchen at the rectory, Maria waved a wooden spoon at Allie. "Caro, you not take care of yourself," she scolded and ladled stew into a bowl. "Mangiare," she demanded. "Eat!"

Allie closed her eyes as the savory scent of vegetables and herbs caused her mouth to water. Her stomach was in knots, but rather than face Maria's wrath, she lifted a spoonful to her mouth.

After finishing her meal, Allie washed the dishes. "I love this kitchen," she said. "I want to come back."

"It not right for you here," Maria said and placed two cherry pies in the oven.

Allie saw creases deepen around Maria's eyes. "Everyone seems to think they know what's best for me."

Sister Margaret entered the room and placed a hand on Allis's forehead. "Sister Pat told me you're ill."

Allie tried to hide her irritation. "I'm not ill."

"Then why are you so pale?" It was meant as a statement more than a question. "Does this have something to do with that young man you're seeing?"

Allie didn't want to talk about Ryan. "No," she answered.

Margaret poured boiling water into a teapot and added loose tea. "Let's sit in the garden. The fresh air will do us both good."

Allie carried cups and saucers and followed Margaret to a gazebo at the far end of the grounds overlooking the cliffs. The sunset glittered on the water with iridescent lights the color of fire, but it did little to fill the empty ache in her chest.

"Tell me what's going on, Allison."

Allie reached into her pocket to touch the letter. To make sure it was real and not her thoughts gone mad. "You know me so well."

"The problem is, my dear, I know you better than you know yourself."

"Why won't you let me come back here to live?" Allie asked.

Sister Margaret patted her hand. "I'm not doing this to punish you."

Allie narrowed her eyes. "It feels like it."

"You need to discover who you are."

Allie sipped her tea. "Did you have doubts about becoming a nun?"

"Of course I did," Margaret smiled with a faraway look. "I lived a normal life. I traveled the world and even fell in love with an artist in Spain." Allie felt her eyes grow large, but she smiled at the knowing glance they shared. "All you know is this institution." Margaret waved her hand to indicate St. Ives. "It's much too safe for you here."

Allie didn't understand. Safe is what she wanted. "Why?"

"You need to learn about life before you make such a commitment." Margaret's tone softened. "You don't want to become a nun, do you?"

Allie regarded the question, knowing Sister Margaret was right on target and said nothing.

"Is that Harper boy upsetting you?"

Allie pursed her lips to keep from smiling. "He's not one of the bullies who picked on me at school, Sister. I'm no longer that child."

Sister squeezed Allie's hand. "I know you're not." Her voice grew wistful, almost sad.

Allie inhaled the warm, misty air. "I made a mess out of things with Ryan," she admitted.

"Why would you do such a thing? He seems like such a nice young man."

Allie shrugged, but didn't comment.

"I know he cares for you a great deal." Margaret's smile was tender. "In fact, he's worried about you."

Allie lifted her gaze to meet Margaret's. "How do you know?"

"He was here the other day asking questions about you."

"What kind of questions?" Allie felt her stomach rebel against the hearty meal.

"He wanted to know about your childhood before you came to live here, but I told him to ask you."

"Oh, did he?" Allie stood to set the cups on the tray. "I'd better head back before it gets dark," she said and kissed Margaret's cheek.

Margaret stood. "Pat can give you a ride if you want."

"I'd rather walk," Allie said as she carried the tray toward the kitchen.

* * *

By the time she reached Ryan's block, her cheeks were flushed from anger.

What business did he have asking Sister Margaret about her past? When she spotted his truck in the driveway, the anger had died to uneasiness. The house was dark except for a dim light. She knocked on the door and paced. She pounded on the door and chewed her nail. She stepped off the porch and looked into the front window. Maybe he went out with someone. Maybe he was with someone in the house. The thought only increased her irritation and she stomped to the door and pounded with both fists so hard, if he were anywhere in the house, he'd be sure to hear.

When she raised her hand to take her frustration out on the door once more, the porch light switched on and the door opened. Ryan stood in the doorway and for a moment Allie forgot her anger. He leaned against the doorframe, wearing jeans and a light shirt that was unbuttoned. His hair was tousled and his unshaven face made him appear mysterious, almost dangerous. He blinked against the porch light. Allie swallowed, gazing at his sculptured chest muscles.

"Hi," he said after a long moment. She'd missed the calming effect of his baritone voice.

"I need to talk to you," she managed over the pounding in her chest.

"Come in." He held the door open and she brushed past him. The room was dark except for a faint light down the hall.

"I hope I didn't interrupt anything important," she said, her muscles growing tense.

Ryan straightened scattered newspapers and grabbed two empty soda cans that he carried to the kitchen. "I'm working in the dark room and need a minute to finish."

She crossed her arms and looked around the room. A large entertainment center held a huge television, stereo equipment, and other electronics she didn't recognize. She admired framed photographs that lined one wall. There were breathtaking wildlife prints taken in every season. One in particular caught her eye and she smiled when she recognized one of the eagles feeding an eaglet.

She turned when she felt his presence and their gaze met. "Is this a recent shot?" she asked.

"I took it last week. There are two eaglets."

Allie looked back at the photo. "I wondered about them," she whispered. She felt her anger slip a notch until she remembered the purpose of her visit. She swallowed the momentary stab of tenderness and crossed her arms to face him. "Why were you asking questions about me at St. Ives?"

Ryan continued to lean against the wall and appeared so casual it fueled her anger. "I'm concerned about you," he said. "Or is it a crime to care?" The sarcasm in his voice cut more deeply than angry words.

"My life is none of your business," she declared.

"You've made that clear enough." He was at her side in two long strides and turned her to face him before she could react. "But, I make it my business when someone I care about is in trouble."

She couldn't move and cursed under her breath because he had the power to render her helpless with one touch. "I. . .I'm not in trouble," she stammered. "I want you to forget about me."

"I've tried to forget." His whispered words held a tinge of tight control. His fingers tightened around her arms when she attempted to move away. "I know you care, but can't get past whatever it is you're hiding from." Allie struggled against his grip. "Whatever it is, I'm strong enough to help you deal with it."

"I don't want to know," she cried and moved to the other side of the room. "I can't go back."

Ryan stepped closer and she moved to the door, afraid she'd reveal more. "I have to go." His expression remained indifferent, but his eyes glowed with anger. "Promise me you'll stop asking about me."

"It's not that simple." His voice was too calm, too controlled.

"You have to stop," she insisted. "Please."

Before she could open the door, she was in his arms and didn't have the desire or strength to push him away. She buried her face against his strong shoulder. He was the only thing right in her world. "I was sent away from St. Ives so I would know what is in my heart. I didn't know it would be broken." She pressed the back of her hand to her lips and gulped back a sob as a tear trailed down her cheek. "I don't remember what happened. But, I can't be with you."

"I don't believe you," he murmured against her hair. "Something from your past is keeping us apart." He kissed her forehead, her temple. "I'm not going to stop until I find out what it is." Then his mouth covered hers, hard and searching. She closed her eyes as heat from his body clouded her reasoning.

She gasped and reached for the door. "I can't do this." She saw the protest on his lips, but stepped outside before he could speak.

Before he convinced her to stay. Before more evil memories surfaced by the way he had of opening her heart and mind.

Chapter Seven

*I*t wasn't like Allison to miss church, so as soon as mass was over, Maria drove to Allie's apartment. Normally, she wouldn't be concerned, but lately Allie had been acting so distant, she wanted to know why.

It took several knocks and when Allie opened the door, Maria was forced to conceal her alarm. Her face was pale and she squinted at the sunlight. "Caro, you sick?" Maria questioned as she stepped inside.

"I was sleeping," Allie said with a yawn. "I can't seem to get rid of this headache."

"When headache come back?" Maria's tone was filled with concern or was it dread?

"A few weeks ago." Allie nodded toward the kitchen. "Should I make some tea?"

"Si`," Maria said and sat at the table to study Allie. "Are you pregnant?" Maria spoke in hushed tones as if they were in the kitchen at St. Ives and wanted to keep the conversation from prying ears.

"No!" Surprise shone in Allie's eyes and a slight bit of color touched her cheeks. "Why would you think that?" she groaned as she set the kettle on the stove.

"This about Ryan, no?" Maria stood to place a hand Allie's shoulder. "What he does to hurt you?"

Allie opened a box of tea bags. "He didn't do anything." Maria felt the tenseness in Allie's shoulders relax, as if to let down her guard. "I hurt him." Her voice faded to a whisper.

"You break him up?" Allie nodded as Maria sat at the table. "Perche?"

Allie hesitated, her eyes glazed with confusion. "Because I must be crazy," she said and plopped tea bags into boiling water.

"Don't you care about him?"

"I care about him too much." Allie set a cup of tea on the table and rubbed her temple. "But, it's better this way."

"Lei sono matto?" Maria waved her hand and uttered a barrage of Italian and although she knew Allie didn't understand, she continued. They sat in silence for several moments. "Now you both unhappy," Maria finally said.

Allie covered her face with her hands. "I never thought I'd care about anyone like this."

Maria scooped sugar into her tea. "It make me happy to see you with him. You need to do what right," Maria said and pointed to her heart.

"That's the problem," Allie told her. "I don't know what's right."

"I think you do, but you no like answers." Maria shook her head. "Stop punishing yourself, caro."

Allie uncovered her face. "I'd give anything to go back to how it was before I met him."

"Time to stop hiding," Maria shouted. "Time to get on with life."

Allie stood to pace and pressed her fingers against the side of her head. "My life was much simpler when I thought I'd become a nun and live the rest of my life at St. Ives." She stared out the window and appeared deep in thought. "That was before I met Ryan." She rested her head against the window pane. "I miss him so much it hurts so bad."

"Then you must tell him, caro."

* * *

When Ryan struck out, he cursed, swung around and stalked to the dugout. He gripped the bat to keep from throwing it. First he glared at his teammates, daring them to say anything, and then tossed the bat against the fence. He rarely struck out and when he did, it was never for a lousy pitch.

He wasn't thinking about the game. His mind was on Allie and her doomed attempt to convince him she didn't care. He knew better, which made it all the more frustrating.

He looked up when Mike joined him at the fence. "Having a rough one?"

Ryan watched the action on the field. "That obvious?" he muttered through clenched teeth.

"Yeah and you're taking your frustration out on the wrong people." Mike leaned against the fence. "Go talk to Allie and figure things out. You're both a mess."

Ryan shrugged as if it didn't matter. As if he didn't care that his life was so affected by a woman who resisted his every move. He wondered if the challenge wasn't the main attraction. Damn, if that's what he needed from a relationship than he was one sick bastard. He'd have to find a way to forget about the way she looked when she tried to tell him she couldn't be with him. She hadn't fooled him, he knew just saying it broke her heart.

He watched the final out of the inning and glanced at Mike before he grabbed his glove from the bench. "Allie wants me to leave her alone, so she's on her own to deal with her problems."

* * *

It was so dark in the house I couldn't see beyond my outstretched hands. My hands were damp and I wiped them on the skirt of my school uniform. My heart pounded as I inched my way toward the stairs and climbed each step.

The railing was cold beneath my grip and the warm polished glow of the oak wood contrasted against the shiny, marble steps.

It was so quiet, but the shrill ring of her scream still clung to the air. I was so frightened, I don't know how I gathered the courage to enter her bedroom.

A dim glow from a night-light illuminated the room just enough that I could see a movement on the bed and the shine of long blonde hair spread across a pillow. It sparkled like gold in the moonlight.

Her eyes were open, but I knew she couldn't see me. I screamed when blood trickled from her extended hand and dripped onto the carpet.

I ran from the room, toward the stairs, but stopped when I heard hurried footsteps. Then I saw him and tried to scream but couldn't utter a sound. Tried to run, but my legs wouldn't carry me.

* * *

When Allie opened her eyes, she was chilled and damp from terror. She struggled to be free from the twisted bed sheets. Above her bed, the curtains flapped from a light breeze. She shut the window and buried her face in her hands. Why couldn't she remember?

She wiped her face on the sleeve of her night shirt as the cold, dark fingers of loneliness wrapped around her chest and squeezed so tight it was painful to breathe. The whisper of Ryan's name still clung to her lips as silent tears streamed down her face. Her heart ached, knowing how much she needed, no wanted him to turn to in the middle of the night to help ease her fears.

* * *

The first planning meeting was called to order for the St. Ives Summer Festival. Allie whispered with Sister Pat during Chairwomen Edith Henderson's winded speech about a Renaissance theme for the event.

"Have you made a decision about seeing your boyfriend or not?" whispered Pat.

Allie glanced at Sister Margaret then back at Mrs. Henderson to feign interest in her speech then turned back to Pat, first making sure Margaret wasn't watching. "I'm not sure," she whispered. Pat raised her eyebrows.

Allie's mind drifted to Ryan and how ridiculous it was to blame him for memories he was not responsible for. She wanted to be with him, it was impossible to pretend otherwise.

She checked the time. Ryan would be warming up at his softball game. Before the meeting, Holly had tried to coax Allie into going to the game.

Allie grabbed the edge of her seat and wondered how much more of the meeting she could endure. She had to find Ryan and tell him how she felt. Maybe it was too late. Maybe he already figured out his life was better without her. She bit her nail, fearing she'd go crazy if she had to sit still one more second. It was a risk, but she'd been much too cautious her entire life. He was worth taking the chance.

When everyone in the room clapped, it jolted Allie's attention and she leaned close to Pat. "Do me a favor and sign me up for the food committee. I have to go."

* * *

Ryan watched the umpire and the batter, whom Ryan had thrown out at home plate, argue with a vengeance. He was ready to join the foray before something caught his attention. When he saw Allie walk her bike toward the bleachers, his mouth went as dry the sun-parched sand.

Sunset hovered over the horizon, setting the sky ablaze with fingers of brilliance more intense than the noon sun. The warm tones accentuated Allie's golden skin and caused highlights in her hair to dance with color. She wore a white sleeveless shirt and a khaki skirt. Her eyes were hidden behind sunglasses, but he knew she watched him as she parked her bike against the fence then climbed the bleachers to sit next to Holly.

The play resumed and Ryan forced himself to block nagging thoughts of why she was sitting in the bleachers looking so pretty and messing up his concentration.

He focused on the game long enough to shag a ground ball and throw the runner out at first base. He forced himself not to look toward the stands, but when he caught a flash of Allie's smile, he turned to see her share a laugh with Holly. His heart thumped when her gaze lingered on his.

The sun faded fast and she'd placed the sunglasses on top of her head. He could see the deep blue of her eyes, but couldn't read the tone of her emotions.

She had no idea how beautiful she was or how his chest tightened from wanting her. All the reasoning he'd done to convince himself he didn't care vanished like a morning fog. All it took was one look at her.

He turned back to the play when Mike hollered his name and dove for a grounder to catch the ball in the tip of his mitt. He threw the ball to second and barely got the runner out.

He glared at Allie and felt like a chump for being such a push over. Why didn't she stay away so he could stop thinking about her? This playing yo-yo with his emotions would stop. He grabbed his glove and trotted toward the bench, determined to tell her how he felt once the game ended.

When all the equipment was bagged and most of the players had departed, he walked over to where Allie stood with Holly and Mike. She looked away as he approached, but he saw her shoulders tense.

"Coming to Mac's with us, Ryan?" Mike asked as he placed an arm around Holly's shoulder.

"Yeah, I'll meet you there."

"You come too, Allie," pleaded Holly.

"No. Thanks." Allie glanced at Ryan, but avoided eye contact.

She watched Mike and Holly as they strolled toward the parking lot. Ryan said nothing while she bit her nail. The silence grew awkward until Allie turned to him. She ran her fingers through her hair to smooth the unruly curls, ravished by a steady breeze. A deep furrow marred her brow and she looked so lost, so small, it wrenched his gut. Light freckles spattered across the bridge of her nose making her seem impossibly innocent.

He clenched his hands to his sides to keep from holding her. "What do you want?" he asked with all the patience he could manage.

"I. . ." She started to pace, but he stepped in front of her to block her path.

"Damn it, Allie," he shouted. "Don't start something and then walk away." The anger he wanted to lash at her vanished when the veil in her eyes lifted, replaced by loss and pain.

"I needed to see you," she replied in a voice so soft he was forced to bend close.

His blood pressure battered against his veins and he gripped his hands into fists as he stepped away when reason told him to get as far away from her as possible. "I can't do this anymore, Allie."

A single tear trickled down her cheek as she looked down. "I don't blame you for hating me."

"Shit," he shouted more out of frustration than anger. "I don't hate you." He wanted to hold her, but instead set his hands on his hips and squared off to face her. "What do you want?"

Her hand shook as she placed it on his cheek and he fought the urge from kissing her palm, helpless sucker that he was. "I was hoping it wasn't too late for us."

Ryan reeled from the impact of her words as if he'd been slugged. He released an unsteady sigh when her gaze lifted to meet his and he closed his eyes, swearing under his breath for her to get the hell out of his life. But, instead he stepped to her.

Someone shut off the stadium lights and he blinked until his vision adjusted to the darkness. The lump in his throat prevented him from speaking.

"I'm sorry I hurt you." She gazed into his eyes with such trust. "Why won't you say something?" she whispered.

"It won't work." He sighed, drained of all energy.

She backed away, visibly wounded. "Why?"

"Because you don't know what you want." He shook his head to clear his thoughts. "I want more than friendship, Allie. But you can't give more."

"I thought you were the reason my life has been turned upside down. I thought I'd be able to forget you and things would go back to normal." She stepped forward but hesitated and her gaze, bright with expectation, met his. "I was wrong."

If she'd kicked him in the teeth, he'd have felt a hell of a lot better than knowing she was at the end of her rope without a safety net. Before he could think of anything to say or all the practical reasons not to, he pulled her against him.

"I'll understand if you've already found someone who's not a fractured lunatic like me." Her hands were pressed against his chest ready to push him away. "If it's too late, please tell. . ."

His mouth pressed against hers to kiss away any doubt and he felt the uncertainty melt away when her arms folded around the back of his neck.

The sky was bright with stars and when he looked into her eyes he saw tears that clung like tiny crystal to the tips of her lashes. "I was afraid you didn't care," her voice shook with emotion.

"Hell, caring about you was never the problem." He lowered his head, determined to kiss away the last tread of resistance that stood between them.

* * *

After placing her bike in the bed of his truck, Ryan sat in the driver's seat and pulled her next to him. She felt a thrill shoot through her like a bolt of lightning as she leaned against him.

"What now?" he asked.

Allie frowned and shrugged her shoulders. "I haven't a clue," she admitted. "I've never done this before."

"Done what?" he asked as her fingers intertwined with his.

"Well, if you don't count the time the sisters matched me up with Freddie Wiltshire for the tenth grade dance, I've never dated before." She caught a lopsided smirk on his face. "What's so funny?"

"Freddie Wiltshire? What was he like?"

"He had sweaty hands and wore braces and he smelled like the gym locker room." Allie laughed at the memory. "I didn't talk to the sisters for a week. That was the extent of my dating experience."

"Sounds serious," he teased.

Allie jabbed him in the ribs with her elbow and stopped smiling. "I bet you've had much more experience."

"I've dated before." His smile softened and his fingers stroked the back of her neck with just enough pressure to send quivers along her spine. "But, I've never felt the way I do about you." He looked into her eyes with such tenderness and Allie believed him without question.

"Do you want to meet Mike and Holly?" she asked.

He shook his head. "I'd rather be with you."

Her heart soared, but she glanced away, feeling over her head in uncharted territory. "You'll have to be patient with me when it comes to. . ." She didn't finish, grateful for the darkness, as her cheeks grew warm.

"We'll take it a step at a time," he assured her. "I'm ready to do whatever it takes to make this work."

Her hands folded around his waist and she sank against him when his soft kiss spoke of promise.

* * *

It seemed like she'd just drifted to sleep when the phone rang.

"Hello?" she said, shaking her head to clear the fog.

"Hi," Ryan said. "Get any sleep?" From the warmth in his voice, she could tell he was smiling.

"A little." Her heart rate settled and she smiled. "How about you?"

"Not a wink," he whispered. "I thought about you all night."

The intimacy of his words rocked her. Words she'd never dreamed would be spoken to her made her skin tingle with an awareness equally as new. "I thought about you all night too," she admitted.

He was silent for a moment and Allie held her breath. "I'm glad," he said. "It's raining this morning. Want a ride to work?"

She glanced out the window, there was barely a sprinkle and her smile deepened along with her feelings for him. "I'd like that."

She dried her hair and dressed so she'd be ready to spend as much time with him before work. Every moment counted. She frowned at herself in the mirror. She didn't understand what was happening about her past, but she vowed to keep it from destroying them. Nothing would come between them again.

She picked up her bag and stepped outside to meet him. When she sat beside him, he pulled her close and she savored the spicy scent of soap. He kissed her forehead and her heart soared when she lifted her gaze to discover the glow of expectation in his eyes.

"You look great this morning" he said and tucked a stray curl behind her ear.

"So do you."

He parked the truck in front of the rectory and they ran through the rain to the back door.

They entered the kitchen and found Jessica, Sammy and Kara seated at the table with Maria and Pat.

Jessie jumped out of the chair and ran to Allie. "Hi, Jess," Allie signed.

Ryan knelt down and signed something Allie had taught him and it brought a smile to Jessie's face.

"`E venire avere la colazione," Maria waved and set two more places at the table. "Have breakfast," she repeated when Ryan frowned.

Jessie pulled Ryan by the hand and signed to Allie. "Jessie wants you to sit next to her," Allie told him.

Ryan sat in the chair Jessie pointed to and nodded to Pat. "Good morning, Sister."

"Hello," Pat said and looked at Allie then Ryan. "Aren't these two beaming this morning, Maria?"

Maria clucked her tongue and served them each a stack of pancakes. "Si`," she said and patted Allie's cheek. "Multo buono, caro."

Allie smiled and searched Ryan's face. "She said it's very good."

He placed his hand over hers and beamed at Maria. "It is very good."

Pat stood and signed for the children to put their plates away. Jessie snuggled next to Allie, reluctant to leave. "I'll pick you up from class," she signed. Finally, Jessie signed goodbye to Ryan and Pat ushered them to school.

Allie began to help with the dishes, but Maria stopped her. "Go with Ryan."

"Thanks, Maria. I'll see you later."

They sat in Ryan's truck until it was time for Allie's class.

"Hopefully, it'll rain all day and my game will be cancelled so we can do something."

"I have to attend a meeting tonight at St Ives." She smiled when she saw him frown. "It'll only take a few minutes."

"Good," he said and bent to kiss her. "I intend to spend as much time with you as I can."

* * *

Allie floated through the afternoon at the library hardly remembering what she was doing from one moment to the next. She couldn't stop smiling and fought the urge from pulling Mrs. Carson into the center of the room and dancing. The thought made Allie giggle, which drew a curious look from Mrs. Carson.

"What's so funny, Allison?"

"Oh, nothing." Allie hurried to scan a stack of books.

She spent her lunch hour at the park and kicked off her shoes and lay back in the sweet grass. The morning rain had disappeared and there wasn't a cloud in the sky so it looked as if Ryan would be playing ball after all. She tossed half of her sandwich to the seagulls.

The afternoon dragged and she wondered if time away from Ryan would always seem endless. She worked on the agenda for the next wildlife session. Maybe Ryan would have photos she could show the children.

"Here's some mail for you, Allison." Mrs. Carson set the parcel on the desk and left the room. Allie stared at the thick, brown envelope and held her breath. Her fingers tingled as she opened the seal and pulled out a watch with an attached tag that read. . . *TIME TO PAY YOUR DUES. . .*

She covered her mouth to stifle a cry and lurched to her feet from the force of panic. On the entrance porch, she leaned over the iron rail and inhaled deeply, slowly to quiet her thundering pulse. Sister Margaret was the only person who knew about the trust money. Allie shook her head and tossed the watch into a trash receptacle by the door.

* * *

That afternoon, Ryan was on assignment at a sports camp for under privileged kids. While he changed a roll of film, his cell phone rang. He didn't recognize the caller's number.

"Hello. This Ryan?"

"Maria?" he asked.

"I get number from card on Sister Margareta desk."

"What's up?" he asked and sat on the bleacher.

"I help you with Alicia." She spoke low and the sound of the children's voices almost drowned out her words. Ryan covered his ear with his hand.

"Allie doesn't want me to meddle in her past." Ryan told her.

"I do this because she like child to me. She need to face past."

"I agree." Ryan rubbed his eyes. "What can you find out?"

"I look for her file."

"Alright," Ryan said and ignored a stab of guilt. "Give me a call if you find anything."

After disconnecting the call, he stared at the phone. What would it hurt if it turned out there was nothing worth investigating? Even though Allie wouldn't have to know, he felt uneasy as he turned to snap pictures of a group of kids on the volleyball court.

* * *

Ryan read the paper at the front door while Allie finished her work. She smiled when she saw him, but the delight in her eyes faded, replaced by turmoil before she looked away. It was as if she wasn't sure how to handle her feelings for him. Damn, he loved that about her. He stood when she walked toward him. Her eyes were cloudy and her smile did little to hide the worry lines etched on her forehead.

He held the door and when they stepped outside she buried her face against his chest. He led her to the truck, and even though the evening air was hot, he felt her shudder.

"What's wrong?" he asked when they were seated in the truck.

"Long day." Her voice was strained.

Ryan frowned but didn't press for answers. "I found a sub for the ball game, so I'm all yours." He took her hand and their fingers intertwined. "What time is the meeting at St. Ives?"

"We can go now. All I need to do is sign up for a committee."

"What are you signing up for?"

"The St. Ives Summer Festival."

He shook his head and smiled. "Don't tell anyone I'm giving up a softball game to attend a church meeting."

Allie rested against him and he pulled her close. "Have you been to the St. Ives Summer Festival before?" He shook his head, but watched her with good humor. "You'll love it. People come from out of state to attend. It's really big."

"Really?" He continued to smile.

She nudged him. "You'll see."

Allie held his hand and led the way through the St. Ives Elementary until she found the sign on a classroom door for the food committee. She wrote her name on a list for cooking duties. When Ryan signed his name beneath hers, she looked into his eyes and smiled as he took her hand.

"Why can't we volunteer to work the beer tent?" He pointed to a sign on a classroom door. "Is Father McLaughlin in charge of that committee?"

Allie laughed as they continued through the crowded hall and passed committee rooms for music, entertainment, parking, set up, craft show, bake sale, rides and costumes and so on.

"The entire town must be here," he exclaimed.

"I told you it's a big deal."

They stopped at the Cottage House to take Jessie out for pizza. There was a video arcade at the restaurant and Ryan and Jessie disappeared together. Allie rested her head against the booth and watched from across the room. It warmed her to see Jessie and Ryan getting along so well. She was falling hard for both of them.

Ryan carried Jessie back to the table. "She's tired, Al."

"So am I," she said as he pulled her to her feet.

At St. Ives, they handed Jessie over to Sister Celeste's care.

* * *

Once outside, Allie led Ryan to the cliff over the water. "Is there something on your mind, Al?"

She glanced at him and he caught a look of fear before it vanished. "I'm tired," she said.

"There's more to it." She looked out at the water with her eyes closed and inhaled deeply. He stepped behind her and felt her ease against him as his arms slipped around her waist. "I know you don't want to face your past, but I think it's something we're going to have to deal with or it'll continue to come between us." He kissed the base of her neck and felt her shudder.

"I won't let it come between us." Her voice rose with emotion and she grasped his hands.

Ryan swung her around so he could see her face in the moonlight. "I don't think it's something you can control."

"I promise." She lifted her chin, meeting his gaze as a single tear slid down her cheek.

"Tell me what you do remember."

"My mother's memory is vague. I. . .I'm having dreams about her lately. I see blood in the dream and someone is after me." She ran her fingers through her hair and inhaled a shaky breath. "Something terrible happened and I'm afraid it's not over yet."

"It's going to be alright, baby." He gathered her close. Her body felt stiff with tension. "I won't let anything hurt you."

Ryan was at a loss for how to help. He couldn't get a handle on Allie's problem, and it really ticked him off. Sure, he could hold her and whisper soothing words. "I'm here when you decide to tell me what's going on," he said, but felt a sinking sensation that it was going to take a hell of a lot more than pretty word to help her confront past demons.

Chapter Eight

Ryan dipped the photos in processing solution while Allie watched. "I hope they come out okay," she said and tapped her fingers against the bin.

"Relax." He smiled. "They'll be fine."

Allie laughed as a faint image came to life that captured Sister Celeste secretly snipping flowers from Father Kotalski's garden.

"Oh, look," she exclaimed and pointed to another photo of Sister Margaret, dressed in her habit with her sneaker-clad feet propped on her desk. "I can't wait to see Sister's face."

Ryan passed her a print and she stretched to attach it to a drying line. "Are you sure you want to come to Sister Margaret's birthday party?" she asked.

Ryan stepped behind her, slipped his arms around her waist and kissed the hollow of her neck. He felt her shutter as she turned to face him. "I'll be there," he promised. The close quarters of the dark room prevented her from moving away, so he took full advantage of the situation and nibbled on the tender spot behind her ear.

She tilted her head to gaze at him with the dreamiest eyes he'd ever seen. "It might be boring for you."

"You don't need to make excuses." Ryan rested his hands at the curve of her waist. "It's your family. I enjoy their company."

"I'm just protective of them." She rested her forehead on his chin. "You're the first person who thought of them as my family," she whispered.

"Speaking of families," he said. "What are you doing Fourth of July weekend?"

She shook her head. "I don't have any plans."

"Would you like to come to my family reunion?" He watched uncertainty cloud her vision as she placed her hand on her stomach. He held her hands, not giving her the opportunity to assault her nails.

"I'm not sure."

He pulled her close. "You'll be fine," he said, overcome with a rush of desire to give back everything she'd lost and more. "I want them to meet you."

Allie cupped her hand against his face. "Are you asking me to go because you feel obligated?"

"No." He kissed the palm of her hand and watched her eyes sparkle in the dim light of the darkroom. "I'm asking because I love you."

"You love me?" Her smile broadened as she traced the pocket of his tee shirt with her finger. "I don't know why you came into my life," she whispered. "I wish it could always be like this."

* * *

Maria set a large pan of lasagna on the counter while Allie hummed and set the table in the adjoining dining room. "Make sure flowers have water," Maria called out.

"I already did," Allie replied.

Kara helped Celeste write a message with yellow frosting on a cake, while Pat tossed a salad and Jessie folded napkins into fan shapes.

It was Sister Margaret's seventieth birthday and although she'd made it clear she didn't want any fuss, the party plans were made in secret.

Allie wrapped the photo album, she and Ryan had assembled, in brightly colored paper and curled an entire roll of ribbon to fashion a bow.

The door opened and Jessie ran to greet Ryan, who entered with two dozen helium balloons. He lifted the child and handed her a balloon.

"Nice touch, Ryan," Pat smirked. "Sister Margaret is going to make us do extra chores for a month."

Allie watched Ryan and Jessica hang the balloons around the dining room. The way he guided the little girl with such patience filled her heart with tenderness. "Thank you, Rye," she said.

He glanced at her and the radiance from the candles caught a glimmer of something in his eyes. Was it happiness? Contentment? She frowned, confused by foreign sensations.

He handed the remainder of the balloons to Jessie and reached out his hand to Allie.

Their hands locked and he pulled her to him. She studied the sparkle in his eyes a moment longer before she recognized the meaning as love.

* * *

Allie opened her eyes during the night, afraid to move. Something woke her. Someone was in the room. It took several moments for her eyes to adjust to the darkness. Shadows of familiar furniture seemed ominous and threatening. What had startled her awake? She didn't see or hear anything, but couldn't shake the tingling sensation that warned her she was not alone. Her heart pounded against her ribs and she held her breath, afraid to make a sound. She lay in the dark for an agonizing eternity before she summoned the nerve to get out of bed to switch on the light and gasped when a balloon from Sister Margaret's party bobbed against the wall.

She grabbed a pottery vase from her dresser and peered into the living room. The vase almost slipped from her hands when she discovered the front door open. She rushed to bolt the door. Hadn't she locked it after Ryan left?

Apprehension coursed through her as she gripped the vase, eased onto the couch and waited.

* * *

It was hours later that a knock at the door jarred her from a troubled sleep. She sprang from the couch and the vase crashed to the floor.

"Ratts," she muttered as she stepped over broken chunks of pottery to answer the door.

Ryan stepped inside and pointed to the tee shirt and boxer shorts she wore. "You'll need to wear more than that." He smiled. "Not that I'm complaining." His voice was soothing and Allie leaned against him. "What happened?" he asked, the merriment vanished from his voice as he pointed to the broken vase.

"I thought someone was in the apartment last night." Allie smoothed her hair. "The door was open. I must not have closed it tight." She bit her bottom lip to keep from crying.

"You're bleeding." He pointed to her foot and led her to be seated in the kitchen. "Why didn't you call me?" he scolded and knelt to hold a paper towel to the cut.

"I'm sure the wind blew the door open," she said. "It's silly."

"Damn it, Allie," he yelled. "It's not silly when you're scared out your mind." The scowl on his face deepened. "I don't care if it's the middle of the night. I want you to trust me enough to help you." She watched the flecks of gold in his eyes glow with frustration. "Promise me you'll call next time you have a problem."

She swallowed hard and nodded.

* * *

"Our property begins here," Ryan said. "These apple trees are Red Delicious."

Allie stared in wonder as they passed endless acres of trees on the drive to Ryan's childhood home and when he turned into a driveway, she searched for the house.

"My dad runs the cider mill and my mom the gift shop," he said and pointed to a rustic building.

The exterior of the shop was decorated with antique farm tools. It appeared warm and inviting and Allie caught the scent of fermenting apples.

"There's the barn." He nodded to a large white building. "I'll take you and Jess there later to visit the animals." He stopped the truck in front of a large yellow, two-story home. A porch that extended across the entire front of the house was adored with wicker chairs, a porch swing and several large pots filled with red geraniums.

"Your house looks like it belongs on a magazine cover." Ryan took her hand before she had a chance to bite her nail and whispered in her ear. "It might be a little overwhelming at first, but I promise you'll love it here."

Jessie stirred in the back seat and opened her eyes. "We're here, Jess." Ryan signed.

Jessie didn't smile and when she looked out the window, her eyes grew large. "Come on girls." Ryan laughed. "It's not like we're going to the dentist." He got out of the truck and opened the door.

Allie stepped out and jumped when a large, chocolate lab trotted toward them.

Ryan lifted Jessie and knelt down to snuggle the dog. "This is Kiki," he announced. "Hi, girl." Kiki licked his face, then Jessie's which sent her into a fit of giggles.

Allie laughed and patted Kiki's head. "Aren't you friendly?"

The front door burst open and a woman hurried down the steps. "Ryan," she called.

"Hi Mom!"

Allie watched them hug and felt a catch in her throat as the woman kissed him on the cheek. "This is Allie and Jessica. This is my mom, Julia." Ryan slipped his arm around Allie's waist.

"Hello, Mrs. Harper."

A warm glow softened Julia's dark brown eyes and Allie noticed a single dimple form at the corner of her mouth. She waved to Jessie and reached for Allie's hands. "Call me Julia," she said. "I'm so glad you could come. We've all been so anxious to meet you."

Ryan grabbed the overnight bags from the truck and followed as Julia led Allie and Jessie toward the house. "Dad took the little ones to the pond and everyone else is out back." She opened the front door. "Come inside."

Jessie squeezed Allie's hand while they followed Julia through the large foyer and up the stairs. "This is Ryan and Jake's room," she said as they passed one bedroom. "You girls can share Emily's room." They entered a sunny bedroom that was larger than all the rooms at the Cottage House put together. A full-sized canopy bed was centered in the room. The walls were papered a soft pink with a floral border. "This is lovely," Allie exclaimed.

Ryan set the bags down and turned when a young woman rushed into the room.

"Rye," she shrieked and lunged at him.

"Hey Em." He laughed and swung her around.

Allie watched the exchange with curiosity and Jessie snuggled close. Although Emily's hair was sandy blonde and her eyes were hazel, the resemblance was striking and Allie knew without a doubt she was Ryan's sister.

"This is my little sis, Emily."

"Finally. Another female in the house!" Emily latched onto Allie and hugged her tight.

Allie felt her checks flush while Emily knelt in front of Jessie. "You must be Jessica."

Jessie buried her face in Allie's skirt. "She's shy at first, but she'll warm up," Allie said.

Julia pulled Emily out of the room. "We'll let you get settled."

Ryan was still smiling when he turned to Allie. "I warned you that my family can be overwhelming. Everyone talks and laughs at the same time. It's a wonder anyone can hold an entire conversation." He knelt down to give Jessie a piggy back ride.

Allie slipped an arm through his. "You look just like your mom and sister," she said. "It's amazing."

"Think you're ready to meet the rest of the gang?"

She squared her shoulders and smiled. "Ready."

He set Jess down and led them through the house to the back yard.

"You're family is bigger than I thought," she said when they stepped outside.

Ryan followed her gaze to a large tent in the yard with enough tables and chairs to accommodate a huge crowd. "My parents always invite friends and neighbors," he laughed. "It's not quite as big as the St. Ives festival, but close."

Allie narrowed her eyes when she realized he was joking.

"Ryan," a little boy shouted and ran toward them. "Look what we caught with Uncle Rich."

Allie smiled and watched Ryan open a plastic cooler to examine a fish. "You caught this by yourself?" he said and tousled the little boy's golden hair.

He smiled at Allie. "This is my cousin's son, Nathan." He turned to Nate. "Can you say hello to my friends, Allie and Jessie?"

The little guy scrunched his face against the bright sun and smiled, revealing a gap where two front teeth were missing. "Hi," Nathan said.

Ryan set Jessie down and she smiled at Nathan.

Ryan pointed to a smaller child carried by an older gentleman. "That's Nate's little brother, Andrew, with my dad."

Allie moved closer to Ryan and slipped her hand into his. "How am I going to remember all these names?"

Ryan's father stepped over and embraced Ryan. "How are you, son?"

"Great, Dad."

"Allie, this is my dad, Richard."

"Hi," Allie said.

When Richard smiled, his hazel eyes sparkled with good humor and the lines around his eyes deepened. "Good to meet you, young lady." He was tall, like Ryan, but with a heavier build. His sandy blond hair was spiked with silver, especially at the temples.

Without much effort, he pulled Allie into his arms and patted Jessica on the head. "Hello, little one." Jessie's eyes opened wide while she studied Richard. "Have you been to the barn?" he asked.

"We're headed there now."

"Can I come?" Nate tugged on Ryan's shirt.

"Sure can," Ryan said. He slid an arm around Allie's shoulder and led the way.

They walked through fields of tall grass and wildflowers until they came to a large corral which held a chestnut mare and a pony.

Ryan hopped the fence into the corral and held out his hand to the mare. "Come here, Nell," he cooed. The mare snickered and tossed her shiny, black mane then trotted toward him. She nuzzled his neck and almost knocked him over with exuberance. "I missed you too, girl." He laughed and patted her neck. Nell nearly ripped his jean pocket. "Where are your manners?" he scolded and produced two apples.

Nell munched on one and Ryan held out the other for the colt. "Hey, Star," he coaxed. "Are you going to be sociable or not?" He continued to hold out the apple as the colt strutted around the pen. "Come here, little guy." Star warily stepped closer, grabbed the apple and darted away with his treat.

Jessie and Nate stood on the bottom rung of the fence and giggled at the antics of the colt.

"Come inside, Allie," Ryan said. "These two are harmless."

Allie shook her head. "I'll watch from here," she said.

Ryan led the mare closer. "Put out your hand," he said. "Nell won't bite."

Nell nudged Allie's extended hand with her nose. "She's soft, like velvet," she said.

Nate held out his hand and giggled when Nell greeted him.

Jessie leaned against Allie and watched.

"Haven't you been around horses before?" Ryan asked.

Allie shook her head. "I've seen the ponies at the St. Ives Festival, but never had the nerve to get close."

"Maybe we'll saddle up so you can go for a ride."

"Me too," Nate hollered.

Ryan took them to the barn and the kids played with Tally, an orange and white cat.

They passed the chicken coop and a pen where goats munched on clover.

Before long, the tantalizing scent of barbeque filled the air. "I think Uncle Rich is cooking dinner," he patted Nate on the bottom. "You better hurry before it's all gone."

Nate ran ahead and Jessie followed.

"What a wonderful place to grow up," Allie said and gazed at the wide open property. "It seems so safe and happy."

Ryan draped his arm around her. "I could give you safe and happy."

Allie's heart lifted as she rested her head on his shoulder and inhaled the sweet smell of fresh cut grass and wildflowers and apples. "I know."

"Then why won't you let me?"

Allie opened her mouth to tell him she needed time to settle the mystery of her past, but before she could answer, they rounded the corner of the house to find an army of family and friends.

"Hey, Matt," called Ryan. He grabbed Allie's hand and pulled her along. "Come meet the rest of my family."

The day proved to be a whirlwind. There were so many aunts, uncles and cousins that Allie lost track of names and faces.

Ryan drank beer and swapped stories with his brothers, Matt and Jake, while Allie sat back and enjoyed watching the family bond. Jessie fit right in with the younger children and appeared perfectly at ease. Nate and Jess became best buddies and shared a communication Allie didn't understand. Her heart filled with tenderness, causing her eyes to mist with tears. How long had she wanted to be a part of a family such as Ryan's?

"Isn't this a madhouse?" Emily slipped into the chair next to Allie and passed her a paper cup of wine. "Don't tell my mom," she whispered.

"I won't." Allie smiled.

"Tell me how you met Ryan."

Allie studied Emily's bright eyes. "I was riding my bike and his neighbor's dog chased me into the path of a car." Emily's eyes grew large. "The only casualty was my bike. I think Ryan asked me out because he felt guilty."

Emily leaned close and nodded toward Ryan. "I've never seen him in love before."

Allie followed Emily's gaze and frowned. "How can you tell?"

"He can't keep his eyes off you," Emily said with confidence. "See for yourself."

Allie's gaze met Ryan's and his smile broadened with pleasure.

"Oh, great," Emily mumbled. "Here comes trouble."

Allie watched a tall brunette with a body-to-die-for walk over to Ryan and his brothers. "Who is she?"

Emily frowned. "Sarah Vanderklein, her royal pain-in-the-highness."

Allie saw Ryan tense when Sarah Vanderwhatshername slid her long slim fingers with beautifully manicured nails through his hair. "Who is she?" she asked again.

"She's the witch." Emily mumbled and pursed her lips in irritation. "Ryan and Sarah dated in high school and she's been trying to get her hooks back into him ever since he developed a brain and dumped her."

Allie drained the cup of wine in one gulp, aware of the sinking sensation in her chest. "She's so elegant and beautiful," Allie said as she self-consciously fluffed her hair and curled her hands into fists to hide her half devoured nails.

"She is not," Emily huffed and turned to Allie. "You're much prettier."

Allie's heart sank to new depths when she saw Ryan point her way. "Oh, Lord," she whispered as he led Sarah to the table.

"Hi, Em." Sarah flashed a beauty-queen smile.

"Hi." Emily sighed, as if bored.

"This is my girlfriend Allison Weston." Ryan sat next to Allie and slipped his arm around her shoulder.

"Hello. I'm Sarah Vanderkline." Allie laced her fingers to keep from biting a nail as Sarah's cool gaze examined her.

"So, what brings you here, Sarah?" Emily narrowed her eyes.

"I wanted to see Ryan." She flashed a suggestive smile his way.

"Well, now that you've seen him, you can. . ." Emily said, but frowned at Ryan when he kicked her under the table.

Allie caught the hateful look Sarah flashed Emily and then turned her sights to Ryan's brother Matt. "Take care," Sara winked at Ryan.

"Watch out, Matt," Emily called and smiled at Allie, then smacked Ryan on the back of the head. "You didn't have to kick me."

Julia came over and sat next to Emily. "Do I need to separate you two?"

"Ryan started it," Emily protested. "Besides, Miss Snotty Pants deserved it." She stood and pulled Allie out of her chair. "Come on, Allie. Let's go find something to drink."

* * *

"I like Allie," Julia said. "She seems pretty special."

Ryan searched his mom's knowing expression and smiled. "She's special all right."

"I can't help asking, but when's the big event?"

Ryan laughed. "I'm surprised you waited so long to ask."

"Am I that bad?"

"You're that great." He rested back in the chair. "I'm ready for the big event," he said, "but, Allie needs time to sort out some issues."

Julia reached across the table and patted his hand. "I know with your help, she'll figure it out."

* * *

After the sky grew dark, Julia and Richard helped the kids toast marshmallows around a bonfire while Jake and Matt set out fireworks.

Allie shared a lawn chair with Ryan and snuggled close.

"Having fun?" he whispered against her hair.

She closed her eyes, content in his arms. "I've never been so happy." Shivers of delight followed a trail of light kisses along the side of her face.

"So, tell me about Sarah."

"There's nothing to tell." Ryan kissed the tip of her nose. "She's old history."

Allie's breath hitched in her throat when his smile caught the light of the fire and warmed her to the depth of her soul before his lips met hers.

* * *

In the laundry room located behind the apartment building, Allie opened the dryer to fold the last load of clothes and caught herself smiling. She was exhausted after the long weekend with Ryan's family, but she'd never been happier. Her head still spun from the closeness and bond that had formed in such a short time.

She picked up Ryan's flannel shirt, held it to her face and drew in a breath. It smelled of fabric softener with traces of smoke from the bonfire and still held a hint of Ryan's spicy scent. She inhaled again and her heart swelled with love.

She hummed as she unlocked her door, not able to rid her mind of the catchy tune Ryan had played on the radio.

All tender thoughts of family and love and spicy scents of after shave vanished when she glanced around the apartment in horror. It was turned upside down. She dropped the laundry basket and shrieked as she tripped over torn and shredded cushions from the couch. Books and papers were strewn everywhere and she ran to the bathroom to splash cold water on her face to clear her racing thoughts.

She closed her eyes, shutting out the mayhem. It was a bad dream. It was a flashback to a spooky movie the kids watched at the Cottage House when she was a kid. She'd hated scary movies. She never liked the thrill of living on the edge of her seat. Allie kept her eyes closed as she gripped the edge of the sink until her head stopped spinning. Slowly, she opened her eyes and looked into the mirror.

It wasn't a dream. She screamed when she read the words written in lipstick. . . *I'm watching.* . . A cold chill tingled on her skin as she grabbed a wash cloth. "Go away," she cried and rubbed the message, smearing the words into oblivion. "Leave me alone." She hit the mirror with her fist. "Who the hell are you?"

She blinked to clear her vision and stumbled to the bedroom. All her clothes were torn and discarded in a pile on the bed. Her yellow graduation dress was draped over the curtain rod and torn shreds of material wafted in the breeze.

Allie lifted the phone to find the line dead. A slow, tingling sensation crawled along her skin until the hair stood up on her arms. She wasn't alone. She whirled around, bracing herself for an attack and covered her mouth to quiet her ragged breaths. She hugged the wall and waited. Waited for the dream to end. Waited for her heart to stop drumming against her chest wall so she could take in a breath. Waited for something dreadful.

"Allie," someone called.

A wave of energy charged through her as she bolted into the hall, to the living room. Something caught her foot, she shrieked as she fell to the floor and saw the torn picture of Grace, the eagle, on the floor next to her. She saw the silhouette of a figure standing in the doorway, but couldn't see the face, only a glint of light reflected off a gun in his hand.

"No," she cried and lunged.

"Allie," he called and caught her. "It's Mike."

"I. . ." She squinted to focus on his face.

"Are you hurt?" She buried her face against his chest and clung to him, but shook her head. "I was on my way to Holly's and heard you scream," he said and led her from the apartment. "I'm taking you next door, okay?"

* * *

Allie sat on the couch in Holly's apartment and didn't move or make a sound. Ryan knelt in front of her and held her hands. They were cold in spite of the stifling humidity. She didn't look at him, only stared downward. "Drink this," he said and held a glass of brandy to her lips, hoping to put some color back on her cheeks.

Mike came into the apartment and sat next to Allie. "Is anything missing?" he asked.

"I don't know."

"Do you know anyone who might be holding a grudge? Someone at work, or a student?"

Allie shook her head and Ryan slipped a protective arm around her.

"What about Scott Farrell?" Mike inquired.

Ryan saw an unmistakable flicker of terror flash in her eyes. "Who's Scott Farrell?" he asked as he looked from Allie's ashen face to Mike's solemn expression.

"Scott Farrell was the groundskeeper at St. Ives years back. He had a thing for Allie."

Ryan tightened his grip on her arm. "What kind of thing?"

Mike waited for Allie to explain, but she started to shake. "You need to get her out of here." He escorted them to the door. "We'll check for evidence. I'll keep you posted."

The drive to Ryan's house was silent and strained with questions. Her eyes were closed and the freckles on her nose stood out against her pale skin. He was angry and wanted to know what the hell was going on, but squeezed her hand for reassurance.

He guided her inside and drew her close. "Tell me about this Farrell guy." Her eyes opened for a moment and his gut wrenched from the agony he detected.

"When I was a freshman in college, he was hired as a groundskeeper at St. Ives." She rubbed her fingertips on her temple. "He seemed nice and always brought cut flowers to the sisters." When a tear slid down the side of her face, Ryan brushed a light kiss on her cheek. "He tried to talk to me, but I didn't feel comfortable around him. Then he started showing up on campus and the library."

Ryan swallowed hard. "Go on," he prompted when her voice faltered.

"Sister Margaret talked to Mike about it. Mike did a background check and found out Scott had a number of misdemeanors, but nothing serious." Allie closed her eyes.

"One night, he came into my bedroom at the Cottage House." Ryan flinched as Allie slid out of his arms. He followed her to the kitchen where she filled a glass with water.

"What did he do to you?" Ryan demanded and cupped her chin in his hand.

"He didn't hurt me," she said. "I screamed when I found him next to my bed and he ran. Mike arrested him for breaking and entering and that was the last I heard of him."

"Do you think he trashed your apartment?"

She shook her head. "I don't think he wanted to hurt me."

Ryan fisted his hand in her soft curls. He wanted to bash the guy's head in, but only Allie would defend a scumbag like him. "Why didn't you tell me about him?" The reserved tone in his voice did little to shield the frustration.

"It didn't seem important." Allie buried her face against his chest and he felt the last bit of energy drain from her.

He smoothed her hair. "We'll talk about this later when you've rested." He led her to his bedroom and covered her with a blanket. "I have to go back to work for a few hours. Will you be okay?"

She nodded. God, it twisted his heart to see her so lost. He leaned over, kissed her forehead and paused at the door, reluctant to leave her alone.

* * *

Ryan snapped a series of photos of the sailboat race on Lake Michigan. He was hired to take pictures to sell as mementos to the boat owners. He rode with a charter service alongside the boats and smiled when he focused his camera on the white sails that contrasted against the cloudless sky. He couldn't imagine a better job.

It wasn't until late in the evening when he dragged himself to his truck. He was windblown and sea weary, but satisfied with the shots he got of the race.

He thought about Allie on the drive home and how withdrawn she'd become since her apartment was broken into. She tried to hide her despair, but at night when she thought he was asleep, she'd slip out of bed. He'd find her alone in the dark on the front porch. He'd lead her back to bed and hold her until her worries ceased long enough so she could drift back to sleep.

His cell phone rang and he reached into his sports bag to find it. "Hello," he answered.

"This Maria."

"Maria. Have you found anything?"

"I not talk now," she answered in a low tone. "Can we meet?"

Ryan checked the time. "I'm on my way back to town. I can meet you in half an hour."

"Si`," she paused. "We meet at Seagull Café, no?"

"I'll be there," he said and disconnected the call.

* * *

Maria waved when he entered the coffee shop. He slid across from her in the booth and rubbed the heavy stubble on his chin. "Sorry about my appearance. I was out all day covering the sailboat races. What have you found out?"

Maria glimpsed around the cafe and pulled an envelope from her purse and passed it to Ryan. "I make copies of everything in her file. You keep."

Ryan stared at the envelope and felt as if she'd passed him illegal documents.

"How's Alicia?" asked Maria.

"Her apartment was broken into and almost everything inside was destroyed."

Maria swallowed hard and her eyes grew large with concern. "Why?"

"I don't know." Ryan shook his head. "But, I think Allie knows more than she's willing to say." He waved off the waitress when she came to take his order. "I'm leaving," he said and stood up. "Thanks, Maria. I'll be in touch."

He opened the envelope in the privacy of his truck and read the copy of her birth certificate. Allison Campbell Weston was born in Detroit, Michigan to parents Sylvia Campbell Weston and Stephen Bennett Weston. The second paper was a copy of adoption papers stating that Dr. Franklin Stark legally adopted Allie when she was nine years old.

He stared at the documents and rolled his shoulders to ease the tension in his neck. He didn't know how he could avoid a trip to her hometown and dig into the vault of her past. He didn't know how the hell he could keep what he was doing a secret, especially when he expected total honesty from her. He folded the papers, placed them in the glove compartment, and locked it tight.

One thing Ryan was sure of. He loved Allie enough to risk losing her if it would help make her whole.

Chapter Nine

Ryan focused his camera while an elk cow and her calf munched tall grass at the forest's edge. He'd waited in vain all day for the eagles to make an appearance. Then the elks roamed by. He snapped a photo, then another and zoomed close to get a shot as the mother elk nuzzled her baby. He worked fast and sure in the element he loved and smiled with satisfaction. There wasn't anything he'd rather do.

Well, there was one exception which involved Allie. He couldn't bring himself to even think about the extent of the involvement at this point. But, he allowed his mind to drift. He wanted to kiss the seriousness from her soft lips until a smile hinted at the corner of her mouth. Then he'd trail kisses along the slim line of her neck until her pulse raced out of control and then. . . his cell phone rang. Both elk darted into the woods and the magical moment was gone. "Blasted phone," he grumbled and connected the call.

"Hello," he barked.

"Ryan Harper, please."

"Speaking."

"This is Sister Margaret Collins at St. Ives."

The elk forgotten, Ryan's attention came to full alert. "What can I do for you, Sister?"

"I'd like to meet with you regarding Allison." Her tone was businesslike.

"When can you meet?" he asked and rummaged in his pocket for a pen.

"How is eight o'clock Monday morning?"

"Fine," he said and jotted the time. He shook his head as he disconnected the call. Things were getting interesting, to say the least.

* * *

Ryan was jarred awake by Allie's soft cry. They'd fallen asleep while watching a movie.

"No," she cried and pushed him away.

"Allie, it's me."

He held her by the wrists to keep her from hitting, which only made her struggle harder.

"Allie." He raised his voice.

Her eyes were open, but glazed. "He was there," she cried, pointing to an empty space in the room.

"It was a dream, Al. No one's here but me."

Ryan pulled her close until her rapid breathing calmed and she drifted back to sleep.

* * *

Allie's dream was still on Ryan's mind when he knocked on the door to Sister Margaret's office promptly at eight.

"Come in," she said.

He entered the office. "Hello, Sister."

"Good morning, Mr. Harper." Sister sat at her desk and folded her hands on an open file. "Have a seat." She waited until he was seated. "I know about the files you acquired from Maria," she told him and peered over half-glasses. "What do you hope to gain with this information?"

"I want to help Allie." Ryan swallowed hard as if he'd been caught in the act of a devious crime. "I'd never do anything to hurt her."

"Perhaps some of the mystery of her childhood is better off forgotten." She paused and taped her fingers on the desk. "When she first came to St. Ives, we consulted many child psychologists. Everyone agreed that she'd blocked the trauma so deeply, it would be more harmful to try to bring the memories to the surface." Her brows knit together, as if she were deep in thought. "They assured me that she'd start to remember on her own when she was ready."

"I think that time has come," Ryan said. "She's beginning to remember fragments of her past."

"Did you know that her parents were brutally murdered when she was ten and we know Allison was there? She's never talked about what happened." Sister's hard gaze met his. "In fact, she didn't speak at all for a few years."

Ryan shook his head and felt his chest tighten as he gripped the arms of the chair, but he braced himself for the disturbing facts of Allie's childhood. "Go on," he said.

Fondness shone in Sister's eyes. "After Allison arrived, she became my shadow. Over six months later, I was working with a small girl who was crying. Allison quieted the child, and then began using sign language. She'd learned how to sign while she followed me." The slight smile on her face faded. "At what cost do you want to help her learn the truth?"

"I don't know." He looked away, uncomfortable about prying into her past. "Perhaps Allie needs to make those decisions."

"Good." Sister Margaret stood, the only indication the meeting was over.

* * *

As soon as Ryan stepped foot on his front porch, a savory aroma made his mouth water. He entered the house, followed the scent and stopped in the kitchen doorway to watch Allie.

She was at the sink with her back to him, peeling vegetables. Her hair was pulled into a ponytail and she wore a sleeveless yellow shirt with floral shorts. Bright polish adorned her toenails and she hummed to a tune on the radio. Her smooth golden skin glowed from the summer sun. God, she was beautiful.

Desire made his senses spin, until visions of the unknown trauma she'd suffered as a child filled his mind and a sick sensation settled at the base of his stomach.

He cleared his throat and she whirled around, holding the vegetable peeler as a weapon, her face was wrought with fear. "Ryan." She breathed deeply, her eyes large with surprise. "You scared me." She held a hand against her chest as if to steady the beat.

"I'm sorry, Al." He stepped to her. "You looked so peaceful I didn't want the moment to end." Guilt gnawed at his conscience as he held her. God, he wanted to help her face her fears so they could move forward, but how could he protect her from reliving the trauma of her childhood? A weak smile touched her lips as she stood on her tiptoes, wrapped her arms around his neck and gazed at him with trust oozing from the depths of her sea-blue eyes. Emotion settled in the form of a hard lump in his throat, but he forced his voice to sound casual. "What's the occasion?" he asked and motioned toward the table that she'd set with flowers and candles.

"I wanted to make something special. My apartment is freshly painted and cleaned. I'm moving back tomorrow," she said in a hushed tone.

Ryan felt his heart sink. "I don't understand why you won't stay here."

"I know who I am when I'm with you." She placed her fingers on his lips when he began to protest. "I need to find out who I am when I'm alone."

* * *

Ryan remained quiet through dinner. He watched every move Allie made and whenever she got up to do something, he was at her side to help.

"What's wrong, Ryan? You're acting like I'm going to break." He held her hand across the table. She could see questions in his eyes. "What's changed?" she asked, fearing the answer might be his love for her.

"Nothing has changed," he answered and helped clear the table. "Last night you had a bad dream," he began. "Do you remember?" She shook her head and placed dishes in the sink. He turned her to him. "You thought someone was in the room."

Allie stared at the dish water. "I don't remember."

Ryan poured two cups of coffee and led Allie outside to the porch. "Tell me what you know about your childhood," he said.

"I attended a boarding school." She stared across the yard. "My best friend was Carly." She turned to him. "I haven't thought of her in years." Her throat tightened with emotion. "I don't understand why my memories are returning in pieces like this."

Her heart ached when his eyes filled with concern. "Maybe you should talk to someone who understands this sort of thing."

"Something terrible happened," she whispered. "What if it's so evil it hurts both of us?"

She stepped off the porch and he followed. "Whatever happened was not your fault. You were just a child." He smoothed her hair.

"You don't know for sure." She released a shaky sigh. "For me to have buried it so deeply, it must be something horrible."

"I'll help you through this, Allie." She saw his jaw set with determination. "No matter what happened, we'll face it together."

"God, I want to believe you, Ryan." She leaned against him.

"Look how far we've come," he said and stroked his fingers along her bare arms. "I'll bet you never thought you'd be standing here with me and that I'd be telling you how much I love you." His arms circled around her and he rested his chin on the top of her head. "But I'm here. . .and I love you."

"Why?"

"For the same reason you keep letting me back into your life when you try so hard to push me away." His lips curved into a reassuring smile.

"I wish I were as sure," she whispered as the rough edge of panic subsided.

* * *

"Allison, you have a phone call on line two," Mrs. Carson said. "I'll take over for you."

"Thanks, Mrs. Carson," Allie said as she checked out the final book for a patron.

She hurried to answer the phone, expecting it was Ryan returning her call. She wanted to meet him for lunch and surprise him with the new lens he'd been eyeing at the camera shop in town.

She smiled when she picked up the phone. "Hi, it's Allie."

"Listen carefully," a muffled, raspy voice uttered.

Allie nearly dropped the phone. "Who is this?" she demanded.

"Shut up and listen," the caller snarled. "If you don't do what I say, I won't have a problem destroying your life the way you destroyed mine."

Allie sank into the chair as waves of nausea assaulted her. "What do you want?" A buzzing noise grew louder in her ears and she strained to listen.

"At noon Friday, tape fifty thousand in an envelope to the underside of the picnic table in the park."

Allie swallowed hard to moisten her dry throat. "Which picnic table?"

"At your usual table under the willow tree."

Allie spun around to search the library, fighting the pressing sensation she was being watched. "If you don't leave me alone, I'll go to the police."

"Do you really want to take the risk of something happening to your loved ones if you involve the police?"

The caller hung up and Allie stared at the phone for several seconds before she bent over to place her head between her knees to keep from passing out.

* * *

Friday came and went without incidence and the days that followed, Allie tried to follow her normal routine as if nothing was out of the ordinary. She didn't pay the money. Her survival tactic had always been to block terrible events and they'd disappear. Why would the demands of the extortionist be any different?

She stopped picking up her mail and asked Mrs. Carson to take a message if there were phone calls for her at the library.

"Are you doing anything special with Ryan this weekend?" Lisa asked while she worked on a project for school.

Allie shook her head. "Nothing special," she said and saw the postman deliver mail to Mrs. Carson at the main desk. She looked away and tried to concentrate on the article she'd found about memory loss. Out of the corner of her eye, she watched Mrs. Carson sort the mail and stand with a letter. Allie shut her eyes, but heard footsteps on the tile floor. She bit her nail and refrained from crying out when Mrs. Carson stopped at the desk.

"Here's a letter for you, Allison."

Allie held the letter and stared at the envelope until the letters blurred. "I'll be right back, Lisa."

Allie waited until she was outside to release a shaky breath. She should have torn the letter into pieces, but morbid curiosity drove her. She stared at another copy of the headline that had been sent to her, but this time, there was a picture of a young girl beneath it. It took several moments until she realized the child in the picture was her.

Allie crumpled the paper and reached for the step rail when her legs threatened to buckle.

The door opened, but Allie didn't dare move.

"Allison, you're as pale as a ghost." Mrs. Carson's words were distant and distorted.

Allie swallowed hard until she was sure she could speak. "I'm not feeling well," she whispered. "Would you ask Lisa to cover the reading session?"

* * *

Ryan raced to her apartment when he discovered Allie had gone home sick earlier in the day. He entered, careful not to make a sound in case she was sleeping.

In her bedroom, the shade was pulled to block the light and the only sound was a steady hum from the fan. He lowered himself to the edge of the bed and touched her hand.

"Do you have a headache?" he asked when her eyes fluttered open. She nodded slightly and when she frowned, he could tell it hurt for her to move. He watched a single tear trickle down the side of her face until it disappeared into her hairline.

"What happened today?" She didn't move, but he saw another tear follow the same track. "Tell me," he whispered through clenched teeth. She made no sound, but shook her head slightly. He knew she couldn't lie to him, so instead said nothing at all.

He balled his hand into a fist and slipped out of the room. Damn, his heart raced. He despised the defenseless agony of watching her suffer. He hated it almost as much as her willingness to allow the demons of her past to consume her. He paced, until his anger subsided.

He brewed a cup of tea and set it on the bed table and brushed a light kiss on the back of her hand. She appeared to be sleeping, so he left the apartment.

If she wouldn't fight, he'd fight for her. He'd show her there were other ways to deal with slimy creatures that hid in dark places.

In his truck, he unlocked the glove compartment and retrieved the papers he'd received from Maria. He'd waited until he could bring himself to look into Allie's past with a clear conscious. Well, the time was long overdue. It was his fight now. He opened his wallet for the phone number of a college buddy who worked at a suburban Detroit newspaper and left a message on the answering machine. He stared at the papers and fought the urge to drive straight to her hometown to take matters into his own hands. It was his fight all right, but what the hell was he fighting?

* * *

Allie giggled as she licked drips of strawberry ice cream from her hand. It was windy at the shore and the ice cream melted fast. "I can honestly say this is the first time I've had ice cream for breakfast."

"Once in a while, it's good for the soul." Ryan threw the remainder of his cone to a flock of squawking seagulls gathered nearby. A flurry broke out and Allie felt sorry for a smaller bird excluded from the feast, so she tossed her cone to him. They laughed as the little guy grabbed the cone and ran from the others.

Ryan took her hand and they lingered at the shore to bask in the surrounding sounds and sights of a perfect summer morning. It was early, so the beach was deserted except for an occasional jogger. The gulls were off to other conquests. Sailboats skimmed along the horizon and the cutters were out in force. It was an idle, privileged scene, and Allie felt a tug in her heart. She closed her eyes and when Ryan stopped, Allie turned to him and laced her fingers behind his neck. She felt the strong beat of his heart which matched the rhythmic slap of the waves against the sand. He was safe and solid, which allowed her to discover secrets she never knew existed.

"I love you," she admitted and watched the gold flecks in his eyes glow with warmth.

"You've never said it before," he murmured against her lips. She tasted traces of chocolate mint with a dash of unforeseen promises and melted against him almost as fast as the ice cream. Then without warning, the extortionist's words pierced through the tranquility and jolted her away from Ryan.

He intercepted her fingers before they reached her mouth. "What just happened?" he questioned.

"Loving you frightens me," she whispered.

He opened his mouth to speak, but a distant blast assaulted the peacefulness.

* * *

Allie screamed as Ryan shielded her when a dark billow of smoke rose above the cliffs. He grabbed her arm when she darted away.

"It's St. Ives," she cried.

"Let's get my truck."

"This way is faster." She shook off his grip and ran toward the cliffs.

He followed her along the beach, past the lighthouse to the path through the rocks to the top of the hill until they were on firm ground. The smoke grew thick and black as they ran closer.

Allie leaned over to catch her breath and when he saw the look of terror in her eyes as sirens cut through the breeze, he pulled her close and led her toward the back of the rectory.

A crowd had already formed by the time they arrived and Ryan held onto Allie when they saw a gaping hole with flames and smoke pouring out of the kitchen area.

She tried to break away. "I have to see if anyone's inside," she shrieked and grasped him until the tips of her fingers dug into the flesh of his arms.

"Damn it, Allie. You can't go in there." She tried to push him away and screamed when he looped his arms around her waist and carried her a safe distance from the building.

"I have to find Jessica and Maria," she cried. "Let me go." He set her down and held her while firemen rushed by.

Allie stared, as if in a daze, while more police and firemen arrived. He felt her tremble and pulled her close, but understood that any soothing words would not penetrate her shock.

"Allison!" They both turned to see Sister Pat with the children. Ryan released Allie as Jessica ran toward them.

"What happened? Is anyone hurt?" There was panic in Allie's voice as she hugged Jessica.

"I was at the cottage. Margaret and Celeste are out front," Pat said.

Water sprayed through the fire hose toward flames that licked from the second story roof above the kitchen.

Allie reached for Ryan's hand and he stepped closer. "Pat, do you know where Maria is?"

Pat shrugged and exchanged concerned glances with Ryan.

They watched while the fire overpowered the constant spray from several hoses and it seemed like hours before the flames died down to smoking ambers from the rubble that was once the kitchen.

"Everyone all right?" Mike stepped up beside them.

"Do you know what happened?" Ryan asked.

"Not yet." Mike reached over and patted Allie on the arm.

Margaret rushed over. "Thank goodness Maria is at the market," she exclaimed. "I don't think anyone was in the kitchen."

Allie held Jessie and rested her head on Margaret's shoulder.

Ryan pulled Mike aside. "What's your hunch?"

Mike shrugged. "Most of the time these fires are from faulty wiring or something left on by accident. This is an old building.

There'll be an investigation, but the cause might not be determined for weeks."

It was late when the crowd dispersed and the children were ushered off to bed.

Ryan walked Allie back to his truck in silence. He held her close, as if it would prevent her from withdrawing.

"No one was hurt, Allie."

She'd stopped walking and searched the distance. "No one was hurt," she repeated and he followed her gaze to the dark haze of smoke that hung over St. Ives like a bad omen.

Chapter Ten

Ryan slept beside Allie, he'd insisted on staying, claiming he didn't want to leave her alone. Didn't he know how the rise and fall of his deep, soft breathing made it impossible to get any sleep? His protective arm curled around her, but it wasn't enough to shield the vivid images of flames and smoke from repeating themselves over and over in her mind. The smell of smoke still clung to their pores like a probing reminder of the chard stench.

Careful not to wake him, she slipped out of bed and once outside, covered her face with her hands, desperate to block away the stabbing guilt. Ryan had pressed her to talk. He didn't understand why she was so upset. How could she tell him she was sure the fire was a message from the extortionist? How could she keep from hurting him? He was so patient and understanding, but she could see how her silence upset him by the way he watched her, the protective way he held her and the way he turned away from her in frustration. She couldn't blame him. He gave one hundred percent of himself without hesitation. How did he do it? How could he trust so freely without question?

In the darkness, she sat on the porch step and rested her head against the rail in defeat, swallowing hard to reduce the vise of panic. It was time to pay the money so the madness would end.

* * *

Allie jumped when the door opened and Ryan plopped down next to her. "Shit," he growled, and rubbed his face. "You just don't get it, do you?" He glared at her and she might have seen the rage in his eyes if it wasn't so blasted dark.

"I couldn't sleep," she said. The night air was warm and humid, making her soft curls tighten. She wore a sleeveless cotton shirt and baggy boxer shorts, all she needed was a teddy bear to complete the image of a little girl.

"Why didn't you wake me instead of hiding?" Clouds passed over the moon which allowed a temporary glimmer of light to reveal a flash of wariness in her eyes. She stood to leave, but he pulled her onto his lap and held her until the tension in her body faded and she fell against him, as if she didn't posses the strength to resist. "When will you learn to trust me?" he asked quietly, even though he wanted to rant and rave.

"I'm trying," she whispered and slid shaky arms around his neck.

* * *

Ryan spent most of the day at his desk to work on a directory of local summer events. Summer was slow in the school sports department, so he assisted in other areas of the paper. He stood to stretch his legs and clear the fuzz from his mind.

Allie couldn't meet him for lunch like he'd hoped. He wanted to take her to a nice secluded spot on the beach and hold her. Since the fire, she'd become more reclusive, if that was possible. He didn't get it. No one was hurt and the insurance would cover the cost of rebuilding the kitchen. It was crazy, but for some irrational reason, she acted like it was her fault.

His phone rang and the caller ID listed his college friend's number at *The Daily Record.* "Jason. It's Ryan Harper."

140

"Sorry I didn't call right back, Ryan. I was out on an assignment. How the hell are you?"

"Great. How's everything with you?"

"Can't complain. What's up?" Jason asked.

Ryan tapped his pencil on the desk pad. "I have a favor to ask."

"Name it."

"I'd like you to dig for information on a Sylvia Campbell Weston Stark, Stephen Bennett Weston and Dr. Franklin Stark. Also, Allison Campbell Weston. They lived in Seabrook Hills twelve years ago."

"Is this a case you're working on?"

"I'm not sure. At this point I'm curious about any details I can find."

"When do you need the information?"

"As soon as possible."

Ryan hung up the phone and tried to shake off the familiar pang of uneasiness that crept over him whenever he dug into Allie's past. Knowing he was doing it for her wasn't enough to ease the guilt.

* * *

When Allie entered the bank, a wave of apprehension crept over her, as if she were about to commit a crime. The security guard stepped over to greet her, and Allie smiled, but avoided eye contact. The palms of her hands were damp and she took several relaxing breaths until her heart rate slowed.

She stood in line to wait for the next available teller, her nerves stretched so taunt, she wondered what prevented her from snapping. She glanced at the bankbook she and Sister Margaret had opened a few months before. She vowed then never to touch the money, but circumstances had drastically changed.

She forced a smile and stepped to the next open window. "I'd like to make a withdrawal from this account please," she said.

The teller, whose nameplate read Janice, smiled and entered the account number into the computer. "How much would you like to withdraw?" she asked with a cheerful smile.

"Fifty thousand dollars," Allie said in a hushed tone as she glanced at the security guard. The last thing she wanted was a scene.

"I'll need your name and social security number please."

Allie obliged and watched the teller's expression change from pleasant to utter surprise when the account information appeared on the computer screen. "I'll need to check with the manager."

Allie watched Janice consult an older woman and flushed when they both looked at her as if she'd slipped a robbery note to the teller.

The older woman walked over to the window followed by Janice.

"Hello, Ms. Weston. I'm Sandra Hamilton. We'll need you to fill out a form and to show further identification."

Allie frowned. "Why can't I just get the money? It's in my account."

The older women smiled with practiced patience. "I understand, but government regulations require you to complete a large currency form. It will only take twenty minutes of your time."

Allie's gaze darted to the clock on the wall, but followed the woman to a nearby desk.

Allie drummed her fingers on the arm of the chair while the manager searched through files behind her desk. "Here it is," she said and placed the paper in front of Allie. "You must indicate how the money is going to be spent."

"My apartment was broken into and I need to replace everything." Allie hesitated. "Does the government actually track how the money is spent?"

"No, but this is your declaration the money isn't going to be used for drug trafficking or other illegal activity."

Allie hurried through the form and as promised, was out the door with the money within the allotted time.

She sat at the picnic table and searched the area to make sure no one watched before she taped the envelope under the table.

She raced from the park and refused to look back, afraid she'd find her past in hot pursuit.

* * *

Allie buried herself into plans for the preschool picnic the following week, as if she were doing research for a college thesis.

She glanced up and her heart lurched to her throat when she saw Mike enter the library, stop at the information desk and Mrs. Carson point to the children's section. His face was grim and Allie's breath caught in her throat as he approached.

"Hi, Mike," she said, but didn't look at him.

He leaned on the counter and raised his eyebrows. "You look a little pale, Allie. Is something wrong?" She shook her head, not able to trust her voice to sound convincing. "I'm sorry to bother you at work, but I wanted to ask you a few questions."

To keep her hands from visibly shaking, she folded them on her lap under the table. Did he know about the money? Had someone alerted him from the bank? She placed her fingers on her temple as a sharp pain shot through her brain. Did something happen to Ryan or the sisters? What the hell did he want? She opened her eyes and judging from Mike's concerned expression, realized she'd better pull herself together.

"Do you want to go outside? I can take a short break," she said.

Mike nodded and followed her to a small patio section located behind the library. Shade from a large oak tree created a reprieve from the stifling afternoon heat.

"What's going on?" She forced her smile to appear casual, but wanted to shake him until he told her what was on his mind.

"I shouldn't be talking to you about this, but I thought you might know something about the fire at St. Ives."

"What?" She could barely conceal the surprise in her voice.

Mike reached across to pat her hand. "Would you relax? I talked to Sister Margaret and Father Kotalski, but they weren't much help." The way he watched her made her squirm on the hard wooden bench. "It looks like the fire was deliberately started." Her pulse began to race. "Do you know who might want to get even with someone at St. Ives?"

Allie stared beyond Mike to a stand of trees across the street. "I don't know anything." She stood to leave, but he wrapped strong fingers around her wrist.

"Allie, there's got to be a connection between your apartment getting trashed and the fire at St. Ives. What is it?"

Allie inhaled deeply and released a tight sigh. "I don't know."

"I ran a check on Scott Farrell. He's serving time in Nevada." He released her arm and paused when she met his intense gaze. "You need to tell me if you know anything."

"I will." God, he knew something. "I have to get back to work now."

* * *

The fire at St. Ives did nothing to dampen the excitement and revelry surrounding the summer festival. Large tents were erected on the grounds at St. Ives the week before the scheduled event. Stages were built and props arrived to transform the setting into a medieval village.

Allie stopped to check out the progress at the food booth. "Maria," she called out.

"Caro, come lei sono?"

"I'm fine. How are you?"

"Multo buono." She rolled her eyes and wiped her brow. "I make over hundred meat pies and pastries."

Allie frowned. "I signed up to make ten apple pies for the bake sale and I haven't even started yet."

Maria clucked her tongue. "In case you forget, the Festival tomorrow."

"Ryan's meeting me here in a bit." She checked her watch. "He doesn't know it yet, but he's going to help me peel apples later."

Maria's smile held a note of approval. "I like man who not afraid to work in kitchen." Allie laughed and followed Maria's nod. "Here come su piccolo un."

Lisa and Jessica ran toward them wearing long flowing dresses and wreaths of wildflowers in their hair with pastel ribbons streaming behind them.

Allie scooped up Jessica and hugged her. She smiled to Lisa. "You look like a princess."

Lisa held out her hand in regal fashion and signed to Jessica. "I'm the queen, Jessie's the princess."

Jessica tapped Allie's shoulder and pointed to the flowers and ribbons that adorned her hair.

Allie kissed Jessie's cheek. "Very pretty," she signed and laughed when Jessie smiled and batted her lashes.

"That one trouble." Maria laughed and passed a generous slice of shortbread to the girls. "Help with chairs around tables." She pointed to the dining area under a large white tent.

Lisa took Jessica's hand and off they went.

"Jessie, she getting attached to you, si`?"

Allie watched Jessie nibble on the shortbread. "She's young and trustful." Allie sighed and felt a tug of emotion when Jessie turned her way and smiled. "I'm getting attached to her, too."

Maria set the last of the pastries into a large ice box. "Caro, maybe you adopt her."

Allie searched Maria's face. "Who said anything about adoption?"

"You understand. You make wonderful mama."

Heaviness weighed in Allie's heart. She'd love to give Jessie a home. "I can hardly take care of myself," she admitted. She watched as Ryan approached over the hill and Jessie ran to him. She placed a hand over her heart when he lifted the little girl high into the air and caught her soundly in his arms.

"I think you find your family, si`?" Maria said and pointed to Ryan and Jessica.

"My family," she repeated and watched Ryan carry Jessie toward the tent. "He deserves so much more than what I can give," she whispered and hurried to him before Maria could respond.

Allie laughed when Ryan swept her off her feet and spun her and Jessie around. Jessie giggled and pointed to her wreath. Allie helped Jessie form the proper sign. "Pretty," Allie spoke out loud for Ryan's benefit.

"Not as pretty as you," he nodded and kissed the tip of Jessie's nose. Allie translated and Jessie's smile deepened as she hugged him, then wiggled out of his arms to join Lisa.

When he turned to Allie and kissed her, his eyes were bright with laughter and love. Allie blinked back tears of happiness. She glanced at Maria who hummed a tune and smiled from ear to ear.

* * *

The night of the festival was perfect. The temperature was warm, but the humidity low. Crowds flocked to the grounds of St. Ives and several times, Sister Margaret commented on how it was the most successful opening night ever.

Allie had little time to see Ryan. There was such a steady demand for grilled sausages, kebobs and hamburgers, it took everyone's constant effort to keep up with the orders. Ryan manned the beverages and kept running to the supply tents for ice and cases of drinks.

Toward the end of the evening, Maria handed Allie a glass of lemonade. "Find Ryan and enjoy what's left of evening," she coaxed. "We finish."

"I can't leave you here with all this mess." Allie started to pick up the full bags of garbage, but Maria stopped her.

"We have clean crew," she scolded. "Go."

Allie glanced in the direction of the beer tent and untied her apron. "Maybe I should before Father McLaughlin gets his hands on Ryan." She hugged Maria. "I'll see you in the morning."

Allie folded her apron and freshened up before making her way to the noisy tent. A band played rock music and the dance floor was lively with folks of all ages.

She worked her way through the crowded tent until she found Ryan.

"Hey Al." He greeted her with a grin and a mug of beer. "You're just in time."

"For what?" she asked and laughed as his hands slipped up her arms, pulling her snugly against him.

"For saving me from getting totally wasted," he whispered against her ear.

Father McLaughlin turned his back and Allie took Ryan's hand. "Let's get out of here while we can."

She led him away from the tent, the music and the crowds. "Where are we going?" he asked and stopped mid-stride.

"You'll see," she hinted and smiled when his questioning gaze met hers. Anticipation drove her as she fisted her hand in his hair and raised herself to meet his kiss.

Footsteps broke the spell and they turned to find Jessica running toward them. Allie knelt down to gather the child close. "What's wrong?" she signed when Jessie started to cry.

"Want you," Jessie signed.

"I'm sorry, Allison," Sister Celeste called out as she hurried over. "She saw you and broke away from me." Celeste held her chest and took several deep breaths. "My goodness," she exclaimed. "I'm not cut out for keeping up with these little ones like I used to be."

"Why don't you take a break?" Allie suggested while Jessie clung to her. "Ryan and I will take care of her." Allie handed Jessie to Ryan and led the way to the Cottage House near the rectory.

An iron fence surrounded the dwelling and a shrill creak of rusted metal sounded when Allie opened the gate.

"Could use some oil," Ryan muttered.

Jessica rested her head on Ryan's shoulder while Allie guided him inside and up the stairs to the second floor bedroom. Sister Pat looked up from the book she read to Kara. "There's Jessica." She stood and held out her arms.

"She wants Ryan to put her to bed," Allie said and found Jessie's folded nightgown under the pillow.

Ryan sat on the small bed and untied Jessie's shoes. She'd stopped crying and leaned against him.

"It's been a long day," Allie said and slipped the nightgown over the little girl's head. "Brush your teeth," she signed and watched Jessie lead Ryan to the bathroom.

Ryan tucked Jessie into bed and Allie placed a worn teddy bear beside her. Jessie pointed to a book.

"What do you say?" Allie signed.

A frown of determination crossed Jessie's brow while her small fingers worked to form the word.

"Good job, Jess," Allie signed.

Ryan opened the book and turned pages while Allie signed the story. It wasn't long before Jessie's heavy eyelids closed and her breathing turned soft and regular. Allie smoothed Jessie's hair and kissed her on the forehead. "She'll be impossible tomorrow night when you aren't here to tuck her in," she said as Ryan reached for her hand.

"This feels so right, Allie."

She swallowed hard when their gaze met and glanced at the child between them, but didn't dare speak, baffled by the scope of her emotions.

Allie led him to a back entrance and outside, to a rope swing attached to a willow tree. She sat on the wooden seat while Ryan pushed her. The night was mild and the still air was sweetened by the scent of roses from the arbor along a path leading to Father Kotalski's garden. Allie laughed and her heart soared when Ryan pushed her so high, she felt as if she could reach the stars.

"I spent many hours here as a child," she said. "I prayed that someday, someone I loved would push me on this swing."

Ryan stepped in front of the swing until it slowed to a stop. She placed her hands in his and he pulled her to him.

"I want to give you everything." His voice was tender as he cradled her against him. "A home, family. A life together." His voice grew heavy with emotion. "Hell, we'll even get a cat and a dog if you want."

A strangled laugh caught in her throat. "I've. . ." she began and he caught her hand before she could bite her nail. "I've never felt this way." She reached to brush a lock of hair from his eye.

"Marry me, Al," he murmured. "I have enough love for you and Jessie."

Allie was certain if anyone could make two broken lives whole, it would be Ryan. "I can't." Her voice was just above a whisper. "Not yet. There's so much I need to learn about myself before Jessica can depend on me."

"You're making it more complicated than it needs to be, Al." The softness in his voice gave her hope.

"Please don't give up on me, Rye."

"Never happen." He brushed his lips on her forehead. "Not in a million years."

He trailed light kisses along the side of her face until his mouth covered hers. Heat radiated through her as her senses sprang to life. It was impossible to will her legs to remain strong and she leaned into him. Still, his mouth crushed hers until her heart pounded erratically.

His hands clenched into fists on her back and his body tensed. She searched his smoldering eyes for meaning before he rested his head on hers and when he stepped back, desperation drove her to fight the risk of losing him. She moved to him. "I want to give you everything, too," she whispered, her words shaking with anticipation. "I just need some more time." She kissed the tips of his fingers before placing his hand over her heart. "I love you, Ryan."

* * *

Ryan agonized over stubborn words that didn't come. He had a deadline to meet and all he could think about was Allie. She seemed more distant than usual at breakfast that morning. It killed him to watch her withdraw, knowing he couldn't get a grip while she slipped away, no matter how hard he held her. It weighed on his mind. Much more than the article he was trying to complete on the softball playoffs. He stepped away from his desk to freshen his coffee when the phone rang.

"Ryan. It's Jason."

"What's going on?"

"I found the information you wanted," he said and released a low whistle. "I'd sell my soul to report a case like this."

"What'd you find?" Ryan asked.

"It was a double homicide that remains unsolved."

Ryan cradled the phone against his chin and reached for a pencil and a pad of paper. "Go ahead."

"Twelve years ago, on the night of August 15th, millionaire Sylvia Campbell Stark was strangled to death and her husband, Dr. Franklin Stark, a renowned cardiovascular surgeon, died as the result of a three story fall from their home."

Ryan gripped the phone and wrote the details as fast as he could. "Any mention of the daughter?"

"Plenty," Jason said. "Their ten year old daughter's picture is plastered over all the newspapers. Allison was found on the balcony of her third story bedroom strangled and unconscious. One headline questioned if she was guilty of pushing the doctor to his death."

Ryan closed his eyes and pinched the bridge of his nose to relieve the building pressure. "Any details in the articles about the investigation?"

"By the looks of it, the case created a media frenzy. Several years before, Sylvia's first husband died in an automobile accident. His name was Stephen Weston, as in Weston Computer Technology. He left his widow a very wealthy woman. Dr. Stark, on the other hand, liked to gamble, among other things and was heavy in debt at the time of his death."

Ryan continued to jot down the information. "Any other suspects?"

"The investigating officer was Detective Vincent Hartig. In one article he mentioned several prime suspects. Hold on a second." Ryan listened to the rustle of paper. "The household staff was gone for the evening and were all cleared. There was a forced entry at the home and there were several theories. Could have been a burglary or retaliation for the money Dr. Stark owed to his, so-called investors. Another theory is that Dr. Stark staged it. He would stand to gain millions with the wife and newly adopted kid out of the picture. Maybe Allison pushed him over the balcony when he attempted to strangle her. Afterwards, Allison was hospitalized for a few weeks. There's a news photo of her leaving the hospital with a nun."

"Damn," Ryan swore. "It's more involved than I thought. Can you send me the articles?"

"Sure. Let me know if there's anything else you need."

He gave Jason the address at the paper. "Thanks for your help."

He stared at the notes he'd scribbled for several moments and wondered how this information might help Allie and more critical, how could it hurt?

Chapter Eleven

Mike entered the library to give Lisa and Jessica a ride and found Allie at the computer. She smiled when she saw him, but he detected a faint flash of concern in her eyes. "Why do you do that?" he asked and leaned on the counter.

"Do what?" She stood to file papers.

"Look at me like I scare the hell out of you."

"I don't."

"Yes, you do."

"I don't mean to," she said and buried her face in the file cabinet.

He searched the room. "Where are the girls?"

"They're helping Mrs. Carson." Allie grabbed at the papers as they slipped out of her hand. "They'll be right back."

"Admit it, Allie, I make you nervous, don't I?" Mike asked as he helped her retrieve the scattered papers. When she glanced at him, he saw the pupils of her eyes dilate. His detective instinct told him she was hiding something. He itched to know what.

Allie took the papers from him. "I'm not nervous," her voice trailed off when Lisa and Jessie joined them behind the counter.

"You could have fooled me." He raised an eye brow. "Do you need a ride home?"

"Ryan's picking me up."

"Uncle Mikey," Lisa said and slapped his raised hand.

Mike knelt down and pulled a sucker from his pocket and Jessie looked at Allie.

"It's all right," Allie signed.

Jessica reached for the sucker and signed to Mike.

"Your welcome," he replied and patted her head. "Ready to go?" He waited while the girls gathered their books and he followed them to the door. "I'll check with Holly, maybe the four of us can get together this weekend," he said.

"Sounds great," Allie said and bit her nail as she watched them leave the library.

* * *

Ryan followed Maria's musical voice down the hall to the temporary kitchen in the convent and stopped in the doorway to observe the tender scene.

Maria leaned against the counter to help Jessie spread jam and peanut butter on bread. Allie's smile appeared soft and relaxed as she stirred a container of lemonade. When Jessie placed the completed sandwich in plastic wrap, her face beamed.

Ryan focused his camera and when he snapped a picture, Allie and Maria looked up in surprise.

Jessie squeaked, climbed off the stool, and hurried to him. He lifted her into his arms. "How's my girl?" he signed. She smiled and pointed to the sandwiches. "Looks like you've made enough to feed the entire town." He laughed and stepped over to brush a kiss on Allie's cheek.

Allie slipped an arm around his waist. "Jess enjoyed herself so much, we got carried away. Hope you're hungry."

"Lo porta molta felicita', si'?"

He detected tenderness in Maria's eyes and raised his eyebrows in question. "Between sign language and Italian, I'm definitely language challenged." Ryan shrugged and turned to Allie. "You want to translate?"

Allie laughed and turned to Maria. "Yes, he makes me very happy."

"If you love him, caro, the memories they fade."

Ryan saw the smile freeze on from Allie's lips. "That's enough sandwiches," she signed to Jessica and turned to load the basket. "Maria, are you sure you won't join us?"

Maria patted Allie's hand and shook her head. "I drink tea in garden and read book."

"Thanks for the lunch, Maria." Ryan lifted Jessica and the basket in one swoop.

* * *

Allie knew the perfect spot for a picnic and led them across St. Ives grounds to the Port River which ran along the edge of the property.

"I didn't know there was a river here," Ryan said as he helped Allie spread the blanket along the river's bank.

Allie set out the sandwiches and poured lemonade into paper cups. "Sister Pat and I used to walk for hours along the river," she said. "I love it here."

Ryan shook his head when Jessie placed a pile of sandwiches on his plate. "I'm afraid my limit is three."

When they finished their lunch, Jessie tugged on Ryan's hand. "Can we walk?" she signed.

He nodded and held out his hand to Allie. "Come with us, Al."

"I'm thinking a nap sounds great." She lay back on the blanket and watched Jessie pull Ryan to the river where he picked up a stone to show Jess how to skip it in the fast current.

Allie closed her eyes, lulled by the steady surge of the river.

Sometime later, she became instantly awake when a twig snapped. She scrambled to her feet and searched for Ryan and Jessie, but they weren't in sight. She heard a rustle in the woods and her skin tingled.

"Ryan," she called and hurried along the path by the river. She broke into a run when he didn't respond. The path narrowed, the embankment became slick and she cried out when her foot slipped into the river.

She heard footsteps pounding on the dirt and when she sprang to her feet she rammed into Ryan.

"Ryan," she cried. "Someone was in the woods."

He positioned himself in front of her and Jessie as he searched the woods. "I don't see anyone. It could have been a squirrel or a deer," he said. But Allie knew he wasn't convinced by the way he kept a wary watch while they packed the remains of their picnic.

* * *

Ryan wasn't sure about opening the large manila envelope he'd received. He'd successfully avoided it most of the day, finding several things to do besides confronting the contents. The return address was from Jason's office at *The Daily Record*. What stopped him from digging deep in the articles? He'd asked for this, hadn't he? He loved a good puzzle and this was a juicy case. Why were his fingers hesitant to rip the envelope open and dive into the mystery?

He spread the contents on his desk and felt his heart sink knowing the tragedy involved Allie and all objectivity went out the window.

A newspaper photo of ten year old Allison stared back at him. Her mournful eyes ripped through his conscience and his chest ached when he read the headline. . .*IS CHILD HEIRESS GUILTY OF MURDER?. . .*

He gathered the material and placed it in the top drawer of his desk for safe keeping and grabbed his keys to meet Allie at the library.

Allie frowned when she saw him. "What is it?"

Her eyes were wrought with concern and she bit her bottom lip. God, he loved her eyes and her mouth. He loved everything about her except for the secrets. Ryan held her hand to his chest and fought the conflicting urge to protect her from harm and shake her until she told him what she fought so hard to evade. "I've had a bad day," he said and avoided her gaze.

"I'll get my things and be right back. You can tell me all about it."

Ryan watched her hurry away and struggled with his conscience. Wasn't he the one who insisted on total honesty? The news photos flashed through his mind. Allie's shell shocked expression as a little girl would be forever imbedded in his brain. How could he tell her about the articles?

When she walked toward him, he knew the answer. Her smile turned his insides to mush and she held out her hand as if he were the only trusting soul in her life. She wasn't ready. There were too many unanswered questions. He needed time to sort things out and so did she. He swore under his breath.

He couldn't bare the painful thought of losing her, selfish coward that he was.

Outside in the cool night air, she slipped her arm around his waist as they walked to the truck. "Did something happen at work?"

Ryan sighed. "It was just a long day, that's all." When she stopped and turned to him with questions in her eyes, he went on. "I'm working on a case I can't get a handle on."

She brushed a light kiss on his cheek. "I'm sure it's driving you crazy," she said. "You like all your ducks in a row."

He detected a twinkle in her eyes and smiled. "You're right about that." He closed his eyes when her kiss touched his lips like a whisper.

* * *

"Mike, you have a call on line two."

Mike looked up from the report he was typing and frowned at the blinking light on the phone. The only thing he hated more than the daily run sheet was getting interrupted while trying to complete it. He pressed the button and grabbed the receiver. "This is Officer Vetrano."

"Michael? This is Sister Celeste."

Mike sat upright, alerted to the alarm in her voice. "What's wrong, Sister?"

"We can't find one of the students. We think she left the grounds."

Mike reached for a pen. "What's her name?"

"Jessica Morgan. We've looked everywhere."

Mike grabbed the badge and gun from his desk drawer. "I'm on my way."

* * *

Allie heard several sirens from her desk at the library. She walked to the window, curious about the commotion.

"Sounds like something big," Mrs. Carson commented. "Maybe it's a drill."

Allie ignored the sinking feeling in her stomach as another police car raced past the library.

"Allie, you have a phone call," Lisa informed her from the counter. "It's Uncle Mike."

When Allie turned, her legs threatened to buckle. She held the phone for a moment, trying to steady her nerves before she answered. "Mike, what's going on?"

"Sister Celeste called from St. Ives."

Allie sank into a nearby chair. She could barely focus on Mike's words over the buzzing in her ears. "Is Jessica Morgan with you?"

"No." She pressed her fingers against her temple. "Why?"

"Ryan's on his way to pick you up," Mike assured her. "I'll explain when you get here."

Allie wiped her brow and swallowed a wave of panic. "When was the last time Jess was seen? How long has she been missing?"

"We're not sure." He didn't hide the worry in his voice. "I have to go."

Allie hid her face in her hands and whispered a silent prayer.

* * *

Ryan stopped his truck at the curb and stepped out to face Allie, who paced on the library steps. The look in her eyes reminded him of the newspaper photo when she was a little girl. Lost and terrified.

She ran to him, collapsed against him and he buried his face against her hair. "Where could she be?" she cried.

"I don't know," he said. The ache in his chest tightened as he led her to the truck. "We'll find her."

Neither spoke a word while Ryan drove like a maniac to St. Ives. Allie gripped the door handle until her knuckles matched the pallor of her complexion.

There was a crowd assembled in front of the rectory when they arrived. Allie sprang from the truck to join Maria while Ryan ran to talk to a police officer who organized search teams.

* * *

Pat rushed over to Allie and Maria. "We were hoping she was with you, Allie," Pat said out of breath.

"I haven't seen her. Are you sure she isn't hiding?" asked Allie.

"We looked everywhere. She's been missing since after lunch."

Allie checked her watch. "That was two hours ago." She glanced at Maria. "Have they searched by the lake?"

Maria nodded. "Mike sent group to look. Why you don't come inside?"

Allie shook her head and turned to find Ryan walking toward her. "I want to help."

Ryan held her hand. "I'm going to look for her, Al. Why don't you wait here in case she returns?"

Her gaze held his and she read the worry on his face. "What if someone took her? What if she's. . ." The words caught in her dry throat.

Ryan kissed her forehead and felt her body tense with fear. "We'll find her," he repeated with determination.

"Be careful," she whispered and watched as he disappeared toward the beach.

She ran to the cottage and up the stairs to Jessie's bedroom. Her teddy bear and favorite books were on the shelf. Allie searched the room and closet to make sure she wasn't hiding. She picked up the music box Ryan had given to Jessie and sat on the edge of the bed. When she opened the box, a small ballerina bear danced to a simple tune and tears blurred her vision. "Where are you, Jess?" she whispered and cradled Jessie's tattered teddy bear to her chest.

She opened her eyes when sirens sounded outside and jumped to the window. "Oh, thank God," she cried when she saw Holly step out of Mike's patrol car holding Jessica.

Her heart pounded as she ran down the steps and outside. Jessie held her arms out to Allie. Streaks from dried tears stained Jessie's checks and her unruly curls were damp.

"Where was she?" Allie held Jessie and looked at Holly.

"I found her wandering through town," Holly said.

Allie looked at Jessie. "What were you doing?" she signed.

"Wanted to find you," Jessie signed and rested her head on Allie's shoulder.

Ryan ran to them and gathered both Allie and Jessie close. "She was looking for you, Allie." His voice broke with emotion and tears glistened his eyes.

Margaret and Maria rushed over. "Thank goodness she's safe," Margaret exclaimed. "Maria, take Jessica into the house. Allison, I need to talk to you."

Jessie cried when she was taken from Allie's arms. "I'll be right in," Allie signed and followed Margaret to the rectory.

"I think we should start limiting your time with Jessica. She's become too dependent on you and I'm afraid your feelings for her are based more on emotion then what's in her best interest."

Allie blinked away the tears. "I care about her a great deal, but removing me as her teacher is a bit extreme."

"We can't have her disobeying the rules." Margaret's voice was stern.

"You can't blame this on me," Allie demanded. "This won't happen again. I'll make sure of it."

Margaret sighed. "Allison, I think you see too much of yourself in her which makes it impossible for you to be objective."

Allie paced and pushed a chair out of her path. "That's what makes me a good teacher, Sister." Her voice shook with rage. "I learned that from you."

Margaret uncrossed her arms and slumped into a chair. "You're right, dear."

Allie wanted to break down and cry, but squared her shoulders. "Ryan and I have talked about adopting Jessie."

Margaret smiled. "It's good to know you're talking about a future with Ryan."

Allie returned the smile and together they walked back to meet with Ryan and Mike.

* * *

Ryan covered Allie with a blanket. Her eyes were closed, her face ashen and he knew the migraine was bad.

Holly capped the pain medication. "This should start working soon."

Ryan walked her to the door. "Thanks for coming over, Hol."

"I'll be home if you need me," she reassured him and stepped outside.

He sat on the edge of the bed and touched Allie's cheek, the skin cold beneath his fingertips. "Do you want me to leave so you can rest?"

"No," she whispered. "Don't go."

A faint whimper escaped her and Ryan felt a cold knot tighten in his chest. "I'm here, baby." He eased his weight next to her and felt her relax against him as the medication took effect.

Long after Allie had drifted to sleep, Ryan stared at moonlit shadows through the curtains. When he skimmed his fingers along the silken skin on Allie's arm, she sighed in her sleep and he wondered if she dreamed of him.

For now she was safe from the pain and the memories and the God forsaken terror she'd witnessed as a child. How he longed for the moment to last, but he knew she'd slip away to her secrets once she was awake and it scared the crap out of him.

Ryan closed his eyes, but all he could see were the headlines and pictures he'd received at the office. He was more determined than ever to find out what happened the night her parents were killed. Piece by piece he was ready to remove each brick from the wall standing between them. He'd chip away at every square inch of mortar until she could live freely and completely. Love him without reservation or doubt and hoped like hell he wouldn't lose her in the process.

* * *

Allie was still drowsy from the medication when she woke the next morning. She showered while Ryan slept. He couldn't have slept much, because each time she stirred during the night, he was awake to soothe her. She sat at the edge of the bed with a cup of coffee and smoothed his hair when he opened his eyes.

"How do you feel?" he asked.

"Just a touch of a headache," she said and kissed him. "Thanks for taking care of me."

He set the cup of coffee on the night table and slipped his hands around her waist and pulled her into his arms. She closed her eyes, filled with a strange excitement. "You still look exhausted. Why don't you stay home and rest today?"

"I have a lot of work to do with Jessica." She looked away when he raised his eyebrows. "Sister Margaret threatened to relieve me as Jessie's teacher."

"Why? You're great with that kid." He leaned against the headboard and drank coffee.

"She's only looking out for Jessie's welfare. She thinks I'm too involved emotionally to be an objective teacher." Allie grabbed a brush from the nightstand and ran it through her hair. "I told Sister that you and I have discussed adopting Jess." She smiled when he looked at her surprised.

He set his coffee on the night stand and pulled her to him. "Does that mean you'll marry me?"

Allie felt the familiar tug of turmoil at the mention of marriage. "I can't imagine my life without you or Jessie." When she snuggled against him, she felt him tense, but he didn't speak. "Just give me more time," she whispered.

* * *

Maria scooped tomatoes out of the boiling water while Allie slipped off the peels. "Whew, it's like a sauna in here," Allie complained and wiped her brow on the sleeve of her shirt.

"'E troppo piccolo." Maria frowned and raised her hand to indicate the small kitchen in the convent.

"When will the kitchen be done at the rectory?"

"I keep change my mind," Maria shrugged when Allie smiled. "Too many new appliances and tiles and colors to choose." Maria put another batch of jars to seal in boiling water then poured iced tea into tall glasses. "Let's go outside."

They sat in the shade on the patio. "How did Jessica sleep last night?" Allie asked as she settled into the cushions of a lounge chair.

"She fine at breakfast. I think she sleep better than you."

Allie pressed the cold glass to her forehead. "I'd never forgive myself if something happened to her."

"It like you to blame yourself." Maria waved her hand in frustration. "What's the matter, caro?"

Allie sipped her tea. "Things are happening so fast, my life is spinning out of control."

"What things?" Maria asked.

Allie watched Maria's dark eyes glow. "Do you know what happened to me before I came to live here?"

Maria drained her glass. "I know something bad. Do you remember now what happened?"

Allie shook her head. "I only remember bits and pieces, but nothing makes sense."

The timer went off in the kitchen, so Maria got up. "You ready to tell me what you remember?"

Allie shook her head and watched Maria hurry inside.

* * *

As Allie walked home from St. Ives, all she could think about was crawling into bed and catching a quick nap before she was due at the library.

She entered her apartment and stared at a letter that had been slipped under the door. She whirled around, angry and ready to confront the sick coward who was responsible for inflicting such horror. Not again. She tore open the letter and almost laughed at the demand for two hundred thousand dollars.

She paced in the kitchen, determined to confront the unknown. She bit her nail while she considered where to begin and realized she couldn't fight the battle alone. She grabbed the note and marched out of the apartment. If it meant getting to the bottom of what happened when she was a child, then she was ready. She would not let anything happen to her loved ones.

She needed to tell Ryan before someone was hurt. She ran to town and by the time she entered the lobby of the *South Harbor Herald*, she almost burst from wanting to share the burden.

The receptionist, smiled to greet her. "Hi, Allison. Ryan's due back any time now. You can wait in his office if you want."

"Thanks, Gwen," Allie said.

She found the small pressroom and sat at Ryan's desk. She didn't have much time before she was due at the library, so she dialed his cell phone. A recording asked to leave a message.

"Rye. It's Allie. I'm at your office, but I have to leave for work. Please call me at the library when you can." She hung up and opened the drawer for a pen to write him a note.

"Oh, God," she cried when she saw the newspaper photo of her as a child. Dazed, she sank into the chair and stared at a copy of the horrible headline she'd received in the mail. Her fingers tingled as she flipped through the papers, finding other articles and pictures. Tears clouded her vision and she closed her eyes as the harsh realization ripped through her heart.

"Ryan," she whispered as the nasty bite of betrayal gnawed at her. It couldn't be. She threw the articles and rushed from the office. How could she have been so blind?

Outside, she blinked against the bright sun and placed her hand on her stomach to press back the waves of nausea.

* * *

"Allie was here, but she had to leave," Gwen informed Ryan when he entered the Herald to drop off film.

Ryan stepped toward his desk and froze when he found the articles scattered across the floor. He gathered the articles and felt a rush of adrenaline surge through him when he realized why Allie had left in such a hurry.

He raced to the library, but was informed by Mrs. Carson that Allie went home. There was no answer at her apartment and Holly wasn't home.

He stopped at the lighthouse, only to find it deserted.

He hurried to St. Ives and found Maria reading the newspaper in the kitchen.

"Maria, have you seen Allie?"

"What you do, Ryan?" The usual fire had gone out in Maria's eyes, replaced by sadness. "She no want to see you."

Ryan ran his fingers through his hair. "I have to talk to her."

"Let her alone. Maybe domani. . .tomorrow!"

"I need to talk to her now." Ryan stalked to the back door. "Is she in the garden?"

Maria glanced at the door, then to him and nodded.

He entered the garden and found Allie sitting alone in the gazebo. She'd been crying. He balled his hands into fists, hating himself for causing her pain. "Allie," he said. "Listen to me."

"Go away," she whispered, her blue eyes ablaze with rage. When he stepped toward her, she stood and grasped the edge of the table, as if she'd crumble without its support. "I want you to leave."

"Damn it, Allie. Don't do this," he pleaded.

She turned away and walked to the door, but he reached her before she entered the kitchen. He swung her around and she hit his chest with her fists. "How could you?" The anger he felt melted away when he saw betrayal in her eyes. He released her arm as if he'd been stung and watched her disappear inside. Watched the door slam and shut him out of her life.

Chapter Twelve

Ryan figured he'd already alienated Allie, he might as well really tick her off by snooping around her hometown.

Seabrook Hills was the most affluent area in Michigan. It was home to famous sports figures, CEOs and presidents of international companies and anyone else who could afford the prestigious zip code.

He stood at the main desk in the Seabrook Hills Police Station and waited for the dispatcher to complete a lengthy phone conversation before she turned to assist him.

"What can I do for you?"

"I'm looking for Detective Vincent Hartig."

Her gaze traveled the length of him before she smiled. "Detective Hartig retired over three years ago."

Ryan passed her his business card, and knew the moment she figured out he was a reporter when her come-hither smile wilted into a frown. "I'd like to ask him some questions about a case he worked on years ago."

"Hartig runs a fishing lodge up north somewhere. I can get a message to him if it's important."

"Is there someone else I can talk to?"

She held out his card. "Write the case information on the back. I'll pass it around. Maybe someone will contact you." She turned her back to him and picked up the phone, a clear indication he'd been dismissed.

He stared out the window of his truck, frustrated that he'd exhausted all his leads without learning one damn thing.

He'd contacted Allie's aunt, the only relative he could track down, but she wouldn't talk to him. He couldn't find the names of the household staff like he'd hoped and it seemed unlikely anyone from the police would contact him about the case.

He reclined the seat and shut his eyes, but when his mind replayed yesterday's confrontation with Allie, he knew it was futile to attempt sleep. He picked up the newspaper articles Jason had sent. There had to be a link to Allie's past. Something he'd missed. He examined each article, every photo until his vision blurred. Ready to write off the day as a total bust, his gaze rested on a news photo of the Weston-Stark estate. It was an English Tudor with massive arches and numerous leaded windows. It resembled a small castle he'd seen in photos of Scotland. Crime tape stretched across the huge entry doors and the front of the house. The photo was taken from a distance, so most of the detail was hazy, including the metal address plate to the right of the entrance. Ryan grabbed his camera, slipped off the lens cover and focused through the zoom on the address until the numbers were clear-3457 Breckenridge Lane. Hot damn. He entered the address into the GPS and put the truck into drive. If he couldn't talk to anyone, the least he could do was snoop round the crime scene.

He parked the truck down the street and walked along the ten foot wrought iron fence that surrounded the estate. The grounds were landscaped with ornamental trees and sculpted shrubs and were well maintained. Acres of lawn resembled a putting green and he'd bet his truck there wasn't a single weed to be found.

He passed the gate house, which was larger than the house he rented in South Harbor. The double gate was locked so he continued along the fence line to the side of the estate. The trees became dense, hiding him well, so he climbed a large beech tree and dropped from a limb onto the grounds.

He stood still and listened, half-expecting a pair of Dobermans to charge through the hedges and tear him apart. He held his breath and waited, but all was quiet, so he hid among the shrubs and made his way toward the house.

Ryan inched along to the back of the mansion, stretched to peer through a window and prayed he wasn't live entertainment on a surveillance system. Adrenaline pumped through his veins and he began to feel a little smug, after all this is what real reporters did all the time. Right? Then he heard the unmistakable click of a gun being cocked and all smugness vanished as his knees turned to jelly.

"Put your arms up real slow, sonny."

Ryan swallowed hard and held his arms above his head. "I'm looking for. . ."

"Shut-up, turn around." Ryan clamped his mouth shut and turned real slow. His eyes crossed as he looked down the cold, black barrel of a rifle held an inch from his nose. "Before I call the police," his captor drawled. "You mind telling me what the hell you're doing?"

"I'm a reporter. . ."

"Holy shit, I should just shoot you right now and get it over with," he sputtered. "You damn people never quit."

The old man's eyes shone with fury and his weathered face turned shades of red Ryan never knew existed.

"I'm not here for a story," Ryan explained. "I'm here to help a friend of mine who lived here."

The old man stared at Ryan with narrowed, angry eyes through the scope of the gun. "What's your friend's name?"

Ryan's arms were getting heavy so he folded his hands and rested them on top of his head. "Allison Weston."

"You lying son of a. . ."

"No," Ryan interrupted. "Look in my back right pocket. There's a picture of Allie in my wallet."

The man placed the end of the riffle against Ryan's temple and retrieved the wallet. He lowered the gun when he studied a picture Ryan had taken of Allie at the beach. Her smile was as bright as the sun shimmering on the lake and her eyes sparkled with laughter. "That's her all right. How do you know her?"

"We were practically engaged until yesterday when she told me to take a hike because I have this nasty habit she hates." Ryan swallowed the bitter taste in his mouth.

"What's that?"

"I want to help her face the terror she suppresses from the night her parents died."

"My name's Jim Quant. I'm the grounds keeper." He disengaged the hammer and lowered the rifle.

Ryan released an unsteady breath and held out his hand. "I'm Ryan Harper."

Like his build, Jim's handshake was solid. "Follow me." He led the way to a garden patio with ivy trailing up and over a domed iron canopy. He pulled out two bottles of beer from a plastic cooler.

"Thanks," Ryan said and sat on an iron bench beside a pool with a statue of a water nymph that poured water from a vessel.

"How's Miss Allison?" Jim asked.

"She's crippled from whatever took place in this house that night."

"She was only a child," Jim said with a wary look in his eye. "She damn near died and both her parents were murdered. That would mess anyone up."

"She's blocked out most of it, but blames herself."

"I don't know what I can tell you that wasn't already printed in the papers. The staff was gone for the night. I was at a poker game. Rose, the housekeeper, was out to dinner with friends and the chauffer, Stan, was on vacation."

"Who contacted the police?"

"Whoever disabled the security system didn't know there was a secondary back up that alerted the cops. Allison's real father, Stephen Weston, had the system installed years before."

"Who owns the house now?"

"Still belongs to Miss Allison," Jim said, and stood to open the cooler. "I'm paid by the estate attorney to keep the place up." He held out a beer for Ryan.

Ryan shook his head. "Who do you think did it?"

Jim lifted the beer to take a drink, but lowered the bottle and stared at Ryan with clear brown eyes. "Doesn't matter what I think."

"I'd like to know."

"At first I thought it might be someone hired to collect Dr. Stark's debts."

"What do you think now?"

"The Doc lost his license to practice medicine because of drug and drinking problems. His connections included some serious criminal types and the only way he could get the money was to kill Mrs. Stark and Miss Allison. But, someone killed him before he could finish the job."

"Do you think Allie pushed him over the balcony?"

Jim studied him for several moments. "Miss Allison was found unconscious. Plus, Doc was a big guy, how the hell could she have the strength to take on someone almost three times her size?" Jim shook his head and polished off his beer. "Someone else had to do it."

Ryan's mouth went dry so he gulped down the rest of the beer. "Have any idea who?"

Jim shook his head. "Nope."

* * *

When Mike entered the back room at Mac's Sports Bar, he was rushed and already late.

171

He squinted to adjust to the dim light and searched the room, crowded with new and returning college students. When he spotted Ryan, he edged his way through the crowd standing four deep at the bar to a corner table.

"Hey, Mike," Ryan said and poured a glass of beer.

"Judging by your rough appearance, I missed a hell of a party last night." Mike whistled while he appraised the stubble on Ryan's face that went beyond chic and the dark circles under red-rimmed eyes.

"Yes sir," Ryan smirked. "I'm having myself quite a time."

Mike frowned. "Seriously, you okay?"

Ryan shrugged. "I spent the night in Seabrook Hills."

"What for?"

"I visited a college buddy."

"Well, that explains the rough edges," Mike said.

Ryan didn't smile. "I also looked into an unsolved murder case I've been working on." He passed a file across the table. "Take a look." He pointed to the folder.

When Mike opened the file, a queasy sensation settled in his stomach as he scanned several newspaper articles. He lifted his gaze to meet Ryan's. "Allie's parents were murdered?"

Ryan nodded. "The investigating detective retired, but I talked to the groundkeeper at the estate."

Mike closed the file and passed it back to Ryan. "What do you hope to gain by bringing all this up now?"

Ryan scowled. "I hope it helps Allie move forward."

Mike shook his head. "I think you're playing with fire."

Ryan tossed the file aside and leaned forward. "Come on, Mike. You know how crippled Allie is by her past. She thinks she's responsible."

Mike detected the fire in Ryan's eyes. "Unless Allie wants to deal with it, I'd leave it alone." Ryan opened his mouth and glared at Mike. "She was a little girl," Mike exclaimed, "hasn't she suffered enough?"

"She's suffering all right. She's blocked it deep and she tries to hide from it, but it still eats at her. Haunts her."

The desperation in Ryan's voice tugged at Mike. "I know you love her, but she doesn't want to face it."

Ryan stared at the file. "I can't rest until I find the answers."

"It's not your fight, Rye."

Ryan stood and glared at Mike. "I thought you would understand."

Mike reached for Ryan's arm. "I do."

Ryan pulled his arm from Mike's grip. "Why does everyone think that pretending the tragedy never happened is going to help her?"

"I know you think you're helping by bringing all this stuff out in the open," Mike said. "But I think it's doing more harm."

Ryan shook his head and turned to face Mike before he left the bar. "I don't think it's possible to hurt her more than she's already hurting."

* * *

Ryan knew Allie would be at church, which was perfect because she wouldn't make much of a scene when he tried to talk to her.

He spotted her with Jessie in the third pew from the back and had to finagle his way past several seated parishioners before he squeezed beside her. She scooted away from him when his leg brushed hers. He waved to Jessie and she smiled brightly. Allie, on the other hand, didn't turn to him. She faced forward, but shot him a sideways dagger glance as her chin lifted. Color sprang to her cheeks and her clear blue eyes turned turbulent, like a gale force storm.

"What are you doing here?" she whispered.

"I want to talk to you."

When she shook her head, her soft golden curls sprang to life. "I don't want to talk to you."

"That's okay." He leaned close until her flowery scent wrapped around his heart. "Just listen."

Jessie moved toward him, but Allie positioned herself between them and signed something Ryan didn't understand.

When it was time to receive communion, Allie gathered Jessie and her things and stormed past Ryan. "Go away," she whispered as she slid out of the pew.

He spotted her outside, walking toward the Cottage House with Jessie in tow and hurried to catch up, falling into step beside her. She whirled to face him. "Stay away from me," she shouted.

Ryan grabbed her arm and spun her around before she could march away. "I want to explain. . ."

"I don't want to know," she interrupted. "I want you to leave us alone."

He glanced at Jessica, who peered around Allie and watched them. "Why are you doing this to us?" he implored.

Allie turned to Jessie, signed and spoke aloud. "Go with Sister Celeste. I'll see you at dinnertime."

He felt a twinge in his gut when Jessie's smile quivered as she waved goodbye.

Allie waited for Celeste to take Jessie's hand, turned and blew past him.

"Come on, Al," he reasoned. She stared ahead and didn't give him the time of day, so Ryan stepped in front of her to block her path. "Please talk to me."

"I mean it, Ryan." Her voice shook with rage. "Get away from me."

He followed her to the sidewalk and when they passed his truck, he grabbed her around the waist and lifted her off the ground.

"Damn you," she yelled and hit him with her purse. "Put me down."

"Allison, what are you doing?"

Ryan turned with Allie in his arms and he heard a faint hiss as she forced a smile to Father Kotalski. When Ryan set her down, she dug the heel of her shoe into the top of his foot.

"Good morning, Father. Sorry about the commotion." Ryan smiled between clenched teeth. "Allison is having a little problem."

Father shook his head and disappeared inside the church.

Allie swung her purse again, but Ryan blocked the blow and hauled her toward his truck. "We're going to talk about this whether you like it or not," he ordered as he pushed her inside and crawled over her to be seated.

"Isn't this nice," she grumbled and straightened her skirt. He started the engine and she glared at him. "I can now add kidnapping to the assault and battery and harassment and stalking charges I intend to file against you."

"You're very funny when you're being a smart ass," Ryan growled.

She glared at him and lifted the door handle, but he'd set the child safety lock. Her mouth opened, as if she was going to blast him, but she clamped it shut and folded her arms across her chest.

He slammed on the brakes and held out his arm to prevent her from hitting the dashboard. "I want to tell you why I have the articles." The anger on her face dissolved to pain as if he struck her. He wanted to touch her and kiss away the doubt until she was soft and willing in his arms.

Her shoulders slumped as she fidgeted with her purse strap. "If you did it for the story, I told you I can't remember anything."

"Shit!" he yelled. "What are you talking about? I did it for. . ."

"If you did it for the money, all you had to do was ask." She turned to face him, the wounded look in her blue eyes twisted the knots in his stomach. "I gave you my heart and trust. I would have given you anything." Her soft voice was heavy with sadness.

"You think I want money?" He wasn't sure how he managed to steady his voice, when inside he shook with rage.

"I don't know what to think anymore," she said in a broken whisper.

"Get out." Ryan unlocked the door. "I want you the hell out of my life," he yelled.

"Great," she shouted and threw open the door. "At least we can finally agree on something."

* * *

Maria climbed the stairs to the small study in the Cottage House. She'd seen the light from the convent and knew she'd find Allison at work. She balanced a dinner tray as she entered. The cool, damp air only added to the dismal sight of Allie sleeping with her head nestled in her arms on the desk. The creak of a floor board jerked her awake.

"L' Alicia, lei ha bisgno mangiare." Maria set the tray on the desk. "Have dinner."

Allie rubbed her eyes and stretched. "I must have dozed off." She frowned and wrapped a yellow sweater around her shoulders. "It's getting dark earlier now." Her voice trailed off as if she didn't have the energy to give life to the conversation.

"The leaves change early this year," Maria said and passed a mug of soup to Allie. "It smell of earth at harvest. Remind me of home in Modena." A puzzled expression clouded Allie's eyes, but she said nothing and tasted the soup. Maria whirled around and smacked her hands on the desk. It got Allie's attention for her eyes grew large. "Tutto il liefa e` il lavoro dall `alba fino a lardi nella notte. . ."

"Maria, I don't know what you're saying."

"I say all you do is work from morning to night."

"I don't want a lecture." Allie set down the spoon.

"Look at you." Allie's eyes were red from lack of sleep and her clothes hung on her small frame. Maria paced the small room. "Stop punishing yourself."

"I'm not punishing myself." Allie met Maria's gaze.

"I worry about you, caro." Maria felt a familiar catch in her throat. "Tell me what trouble you." Allie stared out the window and Maria watched as her shoulders lifted with a heavy sigh.

"I wouldn't know where to begin," she uttered. "It's so jumbled I can't figure it out, let alone talk about it."

"Start at beginning," Maria coaxed.

Allie turned to face her. "Something terrible is going to happen," she said.

"What you mean?" Maria shuddered from the dread that clung to Allie's words.

"I live with this constant fear that something is going to reach out and swallow me whole." Allie covered her face with her hands. "I remember things. Things I don't understand."

Maria was overcome with concern and reached to cradle Allie in her arms. "Caro, you worry so."

"Am I going crazy?" Allie cried.

"No," Maria whispered. "This about your past, si`?"

Allie stepped away and wiped away her tears. "Do you remember when I first arrived at St. Ives?"

Maria led her to be seated and took her hand across the desk. "I remember like yesterday."

Maria pictured the scared little girl with huge eyes that shone with the terror she'd witnessed. "You didn't speak for long time. You'd been released from l' ospedale where you stay before coming here." She watched as the invisible barrier formed between them and swallowed as fingers of shame squeezed around her throat. How much could she reveal? "You like to visit me in kitchen, so I let you help."

"Why can't I remember?" Allie cried and pounded her fists on the desk.

Maria felt an insurmountable pang of guilt. "Lei ricorderia quando. . ." she shook her head. "You will remember when time right," Maria whispered and felt a shudder travel along her spine and rest at the nape of her neck.

* * *

Ryan wasn't thinking about the high school football practice as he put his camera gear away. Instead, Allie's words played over and over in his mind. Where did she get the idea he was after money? She blamed him for trying to help. She was definitely, certifiably delusional.

He threw the camera bag across the front seat. Damn, she'd sucked him in good. If he had a brain in his thick skull he would've walked away from her at the start. But, no. He got all wrapped up in her little-miss-innocent-save-me smile and the haunted look in her eyes.

He cursed under his breath and put the truck in reverse. God, he loved her. He needed therapy to figure out why, but he loved her with a hunger he couldn't satisfy.

He left the high school parking lot and instead of heading for the office, he turned in the opposite direction toward St. Ives. If Allie wouldn't see him, then at least he'd visit Jessica.

He drove the scenic route along the lake and stopped to snap a picture of orange and red leaves reflecting brilliant against the cloudless sky. He lowered the windows and inhaled the crisp scent of late summer as he rounded a curve and turned up volume on the radio. He glanced at his speedometer and stepped on the brake.

Nothing happened as he gained speed down the winding two lane road that meandered by the lake. He pumped the brakes, again with no response.

His heart lurched to his throat when he crossed the centerline and swerved to avoid an oncoming van. The driver of the van blasted his horn as he sailed by.

Ryan flipped on his emergency flashers, laid on the horn and grasped the steering wheel as the truck descended the hill.

Up ahead, he spotted a car in his lane traveling under the speed limit, no doubt enjoying the view. Again, he laid on the horn and swerved around the car. When he looked in the rear view mirror, he saw the driver flash an angry gesture.

"Sorry, buddy," Ryan growled and squinted as beads of sweat trickled into his eyes. Up ahead was a stretch of road with treacherous curves referred to by local bikers as Evil's Pass. He eased the truck against the guardrail and gritted his teeth as the hideous sound of metal scraped and twisted. The speedometer needle dropped a mere fraction, he could see the lake over the side of the rail. He glanced to the opposite side of the road lined with shops and pedestrians. He muttered an oath as the truck hit the guardrail with such force, it bolted upward and over the metal.

The moment seemed frozen, like slow motion replay, while the truck sailed airborne toward the lake.

* * *

A misty rain fell when Mike stepped out of his patrol car in the circular drive at St. Ives School. Allie would be teaching, and as much as he hated to interrupt, this was an investigation.

His heart was heavy as he stepped inside the building and walked the corridor to the office. Sister Pat smiled when he entered. "Hi gorgeous."

Pat rolled her eyes, oblivious to his flirting. "What brings you here this time of day?"

Mike brushed off drops of rain from his face. "I need to see Allison."

The smile on Pat's face faded. "Is there something wrong?" She closed the file cabinet.

Mike paused, not wanting to alarm her. "I need to see her right away," he repeated.

Pat moved toward the door. "I'll take over her session and send her down."

Mike stepped into the hall and paced in front of the cabinet which displayed artwork with a harvest theme.

It wasn't long before hurried footsteps sounded in the hall and Allie rushed toward him. Her face ashen and her eyes wide.

"What is it?" her voice was calm, but she clutched her sweater as if to shield herself from a sudden chill.

"I need to ask you some questions." He looked over his shoulder and saw Sister Pat approach. "Can we go someplace private?"

Allie nodded and walked toward the lounge. "I'll get my coat." She held her head high, but her attitude did not hide how frightened she was as her hand shook when she reached for the doorknob. "I'll meet you on the front step."

Mike continued to pace at the entrance. Man, he still craved a cigarette at times like this. The door opened and Allie stepped outside.

"What's going on?" she asked.

"Ryan's been in an accident." Mike cleared his throat and saw the last bit of color drain from her face. Her mouth formed a tiny circle, but only a faint cry escaped her lips and he reached to steady her when her eyes glazed. "He'll be all right, Allie."

She crumbled against him and he led her to his patrol car. When he sat in the driver's seat, she rested her head against the seat as silent tears spilled from the corners of her eyes. "What happened?"

"He ran his truck into the lake." Allie covered her face with her hands. "He banged up his knee and has a strained neck, but he's lucky."

"Where is he? I want to see him."

Mike opened the glove compartment and pulled out a box of tissue. "He's at the hospital," he said. "From what Ryan told me, it sounds like his brakes failed." He watched her closely. "It's a new truck, so I'm guessing the brakes were either faulty or tampered with." He caught a spark of fear in her eyes. "We won't know for sure until the tech report is complete."

She turned to him. "Will you take me to him?"

"Do you know why someone would want to hurt him?" He asked. She shook her head and reached for the door handle, but he held her by the arm.

"I don't know," she cried.

"What are you hiding, Allie?"

"Nothing." She twisted the tissue in her hands. "Please take me to see him."

The drive to the hospital was quiet. Allie stared out the window and never spoke a word until she thanked him when he stopped the patrol car at the front entrance.

Mike sat in the car long after Allie disappeared inside the hospital. He rubbed the stubble along his chin and vowed to find the link between Ryan's recent visit to Seabrook Hills and the accident.

* * *

Allie left the information desk and hurried past the nurse's station on the second floor in search of room two-eighteen.

She stopped at the open door and smoothed her hair. The curtain was drawn, so she waited until a nurse walked by the room. "Excuse me," Allie said. "I'm here to see Ryan Harper."

The nurse nodded. "This is the room." She pulled back the curtain. "I just gave him a pain shot. He'll sleep for awhile." The nurse motioned to her. "You can come in."

Allie eased into the chair next to the bed. Ryan's eyes were closed and an angry red welt stood out at his hairline. He wore a padded collar around his neck. His right leg was propped on a pillow with an ice pack strapped over his bandaged knee. She hesitated when she took his hand, afraid to inflict more harm. The nurse checked his temperature and blood pressure and left the room.

"Ryan," Allie whispered and choked back a sob. He stirred and groaned, but didn't open his eyes. Allie rested her head on the bed and stroked his hand. "I love you," she whispered.

He opened his eyes, blinked to focus and squeezed her hand.

Allie sat at the edge of the bed to rest her cheek against his. "You were right," she said. "It's time to face my past."

When he moved his leg, his faced twisted in agony. Allie covered her mouth with her hand, overcome with unbearable anguish knowing she was responsible. He could've been killed because she was too weak to face her fears. He'd loved her unconditionally and she let him down. Her stomach muscles twisted, not from terror or memories or dreams, but from guilt.

She closed her eyes and vowed to do whatever it took to mend the pain.

* * *

Allie jerked her head when she thought she'd seen something move. Her eyes adjusted to the dim light from the adjoining bathroom and realized she'd dozed off in Ryan's hospital room. Her head was foggy from the short nap and it took a second to focus on Ryan's face.

"How long have you been here?" His voice was hoarse and he cringed as he reached for the cup of water on the bed tray.

Allie held the straw to his lips. "For a few hours, since you got out of surgery." His gaze never left hers as he sipped water through the straw.

"I'm surprised you even came." Allie swallowed the hurt, knowing she deserved worse, but was glad his eyes closed so he missed the tear that plopped onto the sheet.

She set the cup on the bed tray when she heard a faint snore and reached for her purse. Maybe she'd feel better after a cup of coffee. She studied the strong profile of his face and forced back a sob as a muscle clenched in his jaw. "I'm so sorry," she whispered. His breathing remained steady and she brushed a light kiss on his forehead. "I'll be right back, Ryan."

Allie stood to leave and the first waves of nausea hit when her gaze fell to a folded paper at the foot of the bed. She unfolded the note and cried when she read the words. . .*JUST A FRIENDLY REMINDER. . .*

Allie bolted from the room to search the long corridor.

She leaned against the wall and closed her eyes, dizzy and breathless. She took a step toward the nurse's station and covered her ears with her hands to shut out the loud buzzing sound.

When Allie opened her eyes, Holly was crouched over her and pressed something against the side of her head.

"What happened?" Allie asked.

"You passed out," Holly told her. She pulled the gauze away to examine the wound and when Allie tried to sit, Holly rested her hand on her shoulder. "Just sit tight, Allie. I'm taking you to ER."

"I'm all right," Allie protested.

Holly's smile curled sympathetically. "It won't take long. I can pull some strings," she whispered, "and get you out of there in no time."

Chapter Thirteen

*A*llie jumped from the couch to pull open the drapes when she heard a car door shut. She searched Ryan's living room to make sure everything was perfect. She set out the arrangement of flowers Ryan had received at the hospital, then opened the front door and watched Ryan hobble toward the house while Mike walked beside him.

She rushed to help Ryan remove his coat.

"I can get it," he snapped.

Allie's gaze met Mike's. "All right," she said and backed away to give him space. He slumped onto the couch and reached for the remote control.

"It looks like a frigging funeral parlor in here," Ryan grumbled.

Mike shifted his weight, clearly uncomfortable. "Is there anything you need, Ryan?"

Ryan flipped through the channels and shook his head. "No. Everything's just ducky."

Allie laced her fingers to keep from biting her nails and walked Mike to the door. Outside she crossed her arms to ward off the chill. "Give him some time, Allie. We stopped by the yard to check out his truck. He's upset because his camera gear's ruined."

Allie felt her chin quiver and she looked away to avoid Mike's imploring gaze. "Thanks for picking him up at the hospital, Mike."

Mike hopped inside his patrol car. "No problem."

With a heavy heart, she entered the house to find Ryan staring at the television. "I made a pot of spaghetti sauce. Are you hungry?"

He shrugged, but continued to switch channels with the remote. He ignored her. What did she expect? What an idiot she was to think he'd fall right back into her arms. She was getting what she deserved for accusing him of unspeakable, hateful things. She hurried into to kitchen, leaned against the door and willed the tears to stop. She knew it wouldn't help to break down, but she covered her face with her hands to stifle the sobs as despair and guilt ripped through her like a storm.

"Allie, I need time to sort things out."

She wiped the tears away when she opened her eyes to find him standing at the doorway. "I know," she whispered when he limped back to the living room.

She poured a cup of coffee, determined to break through the barrier she'd created. Telling him how sorry she felt wasn't going to do the trick. She needed to show him.

She paused in the doorway and watched him set a log in the fireplace. Before long, a warm glow flickered around the room. He stared at the fire and she clenched the mug to steady her hands. He was a million miles away and knowing he had every right to be angry made it worse.

She entered the room and held out the mug, as if it were a peace offering.

Ryan blinked and even though his jaw was set, he managed a slight smile and lowered himself to the hearth. "Thanks," he said. She eased herself beside him and gazed into his eyes, longing to see the tenderness of his love that was replaced by indifference.

She took his hand. "I don't know how to move forward, but I know it's time." As much as she wanted to sound convincing, her voice faltered.

Ryan squeezed her hand. "Wanting it is a strong beginning," he whispered. "But I don't know if it's enough."

She lifted her gaze to meet the intensity in his eyes and attempted to smile. "I hope it is." She closed her eyes and held his hand against her cheek. Please, God. Her heart raced. "Will you show me the newspaper articles?"

"Are you sure?"

She nodded. "It's time to start putting the pieces together."

* * *

Maria wrapped the last of the sandwiches and placed them in an insulated bag. "Alicia, I pack lunch for you and Ryan," she offered when Allie entered the kitchen.

"How do you know I'm meeting Ryan?" Allie tried to hide her smile.

"Because you wear same perfume when you see him."

Allie laughed. "Some detective you are."

"I'm right, si`?"

Allie peeked in the bag and her mouth began to water. "Of course you are."

In spite of dreading the task she was about to undertake, Allie hummed as she walked to Ryan's office to review the articles. She hastened her steps when she passed the park and blocked the thoughts of the latest threat she'd received at the hospital. She was done paying the money, driven to confront the helplessness she felt. Since Ryan was hurt, she wanted the person to come out of his slimy hole to confront her. "Never again," she muttered when she spotted the picnic table and shivered when a cold blast of air whipped through her light sweater.

By the time she reached Ryan's desk, she was winded.

He was working at the computer and frowned at the screen. "I'll be right with you." His gaze met hers and when the small dimple at the corner of his mouth deepened, her spirits lifted.

When he squinted at the screen, she knew he'd misplaced his glasses again. Finding comfort in the way they sensed familiar quirks about each other made her smile. Like the way he held her hand when she was about to bite her nails. The way she knew he was about to comment on what a nice picture something would make if only he had his camera. How he placed his arm around her to offer comfort when she grew quiet.

He printed his work and turned to her. "Are you sure you're up for this?"

"I've waited too long," she said. "I need to know what happened."

He pulled a file from his desk drawer and spread the contents across the desk. Allie wiped her damp hands on her slacks and forced herself to look. When she stared at the headline of the article that had been mailed to her, a wave of nausea came and went and her gaze met Ryan's. He watched her with concern etched on his brow. "Are you okay?"

She placed her hand on her forehead and closed her eyes. "I'll be all right."

"It was long ago, Allie. Nothing can hurt you now."

Allie swallowed hard as another wave of nausea hit. He was so wrong. Something waited. Something evil. Something connected to these articles. A small cry caught in her throat when she opened her eyes and picked up a photo of her mother dressed in an elegant gown. "She was so beautiful," she whispered. A handsome man in a tuxedo stood next to her in the photo. Allie scanned the caption. *. . Mr. and Mrs. Steven Weston attend the opening of a charity ball to raise money for Children's Hospital.*

Allie stared at the photo of her real father and felt nothing. No wave of emotion, no connection. She sorted though the articles, but nothing clicked. "Why don't I remember?"

Ryan limped around the desk and she looked up after several moments. "It's like a chunk of my life is carved out of my brain."

"Maybe we should take it slow." Ryan took the paper out of her hand.

"No! It's been too long," she insisted. "It has to be done." Her teeth chattered, even though the room was warm and Ryan draped his jacket over her shoulders.

Allie stared at an article with the picture of a nun escorting her as a child from a hospital. "It's Sister Margaret." She lifted the photo of the house draped in crime tape and another of Dr. Franklin Stark with her mother.

"Do you think. . ." Allie dropped the article and Ryan caught her hand to pull her close. She buried her face against his shoulder, in the safe hollow of his neck. "Do you think I killed him?"

He held her at arms length. "No. I don't," he answered. "It could have been a number of people."

"But. . .I was a suspect." She pointed to the article that questioned her guilt.

"The doctor was heavy into debt from drugs and gambling. He was desperate. The media had a fiesta with this," he said as he held up the same article.

Allie frowned as his words grew faint and she shook her head to clear the hum in her brain. "How do you know?"

He led her to the chair, knelt beside her and held her cold hands. "I went to Seabrook Hills."

"When?" She closed her eyes and pinched the bridge of her nose. "A few weeks ago," he admitted.

"But why?" she whispered and backed away.

"Because I want to know what happened. For you, Allie. For us." He reached for her, but she pushed him away.

"You don't know what you've done," she whispered and ran from the office.

* * *

When he found her, she was leaning against the side of the building breathing deeply. There were no tears, but more distressing was the sheer panic he detected in her eyes. "You don't need to run from me each time you're afraid." He wanted to soothe her, but she backed away.

She shook her head, as if to clear her thoughts. "I think you were hurt because you went to Seabrook Hills. Who knew you were going?"

"Why would you think that?" he demanded. He followed her faraway gaze to a stand of trees, then pulled her to face him before she slipped away to her private world.

"Ryan," she began. "I. . ." She spoke each word as if it were ripped from her heart. "I don't know how to tell you."

"Just tell me," he demanded. "No more secrets."

She raised her head to meet his gaze. "I have to show you something at my apartment."

He reached into his pocket and produced his keys. "The rental car's in back." He pulled her along before she changed her mind.

The ride to her apartment was quiet except for the occasional sound of her anxious sigh. He reached to take her hand and squeezed. She slid close and rested her head on his shoulder. "It's going to be alright, Allie."

Allie looked away and didn't speak. Ryan felt her tense when he stopped the car in front of her apartment and for several long moments she didn't move. "You're not changing your mind, are you?" He'd be blind not to notice how stressed she was. Her face was shades too pale and even though there were no tears, her eyes were bright as they searched his.

"I don't think I have a choice." Allie reached for the doorknob and Ryan followed her into the apartment.

She closed the curtains and he watched while she reached behind the refrigerator to retrieve an envelope.

He frowned. "What's going on?" The envelope shook as she held it out for him. He didn't take his gaze from hers while he removed several pieces of paper.

He led her to the table and sat beside her to read the first letter. "Its extortion," he stated. He read each threatening note. "Christ, Allie," he shouted. "How long has this been going on?"

She opened her mouth, but didn't speak. He hauled her outside to the car and grabbed his cell phone.

"No," she cried and lunged for the phone, but he stopped her.

"What the hell's going on?" He regretted his sharp tone when she flinched.

"I started getting the notes before graduation," she said. "At first I ignored them until the fire at St. Ives." She hesitated and he clenched her hair in his fist, fighting to control his rising anger.

"Go on," he said.

As if she sensed his mood, she lowered her gaze. "There were other notes I destroyed." She spoke the words with her head bowed, as if she were at confession and he lifted her chin with his fingertips. The fear in her eyes had eased a fraction. The tenseness of her body had calmed a degree. The worried tone of her voice seemed to lift a mere decibel and a splash of color had returned to her cheeks.

"Who's doing this?" he asked.

"I don't know."

"You paid some of this money, didn't you?"

"I thought it would stop if I paid." She nodded slightly and covered her mouth to stifle a sob. "Then you were hurt."

"When you first saw the articles in my desk, you thought I sent these notes." She shook her head, but he caught a glimpse of truth in her eyes and slammed his fist on the dashboard, finding no other outlet for his frustration. "Didn't you?" he yelled and fought the urge to shake her until she came to her senses. Damn, his knee ached and he was beyond tired. He eased back against the seat and closed his eyes, but saw blackmail notes, the articles, flames and smoke that poured from St. Ives, the blue depth of the lake as it swallowed his truck.

He met Allie's gaze and it sickened him to know she'd faced the horror alone. He glanced at the door and for a fleeting moment, fanaticized about breaking free from the tentacles of madness that held him locked in its grip. The sound of a car passing by jarred him back to reality and he punched numbers on his cell phone.

"What are you doing?" Allie asked.

He blocked out her anxious expression and completed the call. "We need to turn this over to Mike."

Allie grabbed for the phone, but he blocked her with one hand and held the phone to his ear with the other. "Ryan, please. Someone will get hurt if the police are involved."

"I'd like to speak to Mike Vetrano." He held his hand over the receiver. "People have already been hurt, Allie." His heart wrenched when she sank against him as if she were surrendering to the enemy and he kissed the top of her head. "It's got to stop," he whispered into her hair and after leaving an urgent message for Mike to call him, he cradled her against him. "Now we wait."

* * *

Mike stared at the blackmail notes in disbelief. He looked at Ryan, who stood next to the kitchen counter with his arms crossed. The air was thick with tension and when he looked at Allie, she turned away. Her eyes were red and she appeared to be scared beyond reason.

"What do make of this?" Ryan asked.

Mike shrugged. Allie had told him all she knew, so she said. He referenced his notes. "Why would anyone have reason to extort money from you?"

Allie gathered the sweater tightly against her and touched her temple as if the slightest sound was painful. When she didn't speak, Mike stood and stepped to her. "I asked you a question."

Ryan was quick to slip his arm around her as he faced Mike. "It's obvious someone's after her money and they know Allie well enough to prey on her loss of memory, hoping she'd continue to pay rather than face the truth," Ryan said.

"I asked her." Mike raised his voice and watched Allie for a reaction. "This isn't a game."

"Do you think I'm enjoying this?" she asked and pulled away from Ryan to pace.

"You can't stay here alone. It's not safe," Mike said in a low tone. "Do you want to stay with Ryan?"

She looked out the window and shook her head. "If I stay with Ryan then it puts him at further risk." Her gaze met Ryan's. "I'd rather die than have anyone else get hurt because of me."

Ryan was at her side before she could blink and clutched her hand. "Damn it, you didn't do anything wrong," he said, his voice controlled. "Stop blaming yourself."

"Maybe Sister Margaret will let me move back to St. Ives until this is over." Allie closed her eyes and placed her fingertips on her temples. "Right now, I need to lie down."

Chapter Fourteen

"All the years I lived at St. Ives I never wanted to leave," Allie said as she stared out the window in Sister Margaret's office. "Then you asked me to leave, and my world changed forever." She twisted the cord of the curtain around her finger and turned to Margaret. "Now, it feels like I'm in prison."

"You should have come to me when you started getting the letters." Margaret felt a stab of pain from the anguish she heard in Allison's voice. "Maybe I was wrong to shelter you," she admitted. She was tired and the problems Allie faced weighed heavily on her conscience. She rubbed her hands together, hoping to soothe the ache in her joints. "I'm not so sure it would have harmed you to face the past."

Allie sat down in the chair in front of Margaret's desk and reached for her hand. "I know the decisions you made were to protect me."

Margaret squeezed Allison's hand. "You have always been such a sweet child. I know you'll come out of this ready to face your life with renewed spirit."

"You were right to kick me out of here you know."

Margaret frowned and studied Allison's face. "What do you mean?"

"I never would have met Ryan." A slight smile lifted the corners of Allison's mouth. "You are the most unlikely matchmaker."

"You love him, don't you?" Allie's smile deepened in response and Margaret's heart swelled.

"I never thought it was possible."

Margaret grinned. "When this mess is over, looks like we'll be planning a wedding this place has never seen the likes of before."

* * *

Ryan sat on a stool at the kitchen island and watched Maria knead dough. "How's Allie?" he asked, hoping Maria would shed some light on the secret side of Allie's life. "She's avoiding me."

Maria folded the dough. "Alicia only understand here. . .il cercello." Maria pointed to her head. "Not here. . .il cuore," she said, pointing to her heart. "I know she love you from suo cuore. . . her heart."

"I wish I could be sure." He followed Maria's gaze and stood when he saw Allie at the door holding a floral arrangement. She stared into the room, her gaze hollow.

Ryan jumped to catch the vase as it slipped from her grip, set the flowers aside and led her outside. "What is it?"

She walked to the edge of the garden and watched the lake below. The angry waves crashed against the rocks, sending a light mist into the air. "I thought the flowers were from you." She held out a card.

He gritted his teeth as he read the demand for two hundred thousand and threats to kill Jessica, then Allie if the police were alerted. The anguish in Allie's eyes tore at his heart. She looked so fragile, he reached to hold her for fear a strong wind would send her over the cliff.

"Who's doing this to us?" she cried.

He pulled her toward his truck parked out front, fueled by a blast of anger going off like a rocket. "I don't know, but I'm sure as hell not going to sit by and let anything happen to you or Jessie."

* * *

Mike watched through binoculars from his car while Allie walked toward the picnic table. He scanned the park for anything unusual. A young couple made out under the shade of a willow tree. A man played fetch with his dog. Another couple pushed two children on the swing set. He focused on a man who sat on a bench and tossed crumbs to a flock of pigeons. The man didn't look up as Allie secured the money under the picnic table. Through the binoculars, he could see the tension etched on Allie's face as she hurried away.

"The trap is set," he mumbled through the prep-radio to his partner, Chris Mercer.

"I'm watching from my station," Chris answered.

"She's scared shitless." Mike's heart went out to Allie as he saw her disappear around the corner. "She's not convinced that involving the police was the right thing to do."

"Most people in her situation would feel the same, especially after getting threats. Hell, if it was my family, I'd think twice about going against the demands," Chris said.

"We both know the odds against a good outcome if the law isn't involved."

"Yeah, well sometimes having the law involved really screws things up," Chris responded with a deep sigh.

* * *

Ryan drove in silence. Allie tried to sleep, but he could tell by her restless sighs, she wasn't having any luck. He turned up the volume on the radio and changed stations until a catchy rock ballad filled the air, determined to help her escape the agonizing wait. She held onto his arm and hadn't let go since they left town over an hour before. When she looked at him, he knew her slight smile was only for his benefit.

Jessica played with stickers in the back seat and seemed oblivious to the gravity of the situation. She smiled at his refection in the rear-view mirror and his heart swelled.

It was Mike's idea to get Allie and Jessica away from town until the money was picked up and the slime ball apprehended, so Ryan planned a visit to his parent's orchard for the day.

Allie glanced at Ryan's cell phone. "Are you sure Mike has your number? It's been over an hour," she said. "Maybe he lost it. Maybe we should call him." She twisted her hands and he knew how hard it was for her not to bite her nails. "Is your battery charged?"

"It's charged and Mike has my number, Al," he soothed her. "He'll call."

Allie crossed her arms and looked out the window at mile after mile of farmland. "Are you sure your parents won't mind us barging in like this?"

Ryan patted her knee. "Stop worrying so much, honey. They love having us visit." The crease on her brow didn't ease. "They can't wait to see you and Jessie again."

Allie rested her head on his shoulder. "I won't know how to act when this is over. I've spent my entire life hiding, afraid."

Ryan hummed along to a tune on the radio. "I've seen how happy you are when you allow yourself to relax and have fun."

Allie searched his face. "When?"

"You were dancing with Father Kotalski at your graduation party." A smile tugged at the corner of her mouth. "When you laughed, I fell head over heels in love with you."

Allie's eyes gleamed with pleasure. "You remember the exact moment?"

"Yes, I do." He grinned. "It was like getting bowled over by a freight train."

"You make it sound so gruesome." She laughed and nudged him.

"It was pretty scary." He hummed again and Allie settled against him.

Ryan's parents were out the front door of the big farmhouse before Ryan turned off the engine of his truck. They beamed from ear to ear as they stepped off the porch.

"Hello," Julia said as she embraced Ryan. "I'm so glad you all could come."

Ryan smiled when he looked at his mother. "It's great to be here, Mom."

Rich hugged his son and then Allie. "Hello, Allison. Who have we here?" he asked and knelt down to greet Jessica.

"Hi, Mr. Harper," Allie said and signed for Jessie. "You remember Ryan's parents?" Jessie nodded and hid behind Ryan's leg.

"Come inside for lunch." Julia linked her arm through Allie's. "Then Rich and I can take you on a tour of the cider mill and to see the animals." She turned to Ryan. "Star is anxious to see you."

Ryan lifted his eyebrows. "You mean he needs work."

"Ryan always had a special way with animals," Julia whispered to Allie.

Allie's gaze lingered on Ryan. He held Jessica on his shoulders while he chatted with his dad and her heart ached with emotion. "He has a special way with people, too," she murmured so only Julia could hear.

* * *

After lunch and a ride around the orchard and cider mill, they stopped at the barn.

"Jessie wants to see the cat," Julia said.

"Allie and I will be with the horses." Ryan took Allie's hand and led her to the corral where Star pranced and shook his head.

"Where's Nell?" Allie asked.

"Probably in the barn. Star's on his own now, aren't you boy?"

Ryan stepped into the corral and whistled. "Come here, Star."

Star snorted and made a game of avoiding Ryan. "He's shy," Allie said and leaned over the fence.

"Obstinate is more like it," Ryan said and swiped for the bridle but Star whinnied and danced out of reach.

"I think Star's laughing at you."

Ryan gave up on sweet-taking Star and turned to Allie with a sly smile. It was a total ambush and she screamed when he grabbed her under the armpits and lifted her over the fence and into his arms. Star pranced around them and nudged Allie's cheek with his nose and snorted.

Her eyes opened wide and they both lost it. Allie threw her head back and laughed. Not just a simple laugh, but the kind that comes from the belly. Ryan's eyes stung with tears and his sides ached. Her arms were wrapped around his neck and her head rested on his shoulder. Her smile was bright, without a hint of worry.

"Thanks for bringing me here, Rye." Her eyes grew soft when he turned to her. "No matter what happens, I want you to know that I love you so much."

Ryan eased her body to the ground, her hands rested at his waist and he lowered his lips to hers. Star trotted over and nudged his head between them and Ryan patted him.

"Looks like Star is a little jealous," Rich called out from the barn.

Allie hid her face against Ryan's chest and their laughter was cut short by the chirp of his cell phone.

* * *

Allie's heart leaped to her stomach when her gaze met Ryan's. She watched his smile fade when he answered the call.

She held her breath when he turned his back to her and she strained to hear the soft words that were spoken. When he disconnected the call she saw his shoulders slump.

"What is it?" she pleaded.

When he turned, she knew the news wasn't good. His chin was set and the grim line of his mouth was braced for trouble. Her stomach knotted. "It was Mike," he said. "Come here," he held out his hand for her, but her legs wouldn't move.

She shook her head. "Tell me."

"No one picked up the money."

"They know about the police," she cried and covered her mouth.

"Mike didn't say that." He pulled her to him and circled his arms around her.

"Maybe it's too early. Maybe they're still coming to get the money." She clung to him.

Ryan rested his chin on the top of her head. "They've called off the surveillance. Mike wants us to come back to town right away."

He led her from the corral to his truck. "I'll get Jessie and let my parents know something's come up."

* * *

Mike drummed his fingers on the top of his desk and waited for Ryan and Allie to arrive. Ryan had called him from the road and said they were a few hours away. He checked the time. They should be pulling into the station any moment. He forced himself to concentrate on the daily log which was due hours ago, but his mind was on Allie.

He opened her file to pull out the articles and his notes. Something didn't add up. The murder of her parents was never solved. Nothing new had turned up for twelve years and then out of the blue Allie starts getting extortion notes. He had a feeling the answers were locked somewhere in Allie's memory.

The main door opened, he heard their voice's and waited while they entered the squad room.

"Thanks for coming in," he said.

"Why wasn't the money picked up?" asked Ryan, who stood beside Allie with his arm around her like a shield.

"Could be the scumbag was on to us," he explained. "Which means if there's going to be a follow-up to the threats you've had, Allie, it'll probably be soon."

Allie stared at him as if he were speaking hieroglyphics.

Ryan set both hands on the desk. "How could this happen? Do you think the investigation tipped off the extortionist?"

Mike rubbed his eyes. "Nothing was obvious." He turned his attention to Allie. "I need to know what happened the night your parents died, Allie. You've got to remember." It was hard to ignore the alarm in her eyes, but he persisted. "Tell me what you know."

At first she didn't speak, so Ryan jumped to her defense. "She doesn't remember, for Christ's sake," he yelled.

Mike stood up. "If you don't shut-up, I'll have you thrown out of here."

Allie stood between them. "Stop," she insisted. "I've already told you everything."

"Tell me again."

She sank into the chair and Ryan placed a hand on her shoulder. She glanced at the articles spread across Mike's desk. "I remember bit and pieces. I was doing my homework when I heard my mother scream." Her words were barely audible.

Ryan sat beside her and folded his hands around hers. "Go on."

"I went to her room. There was broken glass on the bed table. There was blood. . ." She closed her eyes and placed her hand on her stomach. "I backed out of the room and heard footsteps. I ran to my room. I don't remember what happened next."

"Did your father come into your room? Did he hurt you?"

Allie shook her head. "I don't know," she whispered.

"Did you push him over the balcony when he tried to strangle you?"

She stared at him and shook her head. "I can't. . ."

"Come on, Mike." Ryan stepped in front of her. "Give her a break. She doesn't remember."

"She knows. She needs to concentrate." Mike sat down and sorted through the articles. "Someone murdered your parents and tried to kill you. I think the person who did this to you and your family is after the money again. Anything you might remember might be the key to the case."

He poured hot water and plunked a tea bag into a foam cup and set it in next to her on the desk. "You recently graduated, which met the stipulations of your inheritance. There's millions of dollars in the trust. Do you know how much?"

"I don't want the money." She shook her head. "I plan to give it away."

"Maybe that's why someone is so desperate to get their hands on it now."

She looked into his eyes. "What can we do?"

Mike sighed. "I want you to think about any detail you may have forgotten. Maybe you think it's insignificant, but it might mean something." He wrote down his cell phone number. "Call me any hour if you think of anything more." He gave her his business card. "In the meantime, you need to stay at St. Ives. I'll post a guard there if you want."

* * *

Ryan walked Allie to her apartment so she could get some clothes to take to St. Ives. The apartment was dark and cold when they entered and he checked out the refrigerator while she packed.

"There's nothing to eat. I'm starved." He opened a bottle of cola.

"We could get something in town before you take me back," Allie answered from the bedroom. Ryan stood in the doorway and watched her fold clothes into a backpack. "Why don't you run out and get something while I finish here?"

Ryan frowned. "I don't want to leave you alone."

"Holly's next door. I'll be fine." She smiled at the look of concern on his face. "Besides, we can spend some time here before I go back to prison."

He checked his watch. "I'll be gone ten minutes." He stopped at the door. "Call and make sure Holly's home," he said and leaned against the doorframe.

Allie dialed the phone. "It's Allie. Ryan's going to grab some dinner, have you eaten?" She set the phone against her shoulder and continued to pack. "You have?"

Ryan waved. "Keep her on the phone until I get back."

Allie nodded and waited until Ryan left the apartment before she ended the conversation with Holly. She zipped the backpack and hurried to the door. With any luck at all, she could be out of town before Ryan returned. She called a taxi to request a pick-up at the drug store. She slipped outside and was on the first step when Holly opened her door.

"Allie, where are you sneaking off to?"

Allie's heart sank, but she turned to Holly with a smile. "I'm going to stay at St. Ives a few more days. Ryan will be back to pick me up anytime now." Allie searched the street, expecting to see his truck.

Holly went on about a concert she and Mike attended, but all Allie could think about was loss of precious time.

Holly finally closed the door when the phone rang and Allie hurried toward the street. Her heart almost stopped when she saw Ryan's truck. She dropped her backpack and ran. She didn't look back, even though she heard the squeal of brakes, a car door slamming and the pounding of footsteps.

"What are you doing?" he yelled when he caught up to her.

"I'm not going to stay here and wait for someone to get hurt!" She quickened her pace, but Ryan swung her around.

"Are you crazy?" he shouted. "Why don't you just wear a big red target on your back?" His fingers dug into her arm as he picked up her backpack and hauled her toward the apartment.

She struggled to get away, but his grip was firm. "Let me go." He pulled her toward the apartment. "Ryan, please."

He swept her into his arms, to the door, but it was locked. "Where's the key?" he yelled, his face twisted with anger.

Allie continued to struggle as he dumped out the contents of her purse until he found the key. "Damn it, stop hitting me," he growled.

He opened the door with one hand and half-dragged, half-carried her inside. He slammed the door shut with his foot, locked it and carried her to the bedroom where he dumped her onto the bed. She sprang to her feet, but he tackled her and they fell back.

"Get off," she screamed.

His hands locked around her wrists above her head and the weight of his body made it impossible to move. "Not until you tell me what that was about," he yelled back. His face was flushed with rage and they both breathed heavily.

Allie closed her eyes. "If I leave town then no one will get hurt. I can't sit here any longer and wait for something to happen." Tears of anger sprang to her eyes. "It's the money they want. If I leave then you and Jessie will be safe. Let me go," she pleaded.

"Over my dead body," he snapped.

"That's what I'm afraid of."

"This is by far the craziest idea you've come up with," he growled and rolled next to her. "I can't let you go. If something happened to you it would kill me."

Tears rolled down the side of her face. She was exhausted and frightened, but she'd do anything, even risk her own life for Ryan and Jessie.

He kissed her, tender at first, but the emotions and desperation of the situation drove her. Allie kissed him as if his breath gave her life. She was desperate to escape the danger. She opened her eyes and his hard, bright gaze met hers. He was angry and tousled and all she could think about was his kiss. She smiled and his mouth claimed hers once more. The touch of his hand made her skin tingle with pleasure. She needed him more than anything. She craved the strength of his love. His strong hands caressed the skin on her back and he ran his fingers along her ribs. Allie began to unbutton his shirt, but his hand clamped down on hers.

"Don't stop," she pleaded.

Ryan kissed her cheek. "We can't."

"I don't understand." She frowned. "Don't you want. . .?"

"Oh, you bet I do." Desire smoldered in his eyes. "But, I want you to come to me out of happiness. Not from pain, not like this." He released her hand and pulled down her sweater.

Allie rested her head on the pillow and started to laugh and cry all at once. "Boy, my timing really stinks."

* * *

Mom cried when she said I needed to go to a school far away because he was a busy, important man. But, I knew better. I was sent away because he didn't like me.

Mom said I was supposed to be nice to him because he was my new dad. He was okay when mom was around. He'd smile and hold my hand. I didn't want him to touch me. Didn't like the feel of his cold, hard hand. When I tried to pull away, he'd squeeze real tight and then his smile scared me. If I shut my eyes I could pretend I was safe.

But, sometimes, I couldn't push the memories away, no matter how hard I tried. . .

I hid in the closet. If I was quiet he wouldn't find me. I tried not to cry. I was scared. I wanted my mom, but she was gone. I opened my eyes and there he was . . .his big hands wrapped tight around my neck. I couldn't breathe.

Someone stood over him. He yelled, let go of me, then stumbled and fell over the edge.

I closed my eyes and there was only darkness.

* * *

Allie sat up in bed and gasped for air. She sprang from the room, down the stairs to phone Ryan. Her heart pounded as she waited. Maybe Ryan had his phone turned off or the battery was low. Please answer. Please.

"Ryan," she cried.

"Allie, what's wrong?" His voice was groggy.

"I remember someone else was in the room. Someone killed him," she whispered. "It wasn't me."

"God, Al." He released a sigh of relief. "I thought you were hurt."

"Ryan, I didn't kill him," she repeated.

"Do you remember who did?"

Allie spun around when a floor board creaked in the hall. "I have to go," she whispered.

Chapter Fifteen

Ryan faked interest as a marketing analyst poured over figures from last quarter. Instead, he thought about Allie's call during the night. He hadn't slept a wink after they'd talked. He questioned whether or not she'd told him everything about her dream.

He glanced at the clock, shifted in his chair and wondered how much more he could endure of the meeting. Allie's words played over and over in his mind until he wanted to bolt for the door.

On a screen at the far side of the room, the analyst pointed out each painful detail of charts and graphs until Ryan's vision blurred. He rubbed his eyes and glanced around the room to see if any of his peers showed interest in the intricate garbage. There was no great surprise when everyone stared, with blank expressions, at the data with the exception of Mick, the accountant. Go figure.

Once again, his mind wandered to Allie's call. She'd always waited until he pried information out of her, but she called him. It was the first time she'd reached out to him. This was what he'd waited for, a sign that she needed and trusted him. It made his head spin.

He caught his editor's attention, held up a finger to indicate he'd be back and after a nod of approval, left the room.

* * *

Ryan found Allie at the main desk working on the computer. Her attention was fixed on the screen, a slight frown and the pallor of her skin was a sure sign she had a headache. Ryan leaned against the counter and waited while she finished her task. Several moments later, her gaze met his. It took a split-second for the recognition to register, and when it did, her eyes softened with unspoken words. He fought the strong urge to gather her against him.

She attempted a smile. "I'll be right with you," she said and printed her work. He watched her pass the papers to a young man. "I hope this helps your research."

"Thanks, Allison," the kid replied and gazed at her, but didn't make a move to leave.

Ryan checked out the dude who checked out Allie and stepped closer. "Can you take a break, Allie?" he asked.

Allie turned to speak with Mrs. Carson and Ryan nodded at Romeo, who shot him a dejected look before he walked away.

"I have an hour," she said and came around the counter. "Maria packed a big lunch, want to share?"

Ryan nodded and waited while she disappeared to the locker room. She returned with an insulated bag and her coat.

"So who was the testosterone marvel making eyes at you?"

Allie frowned. "What are you talking about?"

"You don't even have a clue when someone's coming-on to you," he teased.

"Who?" she asked, her expression clueless.

"The kid at the counter. He has the hots for you."

"Daniel?" She laughed. "He does not."

On the entrance step, he pulled her against him. "I know the hots when I see them."

"Do you see them now?" she asked, giving him a sly, sideway glance.

He laughed and led her to the car. The sunlight made her skin seem more translucent and once inside the car, he studied her for a moment. "Looks like you got as much sleep as I did." He cupped his fingers under her chin and titled her head. "How are you holding up?"

"I'm all right." She opened the lunch bag and pulled out two generous chicken salad sandwiches. Allie's weak attempt to appear as if nothing was wrong faded when she fell against him.

"Tell me about the dream you had last night," he said, softly stroking the nape of her neck.

"I told you everything." She clutched his jacket. "Can't we go away somewhere?"

He closed his eyes and buried his face in the soft, fruity scent of her curls. "Where do you want to go?"

"I don't care, anywhere. I can hardly breathe." Her eyes shone with questions and his heart sank from the weight of her vulnerability. "I can't stand waiting any longer," she whispered. She lifted her gaze and pressed her lips to his and deepened the kiss as if it would chase the pain away.

"Let me help you find the answers." He held her in silence and listened to the softness of her breathing. The wind seethed outside the car, swirling bright colored leaves into a funnel. For the moment, they were sheltered from the wind and could hold the evil at bay.

* * *

There was a chill in the air as Maria descended the stairway so she hugged her robe against her. It was dark, another sign that winter would arrive early. She'd still be asleep, but had heard a sound from the kitchen below her bedroom. Perhaps a soothing cup of tea would help ease the thoughts that twirled in her brain like an endless record.

She entered the kitchen and saw Allison seated at the table, her head rested in her hand. The shrill whistle of the kettle jarred her awake.

"Caro, why you awake this hour?" Maria asked.

211

"I couldn't sleep." Allie stood and knocked over the canister of tea. "I'm as jumpy as a cat."

Maria watched her gather tea leaves into a pile. "Something you need talk about?"

"I'm remembering more about my past."

"Tell me," Maria said and placed her hand against her aching chest.

Allie scooped tea into the canister. "About the night my mother was killed." Maria grasped the edge of the counter for balance and held her breath. "I think there was someone else in the room when he tried to kill. . ." Allie stopped and hurried to the door to search the hall. "Did you hear something?" she asked.

"No," Maria answered and turned away so Allie couldn't read the look of horror she was powerless to hide.

* * *

Allie didn't seem to notice when Pat entered the classroom, so she stood in the doorway for a moment to study the look of concentration on Allie's face. It was obvious she'd spent another sleepless night. Pat moved and Allie jumped, but the brief flash of surprise vanished, replaced by a slight smile. "Pat, you startled me," Allie said and breathed a sigh of relief.

"Sorry about that," Pat said and clasped her hands together to keep from fidgeting as she stepped into the room. "I finished my class early and bribed Celeste to take my next session. I thought you'd like to join me for a run into town before you start at the library."

Allie looked at the incomplete lesson plan and without hesitation, closed the book. "You bet," she said, her eyes dancing with excitement. "I could use a break."

Pat checked the clock. "The shops will just be opening if we leave now." She strained to keep her voice calm, even though she wanted to scream at Allie to hurry.

"Let's go then," Allie said and grabbed her purse.

212

Pat peered into the hall, turned to Allie and smiled. "I feel like I'm playing hooky."

Allie covered her mouth to stifle a giggle. "Who are we hiding from?"

Pat motioned for her to follow. "I told Celeste I wasn't feeling well. How else do you think I could get her to cover my class?" Pat knew she had gullible little Allie right where she wanted when the corner of Allie's lips curled into a smile. All she had to do was get them to the car without being noticed.

Pat backed the car from the garage and when they pulled onto driveway, hidden by the line of tall trees, she stepped on the gas and laughed. "Free at last."

"I've been cooped up at St. Ives for too long." Allie rolled down the window and inhaled fresh, cool air. "This is great."

At the end of the road, Pat stopped and glanced toward town. "When do you have to be at the library?"

"Not until noon."

"If we're going to shop, we might as well do it right and go to Grand Bay." She turned the car away from town and gripped the steering wheel, ignoring the worried frown on Allie's brow.

"Relax. We'll be back by noon."

Pat turned up the volume on the radio and started to hum a song while Allie watched her. She reached over and nudged Allie on the arm. "Come on, Al," she said. "Get into the spirit."

* * *

Allie stared out the window, fighting a sinking sensation as the miles stretched, taking her further from the safety of South Harbor. She wasn't about to tell Pat why she felt so uneasy. No one at St. Ives knew about the threats except Sister Margaret. She dug her hands into the pockets of her corduroy jumper to reduce the temptation of biting her nails.

When Pat stopped the car in the parking lot of the Grand Bay Savings and Trust, the sinking sensation turned to panic.

"I need to make a stop here first," Pat said.

Allie glanced at the bank, desperate to calm her nerves. With everything going on, her imagination was out of control. "Go ahead," she told Pat. "I'll wait here."

Pat rummaged through her purse and when she pulled out a handgun, Allie felt the tremor of a small earthquake. "What's going on?" She waited for the joke to begin. This was Sister Pat. Her friend, her confident.

Pat appeared nervous as she searched the parking lot. "We're waiting for the bank to open."

Allie grabbed the door handle and Pat clicked the safety lock to secure the door. "Why are you doing this?"

Pat gripped the gun and pointed it at Allie's forehead. "Keep quiet," she snapped.

As if slapped by the cruelty in Pat's tone, Allie cringed, but didn't move a muscle. It was only ten minutes before the bank opened, but to Allie it seemed like an eternity. She wanted answers. Instead, she waited, certain that the riddles and fragments of her past would soon surface. Her body betrayed her will to remain calm and she began to shake.

Pat reached into the back seat and tossed a coat at her. "If you do exactly what I say, you won't get hurt."

Allie gritted her teeth. "Tell me why you're doing this. I've never done anything to you."

Wicked laughter rang inside the car. "Oh, you've done plenty." Pat sneered while she opened a small case and pulled out a blonde wig and sunglasses. Allie watched Pat tuck dark hair under the wig then study herself in the mirror. She applied bright lipstick and gazed at Allie through dark lenses.

"Looks like the bank's open." She cocked the gun and grabbed Allie's arm. "I want you to arrange for a withdrawal of one million dollars in cash."

"No," the words escaped Allie's lips before she could think.

Pat lowered the sunglasses. Anger intensified in Pat's eyes as her mouth twisted into a sinister snarl while she placed the gun against Allie's temple. "You don't get it, do you?"

Allie shook her head to clear her racing mind and clenched her hand into a fist. "Why don't you explain it to me?"

"Allison, dear, it's the wrong time to develop a back bone." A smile tugged at the corner of Pat's lips. "Let's say this is interest on a debt your father and I tried to collect years ago."

Allie swallowed hard and shook her head. "You mean my step-father?"

Pat tightened her fingers into the flesh of Allie's arm. "Stop pretending you don't know what you did to him." The hatred in Pat's eyes filled Allie with dread. "He killed your mother and was going to get rid of you, too."

Allie's stomach turned as furious tears sprang to her eyes. "You killed my mother for money?" She felt the flood gates to her emotions open wide as she lunged at Pat and grabbed her around the throat. "You ruined our lives."

Pat yanked Allie by the hair with such force, her head hit the door. "You killed him," Pat shrieked and pressed the gun under Allie's chin. "You ruined everything."

"Someone else hit him over the head before he fell," Allie cried.

"You're lying. There was no one else in the house." She released Allie's hair, but struck her across the mouth. "Damn it," she yelled and grabbed a box of tissue. "Clean off your face."

Allie's hand shook from rage as she dabbed blood at the corner of her mouth. Her mind raced as the depth of betrayal began to register. "How did you know him?" She didn't care if Pat became angry. She had a right to know why her life was destroyed that awful night.

"I was his nurse assistant at the hospital." A gleam in her eye flashed at some distant memory. "We became lovers and the rest is history," she added with a smug smile as she opened the car door.

"How did you manage to fool Sister Margaret into letting you stay at St. Ives?" Allie placed her hand across the knotted mess of her stomach.

"There's a shortage of nuns." Pat laughed. "Sister Margaret believed my story. What can I say?" A stab of pain shot through Allie. "How could you kill for the. . ."

"Enough questions," Pat growled through clenched teeth as she stalked around the car to open Allie's door. "Get out," she demanded. "I'll be watching while you're in the bank." Pat pulled her along. "I won't have any problem using this." Allie saw the flash of metal as Pat slipped the gun into her pocket. "If you alert anyone, you'll be dead before you can blink. Understand?"

Allie nodded and tried to gather her wits as she entered the bank. She forced her nerves to calm as she stepped toward the first available teller. "I'd like to make a withdrawal," she said and opened her wallet for identification.

The teller entered the account information into the computer. "What can I do for you, Ms. Weston?"

"I need to withdraw one million dollars." Allie swallowed hard as she choked out the words. "In cash."

The teller's eyebrows raised a fraction, the only indication of her surprise. "We don't keep that much money on the premises. I'll need to get approval."

Allie smiled to calm the rising spasms of rage as the teller left to find a superior. A creepy chill started at her shoulders and settled at the base of her neck when she glanced at the patron desk and discovered Pat watching through dark glasses. Allie closed her eyes, fighting the queasiness in her stomach. She willed useless tears away and searched the bank for a means of escape. There was a surveillance camera in the corner behind the teller station. Allie stared into the lens and prayed for a connection with anyone who might be watching. Her mind screamed, but her body remained frozen with dread.

The teller returned with a large currency form and Allie hurriedly filled in the blanks. When she was done, she handed the paper to the teller, all too aware of the tremble in her hands. "How long will it take to get the money?"

"It might be here tomorrow, but usually takes two business days."

"Two days?" Allie closed her eyes and wondered how she could survive the wait. She wrote down the number Pat had instructed her to use. "I can be reached at this number when the money is available." She thanked the teller and walked out of the bank with Pat hot on her trail.

Once inside the car, Allie turned to Pat. "I started the process, but it might take a few days," she said.

Pat grabbed the front of Allie's jumper. "You better not bull-shit me."

Allie frowned, not accustom to Sister Pat using fowl language. "A bank of this size doesn't keep large sums of cash available." She watched Pat's pupils dilate with fury. "I was going to ask for a cashier's check, but I didn't know who to make it out to," Allie said, surprised at the restrain in her voice, even though she wanted to smack the haughtiness from Pat's face.

Pat whipped the gun from her pocket and rammed it against Allie's cheek. "Don't get smart with me," she said in a low, threatening voice.

"I'm not," Allie whispered, afraid Pat would splatter her brains all over the front seat of the nun mobile, as it was referred to by the sisters.

Pat started the engine and backed out of the bank lot. "Then we'll have to go about our regular routine and wait, won't we?"

The drive to the library was silent. Allie pretended to sleep, but her mind raced in a thousand directions. Once she was in the library, she'd call Mike. She'd alert Ryan. She'd find Jessica and make sure she was safe. She'd notify the National Guard. Whatever it took.

The quakes in her body began to calm at the thought. She wouldn't sit by and allow a disturbed, malicious lunatic hurt anyone she loved. Not again.

Lost in her thoughts, she jumped when the car stopped in front of the library.

Pat turned to her as if she'd read Allie's mind and a slow, wicked smiled crossed her lips as she opened the door. "In case you're having heroic thoughts," Pat said and pointed to the entrance of the library. Allie turned in horror to see Jessie skip down the steps toward the car. Her soft brown curls bounced and her trusting puppy-eyes sparkled with happiness.

Allie placed her fingers over her mouth, afraid she'd lose her breakfast. Pat nudged Allie's side with the gun and cackled. "Little Jessica and I will be inseparable until I have the money."

* * *

Allie sat on the steps of the library and waited. How she managed to get through her shift without falling to pieces was a mystery. The wind storm had quieted, leaving a light drizzle. She didn't feel the cold rain that soaked through her clothes. Just numbness.

Ryan was busy covering the hectic fall sports schedule. It was a blessing, for he'd know something was wrong and would manage to whittle a confession out of her. A dull ache settled in her chest. She couldn't risk seeing him until the money was delivered to Pat.

Headlights grew bright as the nun mobile pulled up to the curb. She stood, at first shaky, but reigned in her nerves. She'd have to focus, remain calm for the next few days and give Pat no reason to lose control.

She reached for the door and her heart lurched when she saw Jessica in the back seat. "Why don't you leave her out of this?" Allie cried.

"Get in and close the door before someone hears you." Pat pulled the car onto the road. "She's insurance you'll behave and do as you're told."

Allie reached for Jessie's hand. "You haven't hurt her," she asked. "I swear there won't be. . ." She stopped when Pat flashed a warning glance.

"You aren't in any position to make threats," Pat snarled.

Allie felt despair threaten her fragile control as she rested her head against the seat. Her brain throbbed from unbearable tension and her throat ached.

When Pat parked the car at St. Ives, Allie carried Jessie to the Cottage House. As least she could keep an eye on her inside. She helped Jess change into pajamas then tucked her into bed. She settled next to the little girl and they read Jess's favorite book about ballerina bears. Allie's eyes stung with tears when she found Jess asleep moments later. She lingered, not wanting the moment to end. Jess snuggled against her and Allie closed her eyes to absorb the sweet innocence before she switched off the light. She was exhausted, but knew she wouldn't find solace in sleep. Her thoughts raced. She had to think of a way to get Jessie to safety. Could she get word to Mike without risking their lives?

She couldn't sit still, so she slipped out of bed to pace. To plan. There had to be a way.

Chapter Sixteen

Mike stopped at St. Ives hoping to catch Allie before her class. He knocked on the kitchen door at the rectory and was greeted by Maria. His stomach growled when he caught a whiff of something sweet and freshly baked.

"You always know when to visit, si`, Michele?" Maria laughed as she removed a tray of blueberry muffins from the oven.

Mike's mouth watered as he poured a cup of coffee. "Yes, Ma'am," he admitted. "Just like when I was in school and I'd sneak into the kitchen." He smiled when she set a plump muffin in front of him.

"Why you come so early?" Maria asked.

"I wanted to talk to Allie."

Before Maria lowered her gaze, Mike saw an unmistakable look of sadness. "She not yet come for breakfast." Maria fidgeted with the handle of her coffee cup. Mike was about to ask why she appeared so uncomfortable, but Pat entered the kitchen.

"Good morning, Mike, Maria. Great, there's fresh coffee," she said.

Mike nodded to Pat. "Maria always has fresh coffee and something incredible to eat."

He saw a nervous smile cross Maria's face. "Michele, he want to talk to Alicia."

Pat shifted on the stool and sipped her coffee. "She's helping the children get ready for class."

Mike slathered butter on the warm muffin. "I swear I'd weigh three hundred pounds if I lived here." He winked at Maria and watched color tint her cheeks.

"I make sure you work off with chores," she said.

"You'd certainly be a welcome distraction if you lived here." Pat laughed.

Mike frowned when Allie entered the kitchen. Her gaze darted from Maria to Pat, then away. She nibbled on a fingernail and avoided his gaze.

"Good morning," she said, her voice heavy with fatigue.

"Mike wants to talk to you, Allison," Pat said and drummed her fingers against the coffee mug.

Allie buttered a slice of toast. "Oh, really?" she asked. "About what?"

Mike wouldn't discuss the details of his visit in front of Maria and Sister Pat, so he forced his voice to sound casual. "Just wanted to see how you're doing."

He watched Allie's shoulders relax a bit. "I'm fine." She finally looked his way and her brief smile faltered. He saw a riot of unspoken emotions flash in her eyes.

Pat set the cup in the sink. "Better bring your breakfast with you, Allie." She nodded toward the clock. "We'll be late for our meeting."

Allie gulped down a glass of juice and wrapped her toast in a napkin. "I forgot all about the meeting." She followed Pat from the room, but lingered at the door. "Bye, Mike."

Mike finished the rest of his muffin without the benefit of tasting it. All he could concentrate on was the tone of urgency he detected in Allie's voice.

* * *

Although the afternoon dragged, Allie attempted to give her students her undivided attention, but with Pat checking on her every few minutes, it was impossible. Besides, her mind was miles away. In the safety of Ryan's strong, protective arms with Jessie by their side. If she closed her eyes and concentrated, she could almost smell the scent of apples fermenting and drying hay. Her eyes stung with tears hoping it wasn't too late. Had she waited too long? Would she ever have the chance to prove to Ryan how much she loved him?

The instant the final bell rang, she ushered the last of her students onto the bus and raced to the cottage, determined to shelter Jessie from Pat.

She hurried up the stairs and her defiance melted away when she discovered Pat braiding Jessica's hair.

"Hi, Allie," Pat said. "Come in and have a seat. We were just about to watch a movie."

Allie spirits sank further when Jessie's innocent smile contrasted sharply with Pat's menacing glare.

* * *

Ryan dialed the number to the Cottage House and waited for several rings.

"Hello, this is Sister Celeste."

"It's Ryan, Sister. Is Allie available?"

"She has a migraine and asked not to be disturbed." Sister Celeste said.

Disappointment settled over him as he checked his watch. "Will you tell her I'll try to stop by tomorrow at lunch?"

"I'll leave a note on her door."

After he disconnected the call, Ryan stared at the phone and wondered if he should force his way into Allie's room to make sure she was all right. It would be a breeze to climb the tree outside her room and gain access through the window. No one would know.

He could hold her and tell her how much he loved her and how it destroyed him to see her in pain.

He tossed the phone onto the passenger's seat and turned his truck toward Mac's for a beer. He'd let Allie rest and see her at the library the next morning. Maybe take her to lunch and try to convince her to move in with him so he could keep a closer watch.

* * *

Allie pretended to sleep, knowing if she stirred before Pat fell asleep, all hope for escape would vanish.

Below, the chimes from the grandfather clock in the foyer announced it was midnight and her heart rate accelerated with each deep gong.

She listened to a steady beat of rain against the window pane. It was still too early to attempt a move, so she waited in the dark and thought of her mother and the events she had spent a lifetime to blot from her memory. It was time to remember.

She closed her eyes and for the first time, willed her thoughts to transcend to the night when she was ten years old. She fidgeted, but let her mind drift until she pictured the wall paper printed with violets in her childhood bedroom. Could see the soft, white eyelet material cover the canopy above her bed. Could smell the fresh scent of rain that drifted into her room from the open balcony doors. It had rained that night, as well.

Allie clasped her hands together to keep them still. God, she wanted the memories to stop, but forced her mind to move through the details.

She pictured the doll her daddy had brought back from a business trip. Her daddy. Allie had loved him so much. Tears welled in her eyes as her mind began to open. Her head pounded from images and fragmented flashes as her memory returned.

Why had she forgotten her real father all these years? He was so kind and she loved him with all her heart. The trust money wasn't something evil at all. It was given to her from her father.

She covered her face and wept bitter tears of renewed grief knowing the funeral in her dreams had been her dad's. She'd only been five years old when he died in a car accident and her life had changed forever.

* * *

It was Sunday and I was home from school for the week-end. After dinner, my friend's mom would pick me up to drive me back to school. I could hardly wait. I tried to concentrate on my math problems, but the house was too quiet. I was used to the constant chatter of my classmates at the dorm.

My mom was in her bedroom, closed away from the fight she'd had with my step-father. He left the house a few hours before and I closed my eyes to whisper a prayer that he wouldn't come back until after I was on my way to school.

I jumped to my feet when I heard glass break and a piercing scream. My book slipped from my hand and my heart thumped when I reached the stairs. I inched my way up to the third floor and stood in the hallway, afraid to look in my mom's room. I could smell her perfume mixed with fresh flowers.

I peered into the room and screamed when I saw her lying on the bed. Shattered bits of glass glistened on the bed side table from a broken vase and blood dripped from her fingertips onto the white carpet. Her eyes were open, but I knew she could no longer see.

I stumbled into the hall and covered my mouth to silence a scream when I heard footsteps in the room below. I ran to my room, to my closet, my hands shook as I set the lock. I hid in the corner and covered my ears to block the sound of my step-father's angry words as he kicked open the door.

He dragged me toward the balcony and yelled when I bit his arm. He wrapped his fingers around my neck. I could feel the pain, but couldn't scream. The light from the lamp on my dresser began to fade and my thoughts grew fuzzy.

"No," someone screamed and hit him over the head with the angel bird bath from the balcony. Chunks of cement fell around me as he staggered against the rail and was gone. I gasped for air and saw the broken wing of the angel beside me.

"He no hurt you anymore," the soothing voice said as gentle fingers stroked my brow. "Close your eyes, caro."

* * *

"Maria. Oh, my God," Allie whispered and sat at the edge of the bed, her body trembling from the vivid images that played in her mind. She didn't have a moment to dwell on the insight as something moved at her feet.

"Lord, Fran," she cried and reached for Sister Celeste's cat. Francis curled into a ball on Allie's lap and began to purr.

* * *

It was hours later when Allie startled awake. The clock struck one and Allie glanced at the alarm, it was three-thirty. With guarded movements, she rose from bed and dressed, all lingering traces of sleep vanished as her senses jumped to hyper drive.

She placed an extra pillow under the blanket and prayed the flimsy illusion would buy her time.

It was dark in the hall, but she knew every square inch of the house, including each creak in the floor boards. Her steps were cautious, to keep from making a sound and when she passed Pat's open door, she held her breath.

Allie entered the children's room and leaned against the wall behind the door for several seconds.

It was so quiet, even the rain had stopped. All Allie could hear was the thunder of her pounding heart. She closed her eyes and inhaled slowly to ease her taunt nerves.

The door opened a fraction and Allie's heart leaped to her throat. She braced herself, but when Francis sashayed against her leg, she covered her mouth to keep hysterical laughter at bay.

She took one slow step after the other until she lowered herself onto the bed next to Jessica.

Jessie stirred, but didn't wake, so Allie shook her and prayed the little girl would remember how they'd discussed their secret adventure earlier. When Jess opened her eyes, Allie placed her fingertips on her lips.

Jessie nodded and wrapped her arms around Allie's neck. Allie inhaled the sweet scent of baby shampoo and fought the sick chill of panic. There would be plenty of time to fall apart once Jess was safe. She wrapped a blanket around the little girl, gathered her close and stepped into the hall.

With the expert steps of a burglar, she descended the stairs without making a sound. Beads of perspiration dotted her brow as she shifted Jessie's weight so she could hold the banister for support.

When she opened the heavy front door, it screeched. Allie hurried outside. At last they were in the yard, but not free, for when Allie made a dash for the road, she saw a dark silhouette move from the second story window.

She gasped and ran toward the back of the house. If only she could make it to the convent, she could call the police.

She crept along the side of the house, hidden by the shadows. Her lungs burned with each breath, as she slipped around the corner, she bumped into Pat.

She screamed and shielded Jessie, but before she could turn, she felt a burning pain on her neck. "No," she tried to scream, but the words were distorted as the world turned lopsided and blurry. She stumbled to her knees and heard Jessie's cry grow distant.

* * *

On the way to the library, Ryan stopped at the bakery for Allie's favorite oatmeal muffins. He carried them into the children section to spend some time with her before he had to rush off to an all day photo shoot at the middle school.

He waved to Mrs. Carson and frowned when he entered the room to find Lisa at the desk.

"Where's Allie?" he asked and searched the library.

Lisa looked up from a book and smiled. "She called this morning to ask if I'd cover her shift," she said. "I have a date this weekend so the extra cash will come in handy for a new outfit."

Ryan smiled. "Hot date?" he asked.

Color jumped to Lisa's cheeks. "Real hot, but don't say anything to Uncle Mike. He still thinks I'm a baby."

"I won't tell," he promised and set the bag of muffins on the counter. "Is Allie sick?"

"I didn't talk to her." Lisa shrugged. "My mom didn't say."

Ryan pointed to the muffins. "Help yourself."

"Thanks," she said and opened the bag.

He'd try to track Allie down at lunchtime, but an uneasy feeling settled over him as he headed to the middle school.

* * *

Consciousness came in waves and when Allie tried to move, her body wouldn't respond. Her eyelids were so heavy, she felt as if she could sleep forever. A dull ache throbbed in her head and her throat hurt when she swallowed. She forced her eyes open and it took several seconds for her vision to clear. Curled up beside her on the bed was Jessie, deep in slumber.

Allie glanced around the room and the hazy memory of her botched escape flooded back.

She tried to move, but her hands were tied behind her back and her legs bound at the ankles. The heavy drapes were closed, but a trickle of light around the edge revealed daylight.

Allie knew they were in a hotel room by the room service menu on the table next to the bed. She rested her head on the pillow to ease the throbbing pain and looked at Jessica. Her mouth, like Allie's was covered with heavy tape. Allie's heart sank when she saw dried tear stains on the little girl's cheeks.

* * *

It seemed like hours later when Pat burst into the room and came around the bed to untie Allie's hands and ripped the tape off her mouth. "Get cleaned up," she ordered and tossed clothing on the bed. "The bank called. The money's ready."

Pat wore a designer suit and her hair, nails and makeup were styled to perfection. Sister Pat was only a memory.

Allie sat at the side of the bed, her eyes burned and her mouth felt like it was stuffed with cotton. Pat scuffed her across the back of the head. "Let's move," she yelled and Allie clenched her hand into a fist.

Jessie stirred and sprang to her feet to follow Allie, but Pat grabbed her arm and yanked her away. When she ripped the tape from Jessie's mouth, the child started to cry. It was a pitiful wail and Allie knelt down to soothe her. "I'm going to take a shower," she signed and kissed her on the cheek. Jess shook her head and the tears stopped.

After finding nothing in the bathroom to use for a weapon, Allie stood in the shower, allowing the water to hide the sound of her tears.

While Jessie picked at a bagel and juice, Allie sipped coffee. "What do you plan to do with us after you get the money?" Allie asked.

"I don't know," Pat snapped and lifted the edge of the curtain to peer outside.

"You can have the money. Just don't hurt Jessica."

"I'll do whatever it takes to get away." Pat crossed her arms and narrowed her eyes at Allie. "You'd better make sure this goes off without a glitch or you know damn well how it's going to end." Pat pointed a gun at her. "You shouldn't have told your boyfriend and the cop." She lowered the gun toward Jessie. "Keep her under control. We have to leave."

Allie positioned herself between the gun and Jessie as she wrapped the rest of Jessie's breakfast in a napkin. "We can take this with us," she signed and helped Jess with her coat.

Outside, Allie shielded her eyes from the glaring sunlight. She fastened the seatbelt around Jess and handed her the bagel.

"Get in the front," Pat demanded.

The drive to the bank was only a few blocks from the hotel and when Pat stopped the car she turned to Allie. "Don't act suspicious or alert anyone." She nodded toward the back seat. "I'll stay here with her."

Allie opened the door and thought for sure her legs would buckle, but she forced herself to remain strong or someone would get hurt.

She entered the bank, relieved to find the same teller who'd assisted her with the initial withdrawal. While she waited in line, she checked out security. There were two cameras. One positioned behind the counter and the other directed at the customers. The camera behind the desk rotated to view the entire room.

One security guard stood at the end of the counter talking to a pretty young woman. It was obvious he wasn't paying much attention, for he'd yet to look at Allie.

At last, she stepped forward to the window. "I'm here to pick up a withdrawal." She gave the teller her identification and a copy of the paperwork she'd filled out on the last visit.

"How are you today, Miss Weston?"

Allie felt a sting of pain in her head. It hurt to talk, much less look natural, but she forced a smile. "Fine, and you?"

"I'm great," the teller said. "I'll get your money." Allie watched the teller push a buzzer to open a door to the back room.

She shifted her weight and bit her nail as minutes past. What was taking so long? She glanced at the security guard who watched her. Something had to be wrong.

The teller came through the door with the bank manager and Allie's heart sank when she noticed they were empty handed. They approached the window and the security guard moved closer.

"I'm sorry, but there's a freeze on your account," the manager said.

"Why?" Allie exclaimed. "It's my money. I need it today. Right now." She paused to get her voice under control.

"I'm not sure. I'll look into the matter right away."

Allie glanced into the lens of the video camera and signed a message, then turned her attention to the manager. "You have to give me the money," she said through gritted teeth. "Someone will kill my little girl if I don't walk out of this bank with the money in the next few minutes."

The manager exchanged a horrified look with the teller. "I'll call the police." She stepped toward the phone, but Allie held her hand against the glass.

"Don't do that," she pleaded. "I need the money. You can call the police after I leave."

The manager nodded her head and left through the security door once more.

"Are you going to be okay?" asked the teller.

"I don't know," Allie admitted and wrote down Mike's cell phone number. "Call this number after I leave. Don't let anyone come after me." Allie paused to catch her breath. "My little girl will be killed. Do you understand?"

Allie breathed a sigh of relief when the manager returned with a large package. "Remember what I said," she told the teller. With one last look at the camera, she turned and made a quick exit.

Brakes squealed as Pat stopped the car at the entrance. "Get in," she shouted.

Allie threw the bundle onto the seat and jumped into the car.

"What took so long?" Pat yelled as she twisted Allie's arm.

"I. . ." Allie saw the security guard bolt through the open door and aim his gun.

As Pat gunned the car toward the guard, Allie latched onto the steering wheel. "Back off," Pat screamed and struck her on the side of the head with the gun. Allie heard a sickening thud as the guard hit the windshield and rolled off the hood.

The car fish-tailed onto the street and Jessie wailed in the backseat. Allie blinked to focus, but couldn't stop the fingers of unconsciousness from pulling her into the oblivion.

Chapter Seventeen

Ryan managed to sneak away from the middle school at lunchtime. He wanted to make sure Allie was all right. He needed to hold her, kiss her. Needed to see her smile.

He laughed as he took the stairs, two at a time, to the entrance of St. Ives School and thought about the way Allie had thrown herself at him. He must have been crazy to turn her down. Ninety-nine percent of each and every day, he'd thought about making mad, passionate love to her ever since the first time they'd kissed. Ever since he saw her smile, saw her tears, heard her laughter. Christ, ever since the first time he saw her.

He entered Allie's classroom. It was empty, so he headed for Sister Margaret's office. She was in a meeting so he left school to check with Maria at the rectory.

Maria was at the kitchen sink and nearly dropped a glass when she turned to him. "You scare me," she scolded and set the glass in the drainer.

Ryan leaned against the counter. "Sorry," he said. "I came to see Allie, but she's not in her class."

He could see dark circles under Maria's eyes before she looked away. "She still sick. Sister Pat take her tea and toast to the Cottage House."

"When?"

"Early this morning."

He jogged to the house and knocked on the door. The kids would be in school. When no one answered, he opened the door and climbed the stairs. Allie's bedroom was dark and she was covered from head to toe with a blanket.

He eased his weight onto the bed and pulled the covers back to discover a pillow.

"Shit," he muttered. Dread filled him as he raced from the cottage. He was out of breath when he knocked on Sister Margaret's office door.

"What is it, Ryan?"

"When did you last see Allie?" he asked, anxious for answers.

"I don't know, sometime yesterday. I was told she's sick this morning, so I made arrangements for a substitute."

"I think she's gone."

"Gone?" Margaret said with a look of surprise.

"She's not in her room."

"Maybe she's at the convent."

"I need to see her," he said, raking his fingers through his hair.

"Allison's migraine was so bad, Sister Patricia gave her a sedative. Why don't you come back this evening?"

Ryan jumped in his truck, but didn't drive away. He couldn't leave without knowing Allie was safe. He was deep in thought until a light rap on the passenger's window jarred him back to reality.

Maria stood outside the car, motioning for him to let her in. He unlocked the door and she slipped into the passenger seat. "I need to talk," she said, fussing with the sweater around her shoulders.

"What about, Maria?" He didn't have time for idle chat, yet when he saw worry etched on Maria's face, he forced himself to listen.

"I should tell Alicia years ago, but afraid to hurt her with truth. The doctors, they say let her remember."

"Tell her what?"

"I thought she remember over time, but no." Maria stared at her folded hands. "Ero il suo nanny quandro. . ."

Ryan shook his head. "Speak English, Maria."

"I was her nanny when her mama killed. My real name Rosa Maria Masilliamo," she said. "My American friends, they called me Rose. That night, I left house to meet friend for dinner, but came back for coat because it start to rain."

"Holy crap," he said with sudden recognition. "You're Rose the housekeeper."

"I hear Alicia cry, I go upstairs." A tear trailed down Maria's cheek. "Dr. Stark, he choke her. I hit him with statue from balcony." She waved her hands. "He come toward me, but he fall back to rail. Then over side to ground." Maria was silent for a moment before she continued. "When I hear sirens, I make sure Alicia breathing and leave before police come." She covered her face, as if the memories were too difficult to bear.

"Why didn't you tell anyone?" Ryan asked.

"I was afraid no one believe me. I was servant. I wasn't citizen," she admitted. "I was afraid for deportation." She heaved as deep sigh. "I tell this to Sister Margaret when Alicia brought to St. Ives. She let me stay."

Ryan studied her for a moment and placed a hand on her shoulder. "I'm glad you were there," he said.

"You go now." Maria dried her tears and opened the door. "Find Alicia."

"Maria, would you check to see if Allie's at the convent?"

Maria disappeared and Ryan rested his head back, but tormented thoughts raced through his mind. It wasn't long before Maria ran out the door, her hand on her heart. "Non sono qui," she exclaimed. "She not here."

"Damn it," he growled and dialed Mike's cell phone.

Mike answered, but put him on hold for another call. Ryan stepped out of the truck and paced.

"Ryan, I just got a call from Grand Bay Savings and Trust." Even though Mike's voice was steady, Ryan stopped pacing when he detected a sense of urgency. "Allie just left the bank. She asked the teller to call me. She said someone would kill her little girl if she didn't get the money. I'm on my way to Grand Bay," he said and disconnected the call.

"So am I," Ryan muttered. "I've got to leave," he called to Maria as he revved the engine.

"Alicia, she in trouble?"

"I don't know." He gazed into her worried eyes and then raced his truck toward the road.

As he pushed his speed beyond the limit, he opened the glove compartment for his snub nose revolver and slipped it into the inside pocket of his jacket.

* * *

Allie stared out the window as they past open farmland. Jessie's cries had quieted to a whimper.

"Do something with her," Pat barked.

Allie reached over the seat and held Jessie's hand. "It's going to be all right," she signed. "Please don't cry, baby."

Big tears rolled down the little girl's cheeks and Allie started to climb into the back seat, but Pat grabbed her sweater. "Stay in front where I can watch you."

"She's frightened." Allie gritted her teeth. "I'm not going to jump out of the car with her."

Pat released her grip. "Don't try anything stupid."

Allie gathered Jessie close to soothe her. "I know you're scared," she signed.

Allie didn't have a clue where they were or how long she'd been unconscious. They past an occasional farmhouse, but nothing looked familiar. She touched the side of her head to discover it was sticky with blood. She opened her eyes when Jessie tugged at her sweater and signed.

Allie met Pat's gaze in the rear-view mirror. "Jessie needs to use the bathroom."

"We can't stop," Pat muttered and stepped on the gas.

* * *

It didn't take a genius to find the bank. Every patrol car for miles had pulled into the parking lot and their flashing lights signaled like a beacon. An ambulance pulled onto the street and when the siren screamed, Ryan jumped out of the truck and sprinted to the bank.

A deputy sheriff stood guard at the entrance. "Sorry, the bank's closed."

"I'm meeting Officer Vetrano from the South Harbor Police Department."

"He's inside. What's your name?"

"Ryan Harper."

The deputy entered the bank and after several moments, Mike came out. "What are you doing here?"

"You didn't expect me to sit and twiddle my thumbs did you?"

Mike led him away from the officers gathered at the door. "Look, this is police business, Rye. Go home and wait."

Ryan turned and counted to ten before he did something stupid like slam his fist into Mike's jaw. "I know how dangerous this is, damn it. Allie and Jess have been kidnapped. I know what's at stake." His voice was low, but shook with rage.

Mike placed an arm across Ryan's shoulder. "We'll find them. They can't be far. From the security camera video, we've obtained the make of a car that was reported stolen from a Grand Bay grocery this morning. An APB has been sent to all units."

"What happened in the bank?"

"Two days ago Allie requested a million dollar withdrawal. Today she came back for the money, but we flagged the account before she could collect. Allie told the teller someone would kill Jessica if she didn't leave with the money. The security guard followed, but was hit by the getaway car."

Ryan watched a tick in Mike's cheek twitch with anger. "Do you know who did this?" asked Ryan.

Mike glanced around to make sure no one was within ear shot and leaned close. "I viewed the surveillance tape and Allie signed Sister Pat's name."

* * *

"You dragged Jessie into this. You need to stop or she's going to have an accident," Allie yelled.

Allie caught Pat's glare in the rear-view mirror. "She can go by the side of the road." Pat stopped the car and motioned for Allie to get out. "Take her into the rows of corn so you're hidden in case someone drives by."

Allie led Jessie down a path between dried corn stalks.

"This is as good a place as any," Pat snarled and jabbed the gun into Allie's back. "Hurry up."

While Jessie hid behind a corn stalk, it gave Allie a moment to think. She reached through the stalks to hand Jess a tissue and grabbed a hand full of soil.

When Jessie was done, Pat led them toward the car, but before they were out of the field, Allie turned and hurled the dirt at Pat's face. Pat screamed and rubbed her eyes, but held on to the gun. Allie scooped up Jessie and ran through the maze, her heart pounding erratically.

"You bitch," Pat shrieked.

Allie knelt down and signed to Jessie. "Go to the white house." She pointed toward the farmhouse she'd seen before they stopped.

"Run fast and don't come back." Jessie hesitated, so Allie pushed her to move. "Go."

Allie's only thought was to divert Pat's attention, so she ran in the opposite direction until she came to open field. She saw a wooded area about five hundred yards away. Her only hope was to out-run Pat and seek cover in the trees until help arrived.

She didn't dare breathe as she inched along the edge of the corn field. A twig broke behind her and she turned to see Pat charging at her. Allie sprinted into the open field, toward the woods.

"Come back here," Pat shouted.

Allie heard a deafening blast, but didn't look back. Then another shot and felt a searing pain in her arm, but wouldn't stop. She refused to look at the blood she felt soaking through the fabric of her sweater. The woods grew blurry from tears, but by the grace of God she'd get there if she had to crawl.

* * *

When three deputies burst through the doors of the bank, Mike hurried over. "What's up?"

"Just got a call about shots fired at a residence on Hill Top Road off Darkle. The complainant also reports finding a child matching the description of the missing girl."

Ryan jumped toward his car, but Mike grabbed his arm. "Stay here, Ryan."

"No way," Ryan argued and shook free of Mike's hold. "My whole life is out there."

"I'm telling you to stay here." Mike glared a warning.

Ryan reached for the door and when a deputy distracted Mike, he slipped into his truck, floored the gas and peeled onto the road.

Shots fired. The words hung in his mind as a cold, damp fear crept over him like a fever. Allie and Jessie were in danger, possibly fighting for their lives and all he could do was squeeze the steering wheel and hope he wasn't too late. Ten—fifteen minutes max and he'd be there, hopefully before the entire county of squad cars arrived. Christ, he had to do better and he floored the gas pedal.

In the side mirror, he caught sight of Mike's patrol through the dense cloud of dust. Ryan let Mike pass, and ignored the pull-over gesture Mike flashed.

Mike slowed to a stop and Ryan followed when he saw a dark sedan parked at the side of the road.

Ryan jumped out of the truck and pulled out his gun.

"What the hell do you think you're doing?" Mike growled as he searched the rows of corn. "Go to the farmhouse and see if Jessie's safe," Mike said. "I'll search the yard."

Ryan nodded and ran toward the house, but stopped and crouched to the ground when he heard gunshot. He watched Mike grab his side and crumble to the ground.

Ryan crawled to the cornfield for cover and made his way to the edge so he could get a better look at the woods where he thought the shot came from. His heart sank to his stomach as he crawled toward Mike. Beads of sweat dotted his brow and he wiped his forehead with the sleeve of his jacket.

Mike held his side, his eyes were closed, but he was breathing. "Jesus, Rye," Mike groaned. "I told you to get the hell out of here."

Ryan steadied the revolver and felt a sickening chill when he saw a trail of blood lead toward the woods. He zigzagged to avoid being an easy target and followed the blood.

There wasn't even a breeze as sirens pierced the still air. He ducked behind a tree and waited for a sound.

"Sorry, little Allison," Pat taunted. "Such a shame I had to shoot your friend."

Through the woods, Ryan followed the voice, careful to move without making a sound. He inched his way closer and griped the handle of the gun to steady his hand.

"Allie-Allie-un-free," Pat called. "Come out and play."

Ryan peered around a tree when he saw something move. He swung his piece, his finger froze on the trigger and his heart nearly stopped when he discovered Allie slumped against a tree several yards away.

She gasped when their gaze met and he placed a finger on his lips. He swallowed hard when he saw her sweater drenched with blood. *Don't make a sound, baby.*

Pat stepped into view, her gun pointed at Allie's head. "There you are."

Ryan aimed the revolver at Pat and she whirled to face him. "Drop your gun," he yelled.

"I'll kill her before you can get a shot off," she snapped.

"You'll die first." He called her bluff. He saw the gun shake in Pat's hand and kept a watch on Allie from the corner of his eye.

Distant voices grew louder and Pat averted her gaze from Ryan. "Come here, Allie," she ordered. "Now!"

Allie shook her head. When Pat angled the gun at Ryan, he didn't flinch as he pulled the trigger.

Pat fell over and he kicked her gun away before he felt for a pulse. There was none. He rushed to Allie's side, eased her to the ground and tore off his jacket, then his shirt.

"Stay with me, Allie." He forced his voice to remain calm, even though his hand shook as he pulled up the arm of her sweater, twisted the sleeve of his shirt above the wound into a tourniquet and covered her with his jacket.

She opened her mouth and he leaned close. "Where's Jess?" she whispered.

"She's safe." He could only hope. She stopped shaking and Ryan checked to make sure she was breathing. "Damn it, Allie," he cried. "Stay awake. Do you hear me?" In one quick motion, he lifted her, alarmed by the limpness of her body as he carried her to the clearing. *Please God. Don't let her die.*

There were officers running toward them. "The kidnapper's down in the woods about fifty yards," he shouted and carried Allie toward a team of paramedics.

He laid her on a stretcher and stepped back as the EMTs went to work. He crossed his arms to steady his hands. Never had he felt as helpless while he watched tubes, solutions and oxygen being hooked up to Allie's lifeless body.

"Hope you have a permit for that gun."

Ryan turned and saw Mike lying in the back of an ambulance. "You bet I do, Officer Vertrano."

Allie was lifted into the back of another ambulance. "Will she be alright?" he asked as a vice of fear gripped him.

"She's lost a lot of blood," the technician said. "But I think she'll be okay,"

Ryan lowered his head and felt tears sting his eyes as he kissed her on the forehead. "You're going to be fine, Allie. Do you hear me?"

She didn't open her eyes, but a hard lump formed in his throat when she nodded. The ambulance pulled away and he turned to the closest officer. "Where's the little girl?"

"She's with Officer Foster." He pointed to a woman in uniform sitting on the ground holding Jessie.

Ryan saw the grimy streaks of tears on Jessie's face when he approached. She looked so tiny, so bewildered. Then she saw him and ran. Even though she was crying, a bright smile covered her face when he lifted her into his arms and kissed her. "Are you hurt?" he signed.

She shook her head and buried her face against his neck. He inhaled her sweet innocence and knew, at last, that everything would be all right.

* * *

Holly sat at the edge of Allie's bed when Ryan entered the hospital room. Allie had just come out of recovery and flinched as she tried to sit. A sling bound one arm and an IV was taped to the other.

"Not so fast there, girlfriend," Holly ordered and pressed a hand against Allie's chest. "You need to be still for awhile."

When Allie's gaze lifted, Ryan's composure performed a downhill slide. She was pale, but her eyes were clear and a slight smile tugged at her mouth. "Are you all right?" she whispered and reached for his hand.

He nodded, even though he felt like he'd been hit by a steam roller and swallowed around a hard lump in his throat as he kissed the back of her hand.

"I need to check on Mike. Something tells me he's going to give his nurse a hard time." Holly patted Ryan on the back. "She's going to be fine, Rye."

Ryan didn't dare speak, afraid he'd start blubbering, but he wanted to tell her how scared he was when he thought he'd lost her. How empty his life would be without her. How much he wanted to take her home so they could begin a life without secrets or doubts.

He lowered himself to the edge of the bed. He didn't know how to hold her, she looked so frail, but Allie solved the problem by pulling him beside her.

"God, I love you, Allie." His voice broke. "I was so. . . I'm so. . ." His words trailed off as he held her close.

She smiled, even though bright tears shone in her eyes. "I know. So am I," she whispered against his lips before her sweet kiss tamed the wild beat of his heart.

Epilogue

Thanksgiving was a special celebration at Harper Orchards. With the height of apple season finally over, the family could breathe a sigh of relief and give thanks for another prosperous harvest.

Ryan watched the activities from his vantage point on the loft above the great room. He'd gone upstairs to select a CD and enjoyed the scene so much, he grabbed his camera to document the action below.

Emily was home from college and showed Jessica how to style fancy braids in her doll's hair. Jessie looked at Emily with eyes wide and he zoomed to capture the glee as they giggled at a private joke.

Matt, always the most serious of the Harper brothers, was deep in thought over a game of chess with their cousin, Tom. When Matt's fingers lingered on his knight, Ryan framed the image to center the furrow on Matt's brow.

Mom displayed Ryan's soon-to-be published photo-journal, *Flying with Grace,* to his Aunt Carla and Tom's wife, Lauren. He composed the shot and caught the look of pride on Mom's face as she turned the page.

Dad filled Uncle Joe's empty glass with his latest batch of hard cider and while they sipped, Ryan acquired a shot to illustrate the unspoken bond only close-knit brothers could share.

His brother, Jake lay unsuspecting on the floor playing a video game. Ryan chuckled as he clicked to obtain a series of an ambush by Tom's little guys, Nate and Andrew, and the tickle attack that followed.

After much debate, Maria and Sister Margaret convinced Mom that she deserved a break from kitchen duties. While Maria trussed the turkey, she sang a light Italian tune. Sister Margaret sliced sweet potatoes into a casserole and hummed along. He smiled, releasing the shutter when they gazed at one another with a look of mutual friendship and trust.

Allie sat on the hearth and Ryan guessed that the warm glow on her face was more than a reflection from the crackling fire.

Her confidence had blossomed so rapidly over the past month, it made his head spin. Her physical wounds were almost healed along with the mental demons that had haunted her since childhood.

She tucked a curl behind her ear and the engagement ring she wore caught a light from the fire and flashed a prismatic beam of brilliance in his direction.

When Allie searched the room and her gaze rested on his, a surprised smile brightened her face. He depressed the shutter button, knowing he'd captured an image to treasure. After all the heartbreak she'd seen, he'd never grow tired of the serene look on her beautiful face.

She slipped away unnoticed to the top of the stairs where he waited. "What are you thinking?" she asked and slipped an arm around his waist.

He cradled her close, overcome with all he had to be thankful for. "About how I can't wait to spend the rest of my life with you," he whispered before her lips met his.